Praise for Kiki Swinson

"After reading *Candy Shop* all I could say was scandalous!"
—K'wan, *Essence* bestselling author of *Still Hood*

"*I'm Still Wifey* is the truth! Swinson has done it again. This book pulls you from the first page."
—Treasure E. Blue, *Essence* bestselling author of *A Street Girl Named Desire*

"Kiki has written a gripping, 'reality-based' story about living life married to a drug kingpin—which isn't glamorous . . ."
—Crystal Lacey Winslow, *Essence* bestselling author, on *Wifey*

"The eagerly awaited sequel from the author of the bestseller *Wifey*, Kiki Swinson continues to thrill with excitement . . ."
—Anthony Whyte, author of the Ghetto Girls trilogy

Also by Kiki Swinson

Sleeping with the Enemy (with Wahida Clark)

Wifey

KIKI SWINSON

Kensington Publishing Corp.
http://www.kensingtonbooks.com

DAFINA BOOKS are published by

Kensington Publishing Corp.
850 Third Avenue
New York, NY 10022

All Kensington Titles, Imprints, and Distributed Lines are
available at special quantity discounts for bulk purchases for
sales promotions, premiums, fund-raising, and educational
or institutional use. Special book excerpts or customized
printings can also be created to fit specific needs. For details,
write or phone the office of the Kensington special sales
manager: Kensington Publishing Corp., 850 Third Avenue,
New York, NY 10022, attn: Special Sales Department,
Phone: 1-800-221-2647.

Dafina and the Dafina logo Reg. U.S. Pat. & TM Off.

ISBN-13: 978-0-7582-2901-4
ISBN-10: 0-7582-2901-1

First Dafina mass market printing: October 2008

10 9 8 7 6 5 4 3 2 1

Printed in the United States of America

I want to dedicate this book to my two children.
I love you both so much.
And I want you to know that:
"When Mama's Straight,
Y'All Gon' Be Straight Too!"

Acknowledgments

Since God has control over today and tomorrow, I've got to give' Him a shout out, because *He's the Man I love Him to death!*

To Crystal Lacey Winslow who happens to be my publisher and the author of *Love, Life & Loneliness* **and** *The Criss Cross*), thanks for taking an interest in my work. And to my agent, Andre' Kelton, for bringing all three of us together to bring this project to life. To Jonie Smith, I want to thank you for your constructive criticism and some of the editorial work done on this book.

To my mother, Deborah C. White, *who happens to be a skillful government worker.* (Smile) I just want to applaud you for how you manipulated negative situations while being a single parent of four children, living in low-income housing without any financial support from our fathers; to moving into a plush townhouse and driving a 2004 whip (car) parked outside your domain. Yeah, you've been through it all. But, look at you now! You got it going on, *sista*!!! Oh yeah, and I know that I never thanked you for looking out for Shaquira while I was away. So, I want to do it now. Thanks!

And to my father, Loyd Yurgen Drew, *I'm still waiting on you to let me be in your life.*

To my grandmother, Clara P. Swinson, you've always been like a mother to me. And since I'm one of your favorite grandchildren, *I'm, gonna make sure you're straight too!*

To my brothers, Eugene Swinson & Jamon Swinson–aka *Fro. . . . ,* I know ya'll can agree with me when I say the streets ain't like it use to be. But through it all, we were still able to reap some of the benefits. To my sister Sunshine Swinson, you're a Delta now! So, make it happen! Oh yeah, I can't forget my childhood friend Dominique Mitchell who picked me up, took me straight to the mall & bought me a whole new wardrobe the very next day, I came home from doing a five year bid @ the Fed Joint. Oh & I ain't gon' forget you Joe, (Joe Cameron). Because as soon as I got myself a crib, you didn't hesitate to fork out a few G's to purchase my bedroom & living room furniture. That was the best house warming present I got. So, good looking out Cuz! **(smile)**

Now to my best friend Letitia Simmons-Carrington, **(witcha country butt).** I love you for everything you've done for me. And whether you know it or not, your love for me has always had a tremendous impact on my life. You showed me that it's okay to travel the straight & narrow and that I should never <u>lose</u> sight of my dream at becoming a successful novelist. So, I'm always thanking God for placing you in my life. And I also want to wish you & your other half Herman Carrington with nothing but blessing throughout ya'll entire marriage . . . because Tisha, you do be starting up all the ruckus 'round there!!!!!!!!!! (smile) Nah, I'm just playing . . . I love ya'll . . . Much love to my girl Malika Foster from outta the

BX, who is now residing in Maryland! Girl you know I ain't got nothing but love for you. You were there for me from the start. I will never forget how you walked up & down the streets of New York to help me sell my first book **"Mad Shambles."** So, you will be compensated!

Now for you Ms. Kellie Walker, I know you would kill me if I forgot to mention how encouraging you were to me about doing whatever it took to launch my writing career. So, I just wanna say, **"THANK YOU, CHAAAAAA!!!**

To Mrs. Karen Johnson—aka Sunshine, who happens to be the Queen of Divas in the Swinson's family and has always been my favorite aunt. Not to mention, that you are a very strong woman, who I just happen to look up to. And because of your strength & sense of judgment, we *(The Swinson Women)* were able to learn from your struggles. So, we had it easy, when our time rolled around. **THANKS!** I LOVE YOU!!!!!! Oh yeah, you better watch out! Because I'm coming for *your crown! (smile)*

To my favorite cousin Duke Woodley, cousin Xyamara Hines, Reggie Boy, my baby sister Jutta Drew, my cousins out in Atlanta (LaToya & Nikki) & to my favorite uncle Leo-aka-James Drew. I love every last one of ya'll!

To my home girl Tiffany Hoyt: Girl you know I ain't got nothing but mad respect for you. You're a good mother to my niece and nephew. And no matter what obstacle comes your way, you beat it down like a chick in the streets. Plus, you got a good heart. And that alone will take you far. So keep your head up! Because, you know I got your back.

To my peoples: Yoni Wyatt, Chiquita Coleman, Sherry Cherry, Lance & Kim Waters, Kimberlie Flemings from out of Charlotte, NC, Iona Christian & Joan Chisholm from out of Brooklyn, NY, Vandalette WareWatson, Rosalee Evans.

But most importantly, to my home girls Delphine *(Dee Dee)* Johnson, Katrina & Dana Brown, who happened to be my running buddies back in the late eighties when we used to wear *Used Jeans, Damage Jeans, gold-plated Gucci Linx chains around our necks & the 10-carat gold bamboo earrings dangling* from our ears. Plus, the cats back then handed out money like it was falling off trees. Boy! Don't we all remember those days?

I know I do . . . !

Tired of the Drama

It's 4:30 am in the morning and I've been pacing back and forth from my bed to my bedroom window, which overlooked the driveway of my six-hundred-thousand-dollar house, waiting for my husband Ricky to bring dat ass home. Who cared about all the plucks he had to make every other night? I kept telling him, all money ain't good money! But he didn't listen. Not to mention, I had to deal with all his hoes on a daily basis. We've been married for seven years now, and since then I've had to spend a whole lot of nights alone in this gorgeous five-bedroom home he got for us two years ago. That's how his three children came into play. All of them were by different chickenheads who lived in the projects. But one of them had a Section Eight crib somewhere in D.C. and she was ghetto as hell. Just like the other two, who lived not too far from here.

Now, Ricky didn't have enough sense to go out and donate his sperm to women with some class. Every last one of them were high school dropouts, holding eighth-grade educations and an ass full of drama. They figured since Ricky had a baby by them, that he was gonna leave me to be with their nasty tails. Oh, but trust me! It won't happen! Not in *this* lifetime. Because all they could offer him was pussy. And the last time I checked, pussy wasn't in high demand these days like them hoes thought. That's why I could say with much confidence—that *Ricky needed me.* I kept his hot-headed ass straight. And not only that, I've got assets. I'm light-skinned and very pretty with a banging ass body! Niggas in the street said I reminded them of the rapper Trina because both of us favored each other and we had small waists and big asses. And to complement all that, I knew how to play most of the games on the street, as well as the ins and outs of running the hair salon I opened a few years back. Not to mention, Ricky gave me the dough to make it happen. Now you see, he was good for something other than screwing other chicks behind my back. This was why I was always trying to find reasons not to leave his ass.

So, after pacing back and forth a few more times, Mr. Good Dick finally pulled his sedan into the driveway. I made my way on downstairs to greet his butt at the front door. "What you doing up?" he asked as soon as he saw me standing in the foyer.

"Ricky, don't ask me no stupid-ass questions!" I told him with much attitude. Then I moved backwards two steps, giving him enough room to shut the front door.

"What you upset for?" he responded with uncertainty.

I'm standing dead smack in front of my husband, who is, by the way, very, very handsome with a set of six packs out of this world. I'm wearing one of my newest Victoria's Secret lingerie pieces, looking extra sexy; and all he could do was stand there looking stupid and ask me what I'm upset for? I wanted so badly to smack the hell outta him; but I decided to remain a lady and continue to get him where it hurts, which is his pockets. This dummy had no clue whatsoever that I was robbing his ass blind.

Every time he put some of his dough away in his stash I was right behind him, trimming the fat around the edges.

"Kira, baby don't give me that look," Ricky continued.

"You know I'm out on the grind every night for me and you."

"Ricky, I don't wanna hear your lies," I tell him and walk to the kitchen.

And like I knew he would, he followed in my footsteps.

"Baby!" he started pleading. "Look what I gotcha!"

I knew it. He's always pulling something out of his hat when I'm about to put his ass on the hot seat. He knows I'm a sucker for gifts. "Whatever you got for me, you can take your ass right back out in the streets, find all your babies' mamas, play Spin the Bottle and whoever the fuck wins, just give it to them." I fronted like I wasn't interested.

"Shit, them hoes wouldn't ever be able to get me to cop a bracelet like this for them!" Ricky tells me.

"They weren't hoes when you were screwing 'em."

"Look Kira, I didn't come home to argue wit'

you. All I wanna do right now is see how this joint looks on your wrist."

Curious as to how iced out this bracelet was, I turned around with a grit on my face from hell. "You look so sexy when you're mad," he told me.

Hearing him tell me how sexy I looked made me want to smile real bad, but I couldn't put my guard down. I had to show this clown I wasn't playing with his ass and was truly tired of his bull-shit. All his baby mama drama, the other hoes he was seeing and the many trips he took out of town, acting like he was taking care of business. Shit, I wasn't stupid! I knew all them trips he took weren't solely for business. But it's all lovely. While he thinks he's playing me, I'm straight playing his ass, too.

"Where you get this from?" I asked, continuing to front like I wasn't at all excited about this H series diamond watch by Chopard.

"Don't worry 'bout that," Ricky told me as he fastened the hook on it. "You like it?"

Trying to be modest, I told him, "Yeah." And then I looked him straight in his eyes with the saddest expression I could muster. I immediately thought about how I lost my mother to a plane crash just hours before I graduated from high school. I tried talking her into taking an earlier flight from her vacation in Venezuela, but she re-fused to leave her third husband out there alone and wanted to guard him from walking off with one of those young and beautiful women roam-ing around the beaches. So once again, she al-lowed her obsession for wealth to dictate her way of life. I hated to admit it but over the years, I had become the spitting image of her. I wanted nothing to do with a man who couldn't give me all the fine things in life. And since my mother had not been married to her third husband long enough, I got stiffed when his will was read. The only two choices I had was to either move in with my uncle and his family or my grandmother Clara, who were my only living relatives. So, guess what? I chose neither. I did this because I just felt like I didn't belong with any of them. I mean, come on. Who wanted to live in a house that always smelled like mothballs? Who wanted to live with an uncle who forced you to be in church every Sunday? Plus, you had to abide by his rules. And he didn't care how old you were, either. So, it had to be fate when Ricky came into my life.

He got me my own apartment not even a week after we met. The fact that he loved to spend his dough on me made it even sweeter. He tried really hard to make sure I got everything I needed, and I let him. Hell yeah! That's why most of the time when I'm upset, I can make him feel really guilty about how he's been treating me lately.

"Why do you keep taking me through all these changes?" I asked as I forced myself to cry.

"What you talkin' 'bout, Kira? What changes?"

"The constant lies and drama!"

"Tell me what you talkin' 'bout, Ma!"

"I'm talking about you coming in this house two, three, and four o'clock in the morning, every damn night, like you got it like that! I'm just plain sick of it!"

"Come off that, baby," Ricky said as he pulled me into his arms. "You know those hours are the best time for me to work. I make mo' money and get less police."

"Who cares about all of that? I just want it to stop!"

"It will."

"But when? I mean, come on, Ricky. You got plenty of dough put away. And I've got some good, consistent money coming in my salon every week. So, we ain't gon' need for nothing."

"Look, I'll tell you what? Let me finish the rest of my pack and make one last run down to Florida, then I'll take a long vacation."

"What you mean, vacation?!" I raised my voice because I needed some clarity.

"It means I'mma chill out for a while."

"What's a while?"

"Shit, Kira! I don't know! Maybe six months. A year."

"You promise?" I asked, giving him my famous pout.

"Yeah. I promise," he told me in a low whisper as he began to kiss my neck and tug on my ear lobe.

That instant, my panties got wet. Ricky pulled me closer to him. He cupped both of my ass-cheeks in hands, gripping 'em hard while he ground his dick up against my kitty cat. I couldn't resist the feelings that were coming over me. So when he picked me up I wrapped my legs around his waist, only leaving him enough room to slide his huge black dick inside my world of passion. I'm so glad I had on my crotchless panties because if I had had to wait another second for him to pull my thong off, I probably would have exploded.

"Hmmm, baby fuck me harder!" I begged him as I used the kitchen sink to help support my weight. His thrusts got harder and more intense.

"You like it when we fuss and make up, huh?" Ricky whispered each word between kisses. But of course, I declined to answer him. Swelling his head up about how I like making love after we have an argument, was not what I deemed to be a solution to our problems. After we got our rocks off, he and I both decided to lay back in our king-sized bed until we both dozed off.

Around 12:30 in the afternoon is about the time Ricky and I woke up. I hopped into the shower and about two minutes later, he hopped in right behind me. I knew what he wanted when he walked in the bathroom. It's not often that he and I take showers together, unless he wants to bend me over so he can hit it from the back. He knows I love giving it to him from the back, especially in the shower. The slapping noise our bodies make together in the water, as he's working himself in and out of me, turns me on.

After Ricky got his rocks off, he left the shower and returned to our bedroom to get dressed. "What you gon' do today?" I asked him as I entered into our bedroom, wrapped in a towel.

"Well, I'mma run by the spot out Norfolk and see why Eric and them can't get my dough straight."

"Please, don't go out there and scream on them like you got something to prove."

"I'm not. I'mma be cool 'til one of them niggas step out of pocket."

"See, that's one of the reasons I want your ass to stop hustling!" I pointed my finger at him.

"Won't you stop stressing yourself? Believe me,

most niggas out there got nothing but respect for me."

"What about the one who don't?" I continued with my questions as I started to lotion my body down.

"I've got plenty of soldiers out there that'll outweigh that problem."

"Yeah, yeah, yeah!" was my response, hoping he'd catch the hint and shut up.

Unfortunately this wasn't the case. Ricky kept yapping on and on about how good his product was, and how the fiends were loving it. Once I had gotten enough of hearing about his street life, I grabbed a sweatsuit and a pair of Air Force Ones that matched my outfit and threw them both on. I scooped up my car keys and my Chanel handbag, and headed out the front door.

When I pulled up in front of my salon, it was packed. I knew I had at least four, if not five, of my clients waiting on me already. I know they were mad as hell, too, considering I was supposed to have been here three hours ago. My first appointment was at ten o'clock. Hell! I couldn't get up. After waiting up all night for my trifling-assed husband to come home and then after all the fussing I did, I still let him con me outta my drawz. As I made my way through the salon doors, I greeted everyone and told my ten o'clock client to go and sit at the washbowl. "Tasha, girl, please don't be mad wit' me," I began to explain as I threw the cape around her neck.

"Oh, it's alright. I ain't been waiting that long," Tasha replied.

"What you getting?"

"Just a hard wrap. I got two packs of sixteen-inch hair I wantcha to hookup."

"Did you bring a stocking cap?"

"Yep."

"A'ight. Well, lay back so I can get started."

Within the next two hours, I had all four of my clients situated. They were either under the dryer or on their way out the door. Seven more of my clients showed up, but three cancelled. I thanked God for that because I wouldn't be getting out of this shop until around ten or eleven o'clock tonight. That couldn't happen. I had to get home and wash those two loads of clothes I had packed up top of my hamper before I heard Ricky's mouth about it.

He loved for his house to be cleaned at any cost; If his ass wasn't so unfaithful, we could have had a housemaid, because nothing must be out of place. This fetish for absolute cleanliness got on my nerves sometimes. I mean, shit, ain't nothing wrong with leaving a damn dirty glass or a plate and a fork in the sink every now and then. As for certain garments in his wardrobe, I was forbidden to throw them in the washing machine. I was always reminded to read the label instructions for every piece of clothing he had. If it said "Dry Clean Only," then that's where it was going. I got a headache just thinking about it, so, I made a rule to put a big *"H"* on my chest and handle it.

A few more hours flew by and my other stylist's clients started falling out the door, one by one. This meant our time to go home was coming.

"Rhonda," I called out to one of my hair stylists, who happened to be one of the hottest beauticians in the Tidewater area.

"Yeah," she replied.

"You feel like giving me a roller set after I put my last client under the dryer?"

"Girl, you know I don't mind," Rhonda replied as she bopped her head to Lloyd Bank's single, "On Fire."

Rhonda's good people. I knew she was going to tell me yeah, before I attempted to even ask her. That's just her personality. She'd been working with me ever since I opened the doors to this shop four years ago. From day one, she's showed me nothing but love, even through all the drama her kid's father had been giving her. Her kid's father, Tony, is also a ladies' man; just like Ricky. I keep telling Rhonda to get him like I get my husband. Stick him where it hurts: either steal his money or his pack. It can't get any simpler than that. But nah, she ain't hearing me. That's why them hoes Tony's messing with was laughing at her, 'cause she was letting that nigga play her.

Now my other stylist, Sunshine, was working her game *entirely* different. She was your average-looking chick with ghetto-assed booty. Niggas loved her. Every time I turned around she had somebody else's man walking through my salon doors, bringing her shit.

Sunshine was strictly hustler bound. No other kind of man would attract her. You had to be driving a whip, estimating thirty Gs or better. And his dough had to be long. I'm talking like, from V.A. to the state of Rhode Island, to mess with that chick.

Oh, and Sunshine's wardrobe was tight, too. She wasn't gonna wear none of that fake-assed, knock-off Prada and Chanel that these hoes were getting from the Chinese people at the hair stores. No way. Sunshine was a known customer at Saks Fifth Avenue and Macy's.

I've seen the receipts. Sometimes I thought she was trying to be in competition with me, considering I was like a regular at those stores and all. But there can be no contest because when it's all said and done, I am and will always be the baddest bitch.

Since the day had almost come to an end, I sat back in Rhonda's station as she did her magic on my hair. We were in a deep conversation about her man Tony, when Ricky walked through the door. "Good evening," he said.

"What's up, Ricky!" Rhonda greeted him.

"Nothing much," he responded.

"Where you just coming from?" I wanted to know.

"From the crib."

"Our house?"

"Yeah."

"So, what's up?"

"I need to switch cars witcha," he said as he took a seat in one of the booth chairs across from me.

Something must be getting ready to go down. And he wasn't gonna spill the beans while Rhonda sitting up in here with me. I let her finish my hair and in the meantime, Ricky and I made idle conversation until she left. After she finished my hair, it only took her about ten minutes to clean up her station. Then Rhonda said her goodbyes and left.

"So, what you need my car for this time?" I wasted no time asking Ricky the second Rhonda left out the door.

As I waited for him to respond, I knew he

could do one of three things. He could either tell me the truth, which could probably hurt him in some way later down the line. Or he could tell me a lie, which would really piss me off. And then he could throw Rule #7 at me from the *Hustler*'s *Manual*, which insisted that he tell me nothing. A hustler's reason for that was: "The less your girl knows, the better off ya'll be."

"I need it to make a run," he finally said.

"What kind of run?"

"You don't need to know all that!" Ricky snapped.

"Look, don't get no attitude with me because I wanna know where you're taking my car."

"And who bought you the LS 400?"

"I don't care who bought it! The fact remains, it's in my name. Just like the Benz and that cartoon character, Hulk–painted, 1100 Ninja motorcycle you got parked in the garage."

"And your point?"

"Look, Ricky, just be careful. And please don't do nothing stupid."

"I'm not," he assured me with a kiss on my forehead.

"Don't have no bitch in my car," I yelled as he made his way out the door.

While he ignored me like I knew he would, I stood there and watched Ricky unlock my car door and drive off. At the same time, I wondered where he was goin'.

Hustling + $ = Women

On my way home from the salon, I decided to stop by Wendy's for a chicken sandwich. The lady in the drive-thru window rung up my total, so I paid her and waited for my food. After sitting there for about five minutes, she finally handed me my order. But before she said her "Thanks for stopping at Wendy's" spiel, she hesitated. "Ain't this Ricky's car you driving?" she boldly asked.

"Is this who car?" I asked her, wanting this young girl to repeat herself.

"Ricky," she responded. "He's dark-skinned with long dreads. And he keeps them hidden inside this big hat," she continued.

Well, I guess she passed the test. She described my husband to a T.

"Yeah, I know him," I told her. "Why, you mess wit' him?" I threw her into twenty questions mode.

"Nah."

"So, why you wanna know if this is his car?"

"Well, 'cause I ain't never seen nobody else drive it."

"Well, let me be the one to tell you, this is his

car! And the person who's driving this car is his wife."

"Oh, for real!" the young girl said, with a dumbfounded look on her face.

"Yeah, for real!" I waved my five-carat marquise-cut diamond ring that sat next to my platinum wedding band, which was flooded out with two-carat baguette diamonds.

From her reaction, I could tell she hadn't been ready for the curve ball I had just thrown her.

"Oh, I'm sorry," she apologized.

"Nah. Nah. Nah. You ain't got to apologize. Just tell me how you know my husband?"

"Just from coming up here," she explained.

"So, he comes up here a lot?"

"Sometimes."

"Has he ever tried to holla at you?"

"Nah. It's just that whenever he comes through and orders, he always tell me I can keep his change."

"Are you sure that's it?"

"Oh yeah. I'm sure," she tried to assure me.

"Well, the next time he comes through here, tell him you met his wife. Okay?"

"Okay," she replied. I could see by her expression that she was disappointed, but that's her problem. Bitch!

Once I got all the information I could, I drove off. I only drove about a quarter of a mile up Virginia Beach Blvd. and thought about nothing else but my flirtatious-assed husband. He always had to show off. I bet he had all these hoes out here thinking he's the man. And the more I thought about it, I could do nothing else but pick up my cell phone and dial up this nigga's number.

"What's up, baby?" Ricky answered after the second ring.

"I just seen your peoples," I told him.

"Who?" he asked.

"Your little girlfriend at the Wendy's on New-town Road."

"Who?" he repeated the question.

"Nigga, don't *'who me'* witcha slick ass! You know who I'm talking about," I yelled. "I just left from talking to this young-ass girl at Wendy's."

"Kira, you tripping!"

"I ain't tripping! That bitch was the one trip-ping when she asked me was I driving your car, like she's fucking you or something."

"Kira, don't call me wit' that shit right now."

"What you mean, don't call you wit' this shit now? Ricky, you act like I be looking for this mad-ness."

"Look, I'm in the middle of something. So, we gon' have to talk about this later."

"Yeah, what the fuck ever!" I replied sarcasti-cally and pressed the "end" button on my cell.

I got so pissed with him when he acted like I was the one bringing him the drama. I kept telling him all he had to do, was keep his hoes in check. 'Cause, what I don't know won't hurt me. But nah, he couldn't do that. He had so many of them running around, he done lost control. I learned this a long time ago, that when you live with your man and he's a hustler, nine times out of ten, he's gonna have at least one or two hoes he's screwing on the side. Trust me. It's in the *Hustler's Manual.* I don't care how much Ricky lied and told me he wasn't screwing anybody, because he was. So, having to live with this fact, I constantly had to remind myself that I'm the one was living in the big house. I also had the pass codes to the bank accounts and the combination to the safe, which was built into a hideaway place under the floor, under our bed. Now, to know all of this, I couldn't be nobody else but *wifey*.

By the time I made it home, I was still in a pissy mood because of Ricky's lack of concern for my feelings. I did what any other woman would do, and that was going on a manhunt for names and phone numbers. I searched Ricky's car from top to bottom and in every hidden compartment I could find. I couldn't find anything. He must've cleared everything out before he dropped his car off to me.

He thought he was so slick. But I had his number.

Ricky came home about 1 a.m. I was gonna get outta bed and jump dead in his case about the chick at Wendy's, but I decided against it. I mean, what was the use? He wasn't gonna do nothing but deny any dealing with her, anyway. So, I closed my eyes and lay completely still. I could hear everything he was doing downstairs. By the noises he made, I could tell he was in the kitchen messing with the microwave 'cause I heard him pressing buttons.

After staying in the kitchen for a few minutes, I heard Ricky making his way up the staircase. I could also smell the aroma coming from his food. It didn't smell like anything I had cooked all week. After he entered the bedroom, I decided to open my eyes and sit up in the bed.

"Where did you get that food from?" I asked after turning on the lamp from my nightstand.

"I bought it from Ms. Tiny's house."

"From who?"

"You know Ms. Tiny? She's the lady who sells the shots of liquor, beers and dinners after hours."

"Oh yeah, I know who you talking about now. So, what you buy?"

"I got the fish dinner."

"What else did you get wit' it?"

"Some macaroni and cheese and cabbage."

"Did she give you a piece of corn bread?"

"Yeah. But I ate that when I first got the dinner."

"Why didn't you get me some extra pieces?"

"I didn't think about it."

"Well, you should've brought me a dinner home, anyway."

"Ahh, don't even try that one. 'Cause you know when I'm out on the grind, I don't know when I'm gon' come home. So, if I would've copped you one of Ms. Tiny's dinners, and brought that shit home all cold, you would've screamed on me."

Hearing my husband analyze me made me smile. He truly knew me like a book.

"Let me taste your macaroni and cheese," I told him.

"Here." He handed me the styrofoam container.

"Hmm, this shit is good!" I expressed between chews.

As I continued to dig into the mac and cheese, Ricky's cell phone rang.

He pulled the phone from its holster and looked at it to see who was calling him.

"Hello," he finally said.

Judging from Ricky's expression, I could tell he was getting very angry by what he was hearing from the other caller. "Just stay there 'til I get there! I'm on my way now!"

"What happened?"

"My spot just got robbed."

"Which one?"

"The one out Park Place."

"Who was that on the phone?"

"My man Mike."

"Did he say who did it?"

"He said he didn't know."

"What did they take?"

"Every damn thing!" Ricky grabbed my car keys from the dresser.

"Why you grabbing my keys?" I asked.

"Because you gon' drive me to the spot."

"I ain't getting outta my bed, " I told him.

"Come on, Ma. Please!" he begged.

I told him no. He continued to beg me, so I eventually got out of my bed and got dressed. The ride to Park Place only took like twenty minutes or so, considering we lived in the heart of Virginia Beach. Once we were on the block, it didn't take long at all to see how the fiends reacted to Ricky's presence. Some started flagging my car down. A few of 'em even started running down behind us. I got scared when this type of shit went on; that's why I rarely took these types of trips with him. Oh, but in the beginning when we *first* got together, you couldn't pay me not to hop in one of his cars, to drive him around to check on his spots. The feeling of driving a nice-assed whip with a well-known hustler on the passenger side was the shit. But the best feeling of all was when I had all the project bitches breaking their necks, just to see me pushing Ricky's car while they were walking. Hate mode used to kick in like clockwork. And I loved every minute of it. Especially since Ricky was a new cat from out of town, trying to build himself an empire. But after going through a whole lot of unnecessary drama year after year, I was now in another state of mind. I could care less about all this mess going on out here because it didn't concern me. That's why when Ricky asks me to bring him out here again, I'mma tell him no. And I'm gon' stick to that, too!

After I pulled up to the house, Ricky called Mike, his lieutenant, from his cell phone to let him know we was outside. About two seconds later, Mike walked out of the house and hopped in the back seat of my car. In the rear view mirror, I began to watch his expressions. His eyes had a fearful look in them. He knew the consequences for not being on point. He also knew the story he was getting ready to tell Ricky better be on point, too.

"Y-y-y-yo, Ricky, man," Mike stuttered. "Them niggas took everything!"

"You mean all the food?"

"I'm talking the whole shit, dog!" Mike explained. "And they took the four Gs Jay dropped off for you."

"Do you know who it was?" Ricky asked calmly.

"Nah."

"How many was it?"

"Three of 'em."

"Now, tell me how the fuck they got through that steel latch behind that door?"

"Well, when Remo came back from the corner

store, I was in the back taking a shit. And when he came in the front door, he said them niggas came from around the side and rushed him."

"What were they wearing?"

"Black Carhart overalls and masks."

"Did you recognize they voices?"

"Nah. They ain't sound like none of the niggas I know."

"What is Remo saying 'bout this shit?"

"He ain't said nuttin."

"Where ya'll burners at?"

"They took 'em."

"Do you think Remo could've set this shit up?"

"I don't know, dog," Mike said, sounding a bit unsure.

"Well, you know what's gon' happen, right?"

"Yeah," Mike responded in a long sigh.

"A'ight, then. Just shut everything down and I'll hitcha up tomorrow."

"A'ight."

"Oh, tell Remo I want to see him tomorrow, too."

"A'ight."

Mike got out of my car and headed back in the rundown-looking house. "Let's Go," Ricky told me. I put my car in drive and headed back on the highway toward the beach. I jumped on I-264 and drove ninety all the way home. Ricky loved it when I flooded the engines out in our cars. He said it's hot when a chick can whip a car in and out of traffic on a highway. I could do the same thing on his Ninja. He taught me everything there was to know about driving a car and how to get my hustle on, if push ever came to shove. As I pushed my whip to the crib, I noticed how quiet Ricky had become. I knew he was thinking about doing some crazy shit. I hated when he got in this frame of mind.

"I hope you ain't gon' do nothing stupid to Mike and Remo," I commented.

"I ain't gon' do nothing to them. But, they better be ready to work my next load off without pay."

"You think they gon' work off the next pack you give them without getting paid?"

"They ain't got no choice. 'Cause I ain't gon' let nobody take a half of brick and four Gs from me and not pay for it. Hell nah! It ain't gon' pop off like that!"

"You need to be trying to find out who set them up."

"Oh, I will."

Baby Mama Drama

The next day Ricky headed out to meet with Mike and Remo. His meeting with them didn't take as long as I thought it would. He left the house about ten o'clock in the morning and called me about eleven, telling me he wanted me to take his daughter Fredrica to the mall and buy her some new sneakers. Truth be told, I didn't like his daughter Fredrica at all. She was so damn grown, it was pathetic. This little girl was about five years old and acted like she was fifteen. Now, his other two children were kind of cool; but Fredrica was the worst. Every time Ricky brought her by the house, she always gave me a terrible look. I knew her mama was filling her head up with a lot of nonsense 'cause, every time I tried to tell her to do something, she always reminded me that I wasn't her mama.

Anyway, since it was a Sunday and the mall wouldn't be open until noon, I got up and got dressed. I met Ricky in downtown Norfolk, since he had already picked Fredrica up from her mama's house. He was parked and pumping some gas at the BP station when I pulled up.

"Hey Fredrica," I said to her. I was being fake, as I knew how to be.

"Hey," she replied in a very low tone. To hear her, I had to almost stop breathing.

"What kind of sneakers am I supposed to buy her?" I asked my husband.

"I want the new Jordans!" Fredrica blurted out.

"Yeah. Get her the new black and white Jordans," Ricky told me as he peeled off a stack of fifty-dollar bills from the roll of dough he had in his hands.

"You giving me some of that, too?" I asked him.

"Yeah, I gotcha, Ma."

After Ricky gave me the money, I took it and stuffed it in the front pocket of my jeans. "How did your meeting go wit' Mike and Remo?" I asked him.

"I'll tell you 'bout it later," he brushed me off.

"A'ight. I guess I'll see you in a couple of hours."

"Call me when you're done, because I might be in the middle of something."

"We still going out to dinner tonight?"

"Yeah."

"A'ight then," I said to him as I ushered Fredrica in my car and put on her seatbelt.

Military Circle Mall wasn't packed like I thought it would be, but I did run into a few chicken heads who hate my guts. Like Tiffany, who's a stripper at Magic City in Portsmouth. This chick really and truly thought she had it going on. I caught her a couple times, sitting in the passenger seat of Ricky's car in front of the strip club. I went the fuck off, too. I did it because I heard he was fucking her nasty ass. But he wouldn't ever admit to it. Every now and then I gotta remind Ricky that I've got eyes all over the Tidewater area, watching his every move. It ain't all women, either. But he doesn't care because he still does whatever he wants to do. I bet if I told him that the same niggas he be gambling wit', be calling me and throwing salt on his ass, he'd have a damn fit! I ain't gon' do that, though, because, all Ricky's gon' tell me is that the reason why them niggas doing that bitch shit is because they trying to fuck me. So, I ain't gon' waste my time with it!

Now after Fredrica got her sneakers, I copped her a couple of pairs of the latest Roca Wear jeans with the shirts to match. Then we went to my favorite spot, Victoria's Secret. I racked up on all the newest bra-and-panty sets. I even got myself a pair of bedroom slippers with three-inch heels. Ricky loved that type of shit, especially when we were trying to get our freak on. It was a must that I wear something sexy with a pair of heels on. Ricky's dick gets rock hard when he sees me dressed like that. That was probably one of the reasons he couldn't stay outta them damn strip clubs. Hoes in heels with big asses was right up his alley.

On my way out of the mall, I ran into this cat named Brian. He was Ricky's right-hand man. Now, this dude was hella fine. He was dark skinned and his body was on point. He was probably a little over six feet tall. I heard from a source of mine that if you got in the bed with this dude, he was gonna fuck the shit out of you. I believed her too, 'cause hoes be going crazy over this nigga. Now I ain't gonna lie, if I would've met him before I met Ricky, me and Brian's ass would've been together right now. And quiet as it's kept, I also heard he had a humongous dick and some blazing head. Too bad. I'll never be able to find out 'cause screwing a nigga who works for your man was like going against the grain, and that was a no-no! I learned that from Al Pacino's movie *Scarface:* "Never fuck the help!"

"What's up!" I asked Brian.

"Nuttin, I'm just strolling through."

"Don't spend all your dough on *wifey*."

"Which one?" he snickered.

"Look, you can only have one wifey. The rest of the women you got are your stick girls."

Brian laughed at me. I guess he thought I was funny. "Yo, you crazy. Whose daughter you got?"

"This is Ricky's daughter, Fredrica. You don't remember her?"

"Oh yeah. Damn, she done got big!"

"I know," I commented.

"So, Ricky gotcha playing step-mommy today."

"Something like that."

"Well, let me go and check out one of these sneakers stores."

"Alright. It was nice seeing you."

"Nice seeing you too," he smiled as he turned to walk in the other direction.

Fredrica and I got in my car and headed in the direction of my house. Right after I got on the highway, I dialed Ricky's cell phone.

"What's up, baby?" he asked me.

"Where you at?" I wanted to know.

"I'm taking care of some business."

"What you want me to do with Fredrica?"

"Take her home, 'cause, I'm gon' be tied up for a while."

"Wait! I thought we were going out to dinner."

"We are. But it ain't gon' be until about seven or eight o'clock."

"Seven or eight o'clock?" I asked as the tone of my voice escalated.

"Yeah."

"What the fuck you doing that I gotta wait til seven or eight o'clock?"

"I'm taking care of business," Ricky yelled through the phone line.

"Well, if you taking care of business, then why the hell you sound like you tired? What, you just ran from the police? Or are you fucking one of them stinking-ass project tricks?"

"Look," he said, "don't be saying no dumb shit like that in front of my daughter. And hell nah, I ain't fucking nobody. Now, I'm getting ready to hang up on your stupid ass!"

"Yeah, you think I'm stupid," I yelled back at him and then hung up.

Trying to calm myself down after the episode with my husband, I did a detour in the direction of Fredrica's house. To my surprise, Fredrica remained quiet the entire drive. I did notice her rolling her eyes at me when I was talking smack to her daddy on the phone, though. And I knew she was gonna run and tell her mama what Ricky and I were fussing about. But who the fuck cared? I knew that hooker better not say shit to me about it.

When I pulled into Robert's Park Housing Projects, I circled around the loop to get to

Fredrica's building. As I drove up in front of the apartment door, I started blowing my car horn. Fredrica immediately grabbed her shopping bags and got out of the car. The little wench didn't even say goodbye. As I waited for her mama to open up their front door, this young-looking guy, driving an old 1995 Mazda 929 with tinted windows, pulled up in front of me and started beeping his horn, too. Now Frances must've heard him, 'cause her ghetto ass came flying out her front door. When she saw Fredrica walking up the sidewalk toward her, she stopped in her tracks.

"What you doing back so fast?" I heard her ask Fredrica.

I couldn't hear what Fredrica was saying, but I clearly heard Frances' big-assed mouth.

"Oh, hell nah! You going right back to your daddy. He knows he's supposed to have you today! Shit, I'm getting ready to go somewhere," she yelled.

Then she started stepping in the direction of my car, pulling Fredrica by her arm. As Frances began to walk toward me, I wondered what in the hell did Ricky see in this chick? I mean, what possessed him to cheat on me with this trash? She wasn't all that cute. Especially with that whack-assed weave job. Her gear looked outdated. I mean, who still wore Crest jeans? Nobody I hung out with. It couldn't be her booty, 'cause my ass was bigger. So what in the hell was it? To top it off, Frances tried to rock a fake-assed pair of Manolo Blahnik Timbs, knowing dag-gon well she copped them from the Koreans.

"Where's Ricky?" she asked once she approached my car.

"He's somewhere taking care of business," I told her in an even tone.

"Well, he think he's slick by getting you to drop Fredrica back off to me."

"Look Frances, he didn't tell me nothing about he was supposed to have her today. All he told me to do was take her to the mall. And then when we were done shopping, he told me to bring her home."

"Ricky's a lying muthafucka! He knew I had something to do today."

"Look, I'm just the messenger. So, I don't know what else to tell you."

"Come on Fredrica!" Frances said to her daughter, snatching her by the arm. "'Cause I know this bitch lying for him." She continued talking as her words drifted from the direction in which she was walking.

After I listened to every single word Frances muttered outta her mouth, I just sat in the driver seat of my car, pissed off. I was completely about to lose it. I mean, what gave this tramp a right to have an attitude? Shit, I'm the one who should've had the attitude. She fucked around with my husband and got pregnant, not the other way around. So why was she marching her broke ass 'round here like I owed her something? And talking shit at that! I wanted so badly to put my car in drive and run right over her and her grown-assed daughter. But, I remained a lady and brushed the name calling off my shoulders and took a deep breath. Besides, I didn't want to mess up my brand new Lexus putting both of they asses into the hospital. I blew my horn to get Frances' attention. When she looked dead at me, I smiled and said, "I'll let my husband know what you said."

"Well, tell him I said to kiss my ass, while you at it!" she yelled back.

"Okay!" I responded.

When I took off to leave, I drove slowly just to get a look at this nigga Frances was trying to leave with. As my car passed his, he turned in my direction. He was really handsome, but he looked broke as hell with a pair of those one-hundred–dollar, clustered diamond chip earrings the Arabs sold at the mall. And he had a mouthful of gold fronts, wearing a dingy-looking wife-beater. I smiled at him and kept right on driving.

Change of Plans

I drove to my cousin Nikki's house immediately after I dropped Fredrica off to her mama. Nikki was about two years younger than me and very pretty. She was single with no kids and a college student at Norfolk State University. Most niggas who worked for Ricky were in love with her. But, she wasn't thinking 'bout they asses. Besides, she was involved with her sorority on campus and she was green as hell to the game. So, why even bother with the cats that created it? Sounded logical to me.

When Nikki let me into her one-bedroom condo, she had an exhausted look on her face. "What's wrong wit' you?" I asked her.

"I'm just so sick of all these bills I've got," she confessed as she walked over to a table in her kitchen.

"Are you behind?"

"Yeah."

"On what?" I asked as I took a seat beside her.

"My car payment. My Visa. And my student loans."

"How much you need?"

"About six large."

"Don't worry about it. I'll take care of it for you."

"Girl, thanks. I'mma pay you back when my next financial aid check come."

"Damn that financial aid. Your butt needs a job."

"I know. But I can't work with the school schedule and sorority meetings I got this semester."

"Why don't you come down to my shop, a few days a week? We could use another shampoo person."

"How much you gon' pay me?"

"How much will you need?"

"Pay me five large a week and I'll do it."

"Shit, you must be on drugs if you think I'm gon' give you that type of dough to come be my assistant a few days a week."

"Okay, how about three large?"

"How about two?"

"Alright. That's cool," Nikki agreed.

She and I continued chatting until an hour and a half passed and my cell phone started ringing.

"Hello," I said.

"Where you at?" Ricky sounded like he was uptight about something.

"Nikki's house. Why?"

"Have you been in my shoe box behind the refrigerator?"

"Nah. I didn't even know you had a shoe box hidden back there."

"Yeah. A'ight!" Ricky replied, as if he wasn't at all convinced.

"Are you at the house now?" I asked him.

"Yeah, I'm at the house. Why?"

"Are you getting ready to go back out?"

"Yeah. Why?"

"'Cause, I'm hungry and I'm ready to go out to eat. That's why!"

"Well, if you hungry now, then won't you and Nikki go out and get something to eat?"

"Yeah, whatever!" I told him and then I ended the conversation.

I threw my phone back into my handbag and looked back in Nikki's direction.

"And what did he want this time?" she asked me.

"He just wanted to know had I been in his shoe box he had stashed behind the refrigerator."

"Is he missing something?"

"Yeah."

"What was in it?"

"A whole bunch of money."

"Money?" Nikki shouted in a loud chuckle. "Oh yeah, your ass been in it!" She continued to laugh.

"Yep, I sho' have. And if he don't hurry up and hide it in another spot, I'mma hit it again."

"How much he be having in it?"

"I never had a chance to count it. But, it looked like it could be anywhere from forty to fifty Gs."

"Girl, you got to be kidding!"

"No, I'm not. And that's just his play money. That's why I be tearing his fucking head off every chance I get. And you know what's so crazy?"

"What?"

"I don't even feel bad after I do it. And you wanna know why?"

"Yeah. Why?"

"Because of all the shit he's put me through. I just feel like he owes me whatever I decide to take from him."

"Do you think he know you be stealing from him?"

"He might. And he may even hint around about it. But he know I would straight flip out on his ass if he tried to accuse me of anything. So, you know he'll just throw it out there and let me know he knows. But I don't be paying his ass no mind."

"Kira, you are off the chain!" Nikki told me.

"Fuck him! I mean, he don't give a damn about me! So, I'm just gon' do me. And if it means to plan for a rainy day with his dough, then that's how it's gon' be!"

"So, you're planning to leave Ricky?"

"Yeah. One day."

"Girl, you ain't going nowhere."

"You ain't gotta believe me. But, you'll see." I switched the topic from my dysfunctional marriage. "Wanna go and get something to eat?" I continued.

"Go where?"

"I don't care. Just as long as you make up your mind in the next two minutes."

"Okay. Well, come on. We can decide that in the car."

"Well, let's go."

Nikki and I decided to go to the Outback Steak House. We were in the mood to grill our own steaks but, more than that, that place had good mixed drinks. As we were having dinner, a few local hustlers came through with either their girlfriends or a trick they were planning on banging after her belly was full. One guy in particular, who went by the name Gerald, came through with this chick Velda. Gerald was a known weed man. He was about thirty-two or thirty-three, so, he'd been in the game for a minute. He had about a dozen weed spots all around Norfolk and P-town, so everybody knew that his money was long. And everybody and they mama was trying to fuck him. That alone made Gerald think he was the man. Velda was very pretty and a known booster. She could steal anything of value. I remember her coming into my salon about a month ago, trying to sell me and Sunshine these two gorgeous Hèrmes pink diamond watches she had just picked up. Now I can't tell you how the hell she was able to pull that one off, but she did it.

Seeing these two crooks together was like seeing Bonnie and Clyde in a new day and time. I gave her credit that night, 'cause she was definitely rocking that B. Michael top with the slacks to match. I waved at the both of them when they walked by our table.

On my way out, I ran into this nigga I used to fuck with, named Quincy. He rolled up in a silver 2005 seven series BMW with D.C. tags, sitting on twenty-two-inch chrome rims, with some chick I ain't seen around here before. Knowing him, she was probably from Baltimore, MD or the DC area. The way she was dressed put her in a class with the chicks who went to Howard University. Quincy looked like he had lost a few pounds from when he and I used to kick it back in the day. He must've tightened his joint up while he did that ten-year bid at the fed spot in Petersburg. He'd been home for about a year now. And just like that, this nigga was right back on his feet, rocking a hot Sean John sweatsuit and a set of jewels he must've copped from a custom diamond jeweler.

"What's up?" Quincy said as he approached me and Nikki, with his chick on his side.

"What's up wit' you?" I asked.

"Nuttin'. Just chilling!"

"Well, are you gon' introduce your friend?"

"Oh yeah. This is my girl, Chelsea," he stuttered.

"Hi, Chelsea," I said.

"Hi," she replied.

"I'm Kira and this is my cousin, Nikki."

"Nice to meet you guys," she continued.

"Same here," I told her. "So, how you been doing?" I focused my attention back on Quincy.

Before he answered me, he ushered Chelsea into the restaurant to get them a table.

"I'm doing a'ight. How 'boutcha self?" he finally responded.

"I'm okay."

"How's married life treating you?"

"It ain't no different from having a boyfriend, because, I've still gotta deal wit' the hoes."

Quincy laughed at my comment. "You ain't changed one bit," he said.

"Yes, I have."

"Had any kids yet?"

"Nope."

"You still do hair?"

"Yeah. I own a salon off Newtown Road."

"What's the name of it?"

"Millennium Styles."

"Can I come by there and holla at you sometimes?"

"Nah. That wouldn't be a good idea."

"Why not?"

"'Cause for one, I ain't trying to let you run

into Ricky. And two, the chicks who work in my shop talk too much as it is. Which is why I don't need no mo' drama!"

"Well, can I call you sometime?"

"Why? I mean, what in the hell could we possibly talk about?"

"Us."

"Nigga, you ain't changed a bit."

"Yeah, I have."

"In what way?" I asked him.

"Well, I got a little mo' dough to spread around. And now, I eat pussy."

Hearing Quincy tell me he ate pussy nearly blew my damn mind. Me and Nikki's mouths flew wide open. I laughed it off and said, "Too bad you ain't never got the chance to lick on mine."

"It ain't never too late."

"Oh trust me, its way too late!" I told him, as I stepped backwards. "You better save that tongue of yours for Ms. Thang in there." I pointed in the direction of the restaurant.

"So, it's like that?"

"Quincy, you know its been like that since the day I decided I ain't want to play your games no mo'!"

"You know I still love you!"

"Yeah, right," I told him, blowing him off, as I started walking in the direction of my car.

I walked all the way to my car in disbelief after my encounter with Quincy.

"That nigga ain't gon' ever change," I told Nikki after I started up the ignition.

"When were you going out with him? 'Cause, I don't remember him," Nikki inquired.

"We weren't together long, that's why."

"Where you meet him at?"

"I met his ass at the Casablanca Night Club in Norfolk, back in '89. And he was a trip back then."

"What you mean, he was a trip?"

"Well, see, the thing about him was, he had plenty of dough, but he couldn't dress for the life of him. And the hoes knew it. I mean, they were on him like flies on shit. As a matter of fact, the night I met him, he had some chick he was fucking wit', there wit' him."

"For real?"

"Girl, this fool was straight bugging out. Buying everybody I was wit' drinks and shit. And the whole time, he acted like she wasn't even there."

"It couldn't have been me!"

"Shit, me either!"

"So, how ya'll hook up?"

"Well, after the club, he got one of his peoples to give me his number. So, I called him the next day and we met up at the Applebee's on Virginia Beach Boulevard. We had some drinks and ordered some food."

"How long after that day did you fuck him?"

"It took me about two weeks before I let him hit it."

"So, why ya'll stopped messing around?"

"Well, because he couldn't keep his butt still. He was always back home in D.C. And we never really got to spend time together. And then on top of that, he had too many hoes for me. Plus, he had too much shit wit' him."

"What you mean?"

"Well, when we used to go out in public together, he would never want us to hang out in certain places like the Hampton Coliseum Mall or any of the IHOPs."

"Did he say why?"

"Yeah, he said he just had some bad experiences in those places. But I ain't believe that shit! I knew he was trying to keep us from bumping into one of his other hoes. So, to get away from all his drama, I told him to carry his ass!"

"I would've done the same thing," Nikki told me.

Our conversation about Quincy came to an end when I reached Nikki's apartment. She was ready to turn in. I told her I would holla at her in the a.m. She told me that was cool and sent me on my way.

$$$The Delivery$$$

It was a Monday morning, but it felt like a Sunday for me since I ain't have to go to the shop that day. I got up about nine-thirty, so I could watch some of my favorite *Court TV* shows. I fixed myself a bowl of Fruity Pebbles and tore 'em up. Being as though Ricky didn't come in the house last night until after I fell asleep, the first I heard of his voice was around noon time. And that's because his cell phone started ringing. After hearing him scream through the phone for about ten minutes, I finally figured out he was talking to Remo. And from Ricky's tone, I figured Remo either screwed up a delivery or the money count was off, because Ricky was chewing his ass out.

"That nigga can't do shit right!" Ricky yelled as he slammed his cell phone down onto the coffee table.

"What happened now?" I asked him.

"Remo is forever fucking up."

"What he do?"

"Yo, this nigga gots to be the dumbest nigga I know."

"What he do?" I asked Ricky again.

"He fucked up my delivery."

"How he do that?"

"He was supposed to get his girl Pam to drop off some work to three of my spots early this morning, out P-Town. But, since he didn't go to the crib last night, she told him she wasn't doing shit."

"Well, tell 'em to get the chick he was chilling wit' to do it."

"For real. Right now, at this moment, I don't give a fuck who does it. Just as long as it gets done."

"Make Remo do it."

"Hell nah! Remo too hot! I can't risk losing two bricks behind his ass."

"So, what you gon' do?"

"I'm trying to figure that out now."

"Who usually does it?"

"Damn, what is this? Twenty questions?" Ricky snapped at me.

"Well, I was just trying to help," I yelled back.

"Well, help me by finding somebody to run this food over to my spots."

"How much you paying?"

"One yard for each drop off."

"So, that's three hundred," I said, holding up three fingers.

"Why, you know somebody?" Ricky desperately asked.

"I might."

"Well, find out. Shit, call 'em!"

"But wait. Before I call her, she gon' want to know when you want this done."

"Tell her, now."

"She gon' wanna know how she gon' have to carry it, too."

"Wait, hold up! Who you getting ready to call?"

"I'mma call Nikki."

"Well, look Kira, just see if she gon' do it first. I'll get into all that wit' her when I see her."

Trying to be a trooper and help my husband hold his shit down, I got on my cell phone and called Nikki. I briefly told her about the job and how much she could get from doing it. She agreed to do it, so I told her to come by my crib a.s.a.p. She arrived about thirty-five minutes after I hung up the phone with her. This dude named Shampoo pulled up about five minutes after Nikki did. Ricky had Shampoo drop off the tools Nikki needed to successfully complete the job. Shampoo dropped a large black duffel bag onto the coffee table and headed back out the front door.

"I gotta carry all that?" I heard Nikki ask Ricky.

"Nah. What you got to carry ain't this big."

"So, what's all this?" Nikki wanted to know.

Ricky unzipped the duffle bag and pulled out all the stuff in it.

"What's all that stuff?"

"This is the stuff you gon' use," Ricky told Nikki.

I took a seat in the dining room, which was only a couple of feet away from my living room, and watched Ricky put his plan to work.

Nikki was told she was gonna wear the red pizza delivery T-shirt and cap. Ricky also told her she was gonna drive her car with the delivery sign bolted down on the roof of her car. And the three packages she was going to deliver would be duct-taped down inside the three pizza boxes.

"So, when am I gonna get paid?" she asked Ricky.

"When you take the pizza boxes to each house. Whoever answers the door is gon' pay you after you hand them the box."

"That's it? I mean, that's all I gotta do?"

"Yep. That's it."

"Well, I'm ready," Nikki said anxiously.

Just like Ricky had anticipated, everything went smoothly. Everybody, including Nikki, got what they wanted, so making that trip was kind of easy. It felt so easy, Nikki became Ricky's permanent driver. And by the week's end, my cousin started pulling in nothing less than a grand or more. That alone sent the idea of her being my assistant at the salon right out the window. She got caught up on all her credit cards and she even paid her little Honda Accord off sooner. Now, after about two mouths of being on Ricky's payroll, I began to notice a change in Nikki's personality. Her attitude started getting really snotty. And then she started fucking around with Brian, Ricky's right-hand man.

When I found that shit out, I nearly flipped. I tried to school her about this nigga and about all his hoes, but she wasn't trying to hear me. And judging from how defensive she was getting, I knew he had already put the dick on her. Yeah, my cousin was sprung over this nigga already. I guess what everybody said about him was true. Too bad a bitch like me couldn't find out. And quiet as kept, I never told Nikki how I desired to fuck him. I couldn't tell her because the instant I spilled the beans about that, she was gonna swear up and down that I was trying to throw a monkey wrench in her shit. So, I kept my mouth closed and let her be a big girl. The least I could do was be happy for her.

For Ballers Only

Once a year, around Christmas time, this cat named Bishop threw a soiree for niggas he know that be holding shit down like Bill Gates. I'd been to every one of his parties and he be making sure his shit was on point. Bishop was a rich-assed cat from outta Newport News, who be having his hands in everything. Everybody knew him. He sold everything from drugs to real estate. I heard some people say he had a couple of attorneys and po-pos on his payroll, just so he could keep his ass on the streets. I also heard he lived in one of them two-million-dollar cribs out in Williamsburg. Only a handful of niggas done seen it. Bishop was a razzle-dazzle type of cat. In the daytime, he could be found at a golf course and at night, he could be found at any of them award shows you saw on TV. I never saw him with none of the local tramps 'round here. He be on them model types like Naomi Campbell and Shakira. And he made sure they on point, too.

So tonight I made sure I was on point as well. When me and Ricky walked through the double doors of the hotel ballroom, every eye in the place was on us. And the fact that we were wearing his-and-hers Harlequin mink jackets, turned the heat up real high. But since Bishop was the host of this party, he wasn't about to let no one else outshine him. That's why when he finally made his entrance; he walked up in the spot wearing a silver Russian sable. And just like us, everybody had their eyes glued to him, too. This, of course, had to be flattering because Bishop was smiling from ear to ear.

After he had soaked up all the attention he could hold, Bishop pulled his head back down from out of the clouds and realized Ricky was sitting at a table among the crowd. He came on over with this cat named Papi walking alongside of him, to pay his respects and then he walked off so he could greet his other guests.

However Papi, who used to do business with Ricky back in the day, took a seat at our table. Then he and Ricky started talking. I couldn't hear exactly what they were saying, but I knew it couldn't be about anything legal because Papi was like an uncle to Ricky. He basically put Ricky on his feet and introduced him to the connect Ricky got now with these gangsters from South America. Every now and then, they'll get together with some of the older Spanish heads to play dominoes for a little play money.

After only sitting down for two minutes, Ricky and Papi jumped into a deep-assed conversation. All was left for me to do was sit back, look gorgeous, and sip on my glass of Taittinger.

From the looks of the crowd, it seemed like anybody who ever did a few plucks in their life was there with either their wifey or baby mama, dressed in their most expensive attire. I mingled with a few chicks I knew who messed with the cats that worked for Ricky. This one chick named Sandy, who had a baby by Mike, watched Ricky almost the whole night. Ricky smiled at her a few times, but he kind of brushed her off. He probably did that because he saw me peeping all her moves. I ain't trip, though, but I did question Sandy's ass about it when we were in the bathroom together. And like I thought, she denied even doing it. She probably thought her half-breed ass was gonna get Ricky to bite at her bait. However, I made it known that I wasn't having it. She must've taken heed to what I said, because I ain't have no problems from her for the rest of the night.

Now around eleven-thirty, Quincy decided it was time for him to make his appearance. He stepped in the place wearing all the ice he owned and this proper shit by Armani. The chick he had walking in beside him was Chelsea, the same chick from the restaurant back a couple months ago. She must've been doing something right, 'cause Quincy wasn't in the business of keeping the same woman around for too long. Chelsea was small and petite, like he liked his women, but that dress she wore looked truly hideous. I didn't care who the designer was; the shit looked bad. Maybe before the night was over, I'd give her the number to my tailor.

Now since Ricky and Quincy knew each other, I had to go into my fake mode. I mean, Ricky would scream on me if he caught me within one foot of Quincy, being as though me and him used to fuck around. So, I've got to act like I didn't even know he was here. That also meant avoiding eye contact at all times. This only meant I would put my peripheral vision in overdrive just in case Quincy decided to look in my direction. That's when I was gon' strike a pose for his ass and make sho' I showed off the diamond bracelet Ricky got for me not too long ago.

Before the night was over, I was able to sip a few more glasses of Taittinger and get an earful of Ricky and Papi's plans to make a few more plucks together. On our way out, Ricky and I said our goodbyes and headed on home. By the time we made it into the driveway, it was almost four a.m. I was real tired and so was Ricky but after we got in bed, he made sure he got his nut off. He damn near tried to kill me, the way he was jumping up and down on me. It wasn't nothing but all that Armadale he'd been drinking the whole night, which had him like that. Sometimes I liked the drunk dick, but tonight I really wasn't feeling it. After Ricky's usual three-to-four-minute playtime was up, I turned over and went right to sleep.

The next day kind of started off slowly. First of all, I woke up late and after I noticed it was one o'clock in the afternoon, I still couldn't pull myself outta bed. To my surprise, Ricky had already gotten up and left. I knew he wasn't nowhere else but on the streets, checking on his money. I picked up the phone from the nightstand and called him up. This time, he ain't answer his phone. His voicemail came on, on the first ring. That meant his ass turned it off. Ricky knew I got crazy when he turned his cell phone off. He had no other reason to turn it off except that he was out there creeping, and he didn't want me interrupting him by calling and asking him a lot of questions. I already knew what he was gonna say when he stepped through the front door, 'cause his famous line was, "Damn baby, I didn't hear the phone ring," or "My battery went dead. That's why it was off." I always replied, "Yeah. Yeah. Yeah," and walked in the opposite direction. I did that to keep from smacking the cowboy shit outta him.

After I hung up the phone, I got out of my bed and headed to the shower. On my way out, I heard my cell phone ringing, so I threw a towel around me and rushed back into my bedroom to get it.

"Hello," I said.

"Hey, Kira," Nikki said.

"Yeah."

"I gotta problem."

"What's wrong, Nikki?"

"I got a couple of fucking narcos following me down Granby Street."

"How long they been behind you?"

"Ever since I dropped off the first package."

"How many you got left?"

"Two."

"Well, just stay calm and do the speed limit."

"I'm doing that."

"Well, just keep driving."

"And go where?" Nikki asked me. She was starting to panic.

"I don't know."

"Why don't you call Ricky on three-way and ask him what he wants me to do?"

"I just tried calling him right before you called, but he didn't answer. He turned his cellie off."

"Shit!"

"What's wrong?"

"I don't know what the hell to do, 'cause I can't drop these other two packages off."

"Nah, you sho' can't. They'll really have a reason to mess wit' you, then."

"Oh shit! It's too late!"

"What they doing?"

"They just turned on their blue lights."

"You sure it's for you?"

"Yeah, I'm sure."

"Okay. Don't panic. Just calm down."

"Kira," Nikki's voice started trembling, "I know I'm going to jail, now."

"Look Nikki, don't say that. Just stay calm and please don't let them search your car."

"But, what am I supposed to say?"

"If they ask you, just ask them if they got a search warrant."

"And what if they got one?"

"If they had one, they wouldn't have been following you all this time."

"They're getting outta their car."

"Where they pull you over at?"

"I'm over here by 35th Street and the Norfolk Zoo."

"Well, hold on, I'mma call Ricky back on three-way and see if he'll answer his cell this time."

"Please do something!" Nikki pleaded.

"Okay. Hold on," I told her.

Hearing my cousin like that got me pretty

upset. Hearing her wanting to just cry out to me, and me not being able to do anything to help her, really made me feel helpless. I knew deep down inside Nikki wasn't built to handle what them narcos was about to dish out to her. I just hope she held up and didn't give them a reason to search the car.

Meanwhile, I started dialing Ricky's cell phone again, hoping this time he would answer. As I suspected, he still had it turned off. I clicked back over to Nikki, but she had already hung up. That's when I nearly lost it.

The fact that Nikki was about to go to jail got my stomach upset. I sat there numb, not knowing what else to do. Yet I knew in the back of my mind I had to do something. I got back on my cell phone and dialed up Brian's cell number. I mean, if anybody could get in touch with Ricky, it would be him, since they had that two-way radio shit.

"Yo, who this?" Brian answered.

"This is Kira, Brian. I'm trying to get in touch wit' Ricky. So, can you call him over your radio for me?"

"I just tried to call him 'cause I got this youngen wit' me that's trying to holla at him. But, he must've had his radio off, 'cause he ain't responding."

"Outta all the times this nigga wanna turn his phone off!" I said, frustrated.

"What's up?" Brian asked me.

"Nikki just called me and told me a couple of narcos got her pulled over out Norfolk."

"What?!" Brian shouted.

"Yep. I just tried calling Ricky on his cell

phone, so he could tell her what to do. But he turned his shit off. That's why I called you."

"Did she say how much food she had on her?"

"Yeah. She said she only dropped off one box."

"Ahh man! That means she still got two of them joints left."

"Yep."

"Where they got her at?"

"Over there off 35th Street, by the Norfolk Zoo."

"A'ight. I'mma hit you back."

"What, you going by there?"

"Nah. I'mma send somebody else."

"Well, call me back after you hear something."

"A'ight."

The Test

I got up and got dressed after I hung up with Brian. Since it took him too long to call me back with an update, I decided to drive uptown myself and hopefully be able to find out what was going on. By the time I got there, Nikki was nowhere in sight. Not even a crowd of people was out there. I pulled out my phone and tried calling her cell phone, but it just kept ringing. This, of course, got me really worried.

The knots in my stomach started jumping around like crazy. Then I pictured Nikki hand-cuffed in a cold room by herself, waiting for them narcos to ask her a whole bunch of questions about who she was working for.

Boy! Boy! Boy! I sho' hoped, for her sake, she didn't go up in there talking crazy. Ricky would go the hell off if he found out Nikki snitched on him. And what the hell could I do about it? Shit, he was my husband and she was family. I couldn't turn my back on her. I mean, me and Nikki was brought up together. We used to had to sleep in the same bed growing up. And most of all, we were blood. So, I had to make this shit right.

After getting my thoughts together, I put my foot on the gas pedal and drove straight to my salon. It was a Monday, and nobody was supposed to be working. I knew I could make a few phone calls there without any interruptions.

Now it normally took me anywhere from twenty to twenty-five minutes to drive from uptown to my shop, but somehow I made it there in fifteen. During that time, I was able to think of everybody possible to call about Nikki's situation. Before I could dial out on my cell, it started ringing. I looked at the caller ID to see if I recognized the number, but it didn't show up. I started not to answer it, but something told me to answer it, just in case it was Nikki.

"Hello," I said as I took a seat in one of my salon chairs.

"You just called for Nikki?" a man asked me.

Now, I ain't gonna lie. Hearing this unfamiliar voice scared the shit outta me. And to know it was a cracker, ain't make me feel no better. I asked him who the hell he was, asking me if I was calling for Nikki.

"Who are you?" he asked me, instead of answering my question first.

"Wait a minute, now! You called my phone," I began to tell him. "So, don't be asking me who the hell I am." I waited from him to respond.

"I'm Detective Connors with the Narcotics Unit of the Norfolk Police Department," he said boldly.

I couldn't believe my ears, but it was true; this white man just told me he was a narco. And on top of that, he had Nikki's cell phone. There was no doubt in my mind that they had her. That was the answer to my question. Now I had to figure out how I was gonna get her outta this mess, 'cause, I knew she wasn't gon' be able to handle it.

Plus, I had to figure out a way to explain to my uncle what happened. I knew he was gonna flip 'cause he didn't want Nikki affiliated with none of these niggas out here who sold drugs. And to know she was working for my husband was gonna really make him go off the deep end.

"Where's Nikki?" I boldly asked.

"I got her in custody."

"For what?" I asked him, trying to play dumb.

"She'll be able to call you in about two hours, after we process her."

"On what charges?" I yelled through the phone, but didn't get an answer 'cause the phone line went dead. I just sat there and thought, "What am I gonna do next?" But before I could gather my thoughts together, my cell phone started ringing again. I didn't bother to look at the caller ID this time. I just answered it.

"What?" I said, like I was aggravated.

"Yo, Kira!" Ricky said. "I just heard Nikki got bagged up today."

"I already know what the hell happened to her!" I snapped at Ricky.

"You talked to her yet?"

"Why? I mean, where the fuck were you earlier when I was trying to call you?"

"I was at the gambling spot."

"Well, why was your phone turned off?"

"'Cause, my battery was dead."

"Yeah. What the fuck ever! I ain't stupid."

"Yo, look, we can talk about that shit later. Right now, I need to know what's up wit' your cousin."

"Well, you need to call down to the jail 'cause they can probably give you mo' answers than I can."

"Where you at?"

"I'm at the shop."

"Well, stay there, 'cause I'm on my way."

"Yeah. Whatever!" I told him and hung up my phone.

In the time it took Ricky to get to me, I was able to make one phone call. That was to Mitch, the bail bondsman. He was well known around Norfolk. Everybody used him to get their asses outta jail. He'd even bond out certain hoes, if they promised to fuck him. But, he'd tell you, they had to look like something, and they had to have a big ass. So, I knew it wouldn't be a problem for him to check on Nikki. Mitch was just gully like that. I gave him all her information and waited patiently for him to call me back.

Meanwhile, Ricky came strolling through the salon door. I was sitting down when he walked in.

"Heard anything yet?" he didn't hesitate to ask.

"Nah," I told him, then rolled my eyes at his ass. He didn't pay my ass no mind 'cause the questions kept right on coming.

"You think they gon' give her a bond?"

"They should. I mean, she ain't ever been in trouble before. And I just got off the phone wit' Mitch. He said he gon' find out what they charged her wit' and if they gon' give her a bond or not."

"Do you think she gon' roll over on us?"

"What you mean, 'us'?" I snapped at Ricky. "Wasn't none of that shit she had mine!"

"So, what you saying?"

"What you mean, 'what I'm saying?' Shit! What you saying?"

"Look Kira, you know the game. The police just don't want the nigga who the shit belongs to. They want everybody who's involved. Even the ones who just sit around and spend the money."

"Yeah. Whatever. I ain't trying to hear that dumb shit."

"Well, you better hear it, 'cause, you don't know what your cousin is down there telling them crackers."

"Oh trust me; my cousin ain't down there telling them shit."

"Yeah. I hope not. But I ain't gon' take no chances. That's why I called all my peoples and told them to shut down everything and clean house."

"Well, I guess you gotta do what you gotta do."

"Are you supposed to call the bondsman back? Or is he supposed to call you?"

"He said he gon' call me back."

"Well, call me and let me know what he said."

"Where you going?"

"To the house."

"For what?"

"To take my money outta there."

"Yeah. A'ight," I said with an attitude.

Instead of sticking around at the shop, I jumped in my whip and drove on to the crib. I figured if

Nikki was gonna call me, she would call me at the house, being that I can only accept collect calls there. When I got home, Ricky was still there. He was in the kitchen, talking on his cell phone when I walked in the house.

"Ain't nobody heard from her yet," I heard him say.

"A'ight, then. I'll call you when I hear something," he said and then he ended his call.

"Who was that?" I asked him.

"Mr. Robinson."

"Who? Your lawyer."

"Yeah. "

"What did he say?"

"He just told me to keep my nose clean."

"That's it? I mean, he ain't say nothing about Nikki?"

"Nah. 'Cause I was the one doing all the talking," Ricky began to explain to me. Before I could make a comment, my cell phone rang.

"Hello," I rushed to say.

"Hi Kira, this is Mitch."

"Hey, what you find out?" I asked nervously.

"Well, first off, your cousin doesn't have a bond."

"What!" I screamed. "But why?"

"My contact downtown couldn't say. But I would bet money it was because she didn't give them any information. Judges and magistrates hate when they get people down here who don't talk."

"What did they charge her wit'?"

"Possession with intent to distribute five hundred and four grams of crack cocaine."

"How many ounces is that?"

"Eighteen of them," Mitch explained. "And I

wouldn't be surprised if the Feds pick her case up, either."

"Wait! You can't be serious."

"No. I'm dead serious. So, I suggest that you get her a good lawyer 'cause she's gonna need one."

"Do you know any good ones?"

"Yeah. I know a few."

"Which one would you recommend to be the best?"

"Glen Shapiro. But, I heard he can be pretty expensive, especially for a case like that."

"The money ain't no problem."

"Well, then, he's your man."

"You got his number?"

"Nah, not on me at this moment. But he's listed in the phone book."

"Okay. Well, thanks."

"Call me if they ever give her a bond."

"Okay. I will," I told Mitch and hung up.

I walked over to my living room sofa and took a seat so I could absorb everything Mitch had just told me. Ricky rushed over and took a seat right beside me. His face had a look of desperation plastered on it. I knew he was waiting for some answers.

"What he say?" he asked me.

"He said they didn't give her a bond," I wasted no time in telling him.

"What they catch her wit'?"

"A half a brick."

"Damn!" Ricky yelled and then he jumped up from the sofa like he was on fire. I watched him as he walked nervously over to the living room window.

"So, what we gon' do?" I asked him.

"We gon' wait."

"Wait?! Wait for what?"

"We gon' wait for Nikki to call and then we gon' figure out what to do, together."

"Well, you better. 'Cause Mitch said with a case like Nikki's, the Feds might pick it up."

"You bullshittin'!" Ricky snapped at me.

"Nah. I ain't bullshittin'!"

"Well, why you jus now telling me this?"

"'Cause, I wasn't thinking about it."

"Kira, how can you not think about that?"

"Look Ricky, my mind is on my cousin right now, if you don't mind."

"Well, your mind needs to be on more than that!" Ricky responded sarcastically.

He grabbed his coat outta the living room closet and walked out the front door. I heard him back his car out of the driveway like a bat outta hell. God knew where he was on his way to. He just better hope he got there in one piece.

The Next Day

The ring of the telephone was what woke me up. It rang about eight times before I reached over to the lamp stand and answered it. As I picked it up, I looked at the clock on my entertainment center in my living room and it clearly read 8:00 a.m. That's when I realized I had fallen asleep on my couch and was fully dressed in yesterday's clothes. It also became clear that Ricky hadn't come home last night, either.

"Hello," I said.

"Caller, you have a collect call from *Nikki*, an inmate at the Norfolk City Jail. If you accept the charges, press 7 now," the automated system told me. After hearing the prompt from the recording, I pressed the button to accept the charges.

"Hello," I said again, anxiously.

"Kira," Nikki replied, giving off a sound of relief.

"Yeah, it's me," I told her.

"Girl, do you know these people just put me in a block so I can use the phone!"

"You mean to tell me this is your first time using the phone?"

"Yeah. And you know I am pissed, too!"

"So, why didn't they give you a bond?"

"I don't know."

"Well, what did the magistrate say to you?"

"He just stood there behind the glass and told me he was denying my bond."

"Did he give you a reason why?"

"Well, he asked me if I had cooperated with the police. So I told him, no. And that's when he told me my bond was denied."

"That's wrong! He knows he can't do that shit!"

"Well, he did it. And I couldn't say shit about it."

"Well, tell me how the narcos found the stuff."

"When they came up to my car, they asked me which Sal's Pizza store was I delivering for."

"What did you say?" I asked her. She asked them why they wanted to know. And that's when they informed her about the two calls they got about her faking to be a pizza delivery person, delivering drugs to different spots out Park Place. She told me that they told her they knew everything and if she didn't hand over the drugs, she was going to be in a lot of trouble. She acted as if she didn't know what they was talking about, so they told her to get outta her car, since she wasn't telling them what they wanted to hear. And then about fifteen minutes later, two more narcos pulled up with search warrant papers. So, that's how they got the stuff. The search warrant stated that the owner of both Sal's Pizza restaurants had no record of any deliveries in the area Nikki was driving, nor did he have any female employees delivering pies on his day shift.

Nikki told me how scared she was about the whole thing and wanted it all to just go away. I tried to calm her down and make her feel like everything was gonna be fine. I also tried to convince her that I was going to be on top of things, which meant she would be outta there really soon. Before we hung up, Nikki made me promise not to tell her dad where she was. I gave her my word and gave her the okay to call me back later on.

Feeling a sense of relief after Nikki's conversation, I wasted no time dialing Ricky's cell phone number to give him the news. I was surprised to hear him answer his phone on the first ring.

"Yo," he said.

"Where you at?" I asked him.

"Pulling up into the driveway."

"Well, hurry up and come in the house, so I can tell you what Nikki said."

"A'ight. I'm coming."

Three minutes later, Ricky came walking through the front door. Immediately I noticed he didn't have on the same clothes from yesterday, even though he ain't make it home last night. I was tempted to question him about whether or not he had clothes stored away in somebody else's closet. But I wasn't in the mood to hear a whole bunch of lies, so I buried the thought of him spending the night over one of his hoe's house and forced myself to discuss Nikki's situation.

"We gotta get her a lawyer," I told him.

"What did she say?"

"She said basically the same thing Mitch said."

"Do you think she told them anything?"

"She said she didn't. That's why they ain't give her a bond and took a long time to process her."

"Did she tell you how they found the stuff?"

"Yeah. She said they told her somebody called and tipped them off about what she was doing. And she told me they had a search warrant, too."

"They lying! I know ain't nobody called and told them no shit like that!"

"Well, somebody had to say something. And I wouldn't be surprised if it was one of them grimy-ass niggas that work for you."

"Nah. None of them niggas wouldn't do no shit like that!"

"Well, who you think could've done it?"

"I think them narcos lying! They just trying to make Nikki think somebody ratted on her, so she can turn around and get the weight off herself. I mean, it ain't nothing new. Them narcos do that type of shit all the time."

Listening to what Ricky just said made a lot of sense. But what's done is done. Nikki was locked up, regardless of how she got there, so a plan needed to come together.

"Okay. You might be right about the whole thing. But the fact remains that my cousin is on lock. So, we need to call her a lawyer and see if he can get her a bond hearing or something."

"Well, call one."

"You paying for it?"

"Yeah. Just as long as she keeps it real."

When Ricky gave me the cue, I hopped my ass on the phone and dialed *411* to get Glen Shapiro's number. The operator gave me his office number and connected me for an extra fifty cents. I spoke to the secretary and she told

me I had to make an appointment, which I did.
I had her schedule me for the next day, since Mr.
Shapiro was was gonna be outta the office for the
rest of this day. By the time I wrote down the address and directions to the office, Ricky had already took his ass upstairs to our bedroom. He
must've been up all night with that hoe he stayed
with last night 'cause he don't come in the house
and take a nap during the day unless he been up
the whole night before. I wasn't gonna say shit to
him about it, 'cause his time was gonna come.
And when it did I was gonna be off in the sunset,
drinking me some Cristal with my new man chilling right beside me.

The next day I got really anxious to meet with
Mr. Shapiro, so I wasted no time getting all four of
my clients in and outta my salon. As I made my way
out of the shop, I left brief instructions with Sunshine. She was the only person working with me
that day, so I told her to call me on my cell if somebody came by looking for me while I was gone.

On my way uptown to see the lawyer, I stopped
by Nikki's apartment 'cause I promised her I
would pick up her mail and check her messages.
Her mailbox was filled with junk mail, nothing of
importance. Her answering machine had two messages on it. One was from our grandmama Clara,
who wanted Nikki to come by her house and run
her to the supermarket. Another message was
from Nikki's daddy. He called to see if Nikki got his
mama's message about the supermarket. Both
messages had been recorded yesterday.

Now I had to make it my business to put Nikki

on a three-way call to her daddy before this shit hit the fan. Lord knew I was truly not ready for that to happen.

My waiting time to see Mr. Shapiro wasn't long at all. I was in his office not even ten minutes before the secretary led me in. He wasn't all how I pictured him to be. I thought I was going to be meeting with a short, fat, Italian cat, but this man I saw as I walked in the big oval-shaped office was a fine-assed brother. He put me in the mind of the actor Morris Chestnut. As I got closer to him, he seemed to look better with each step.

When I approached Shapiro's desk, he stood up, shook my hand and told me to have a seat in one of the two chairs in front of his desk.

"Are you Mr. Shapiro?" I asked him and looked at him really funny.

He laughed at me and said, "I get that all the time. You thought I was Italian, huh?"

"Yeah, I did."

"Shapiro is my adopted name."

"Oh, okay," I replied.

"Don't worry. I'm still a dynamite attorney."

"I heard. You came highly recommended."

"That's good to know. And please, call me Glen. Now, how can I help you?"

"Well, I have a cousin who's locked up in Norfolk City Jail without bail. And I need to know if there's something you can do to get her out."

"What's your cousin's name?"

"Nicole Simpson."

"What was she charged with?"

"Possession wit' intent to distribute eighteen ounces of crack cocaine."

"How did she get caught with it?"

"She told me a couple of police pulled her over in her car and found it."

"Where did they pull her over?"

"Off 35th Street and Granby. Right across from the Norfolk Zoo."

"Has she ever been arrested?"

"No."

"Does she work for a living?"

"Well, yeah. She works at my hair salon. And she's a full-time student at Norfolk State."

"Okay. Let me ask you another question."

"Yeah. Go 'head."

"The car she was caught driving, was it registered to her?"

"Yep."

"Has she admitted to owning the drugs found in her car?"

"She told me she didn't tell them anything. That's why they took a long time to process her and didn't give her a bond."

After answering all of Mr. Shapiro's questions, he sat back in his chair and thought to himself for a moment. "Well, first off, your cousin is going to need me to set up a bail hearing for her. And I charge fifteen hundred dollars alone for that," he explained.

"That's no problem."

"Okay. Now, to retain me to work her case will run anywhere from ten to fifteen thousand."

"That won't be a problem either," I told him. "All I'm concerned about is if you can get her out of this jam or not."

"That all depends on your cousin and the evidence from the arresting officers."

"What chances you think she might have?"

"I'll let you know after I speak with her."

"Well, when do you think you can go see her?"

"As soon as you pay your retainer fee, I'll notify the courts. And then I'll contact the jail."

"How much do I have to pay today?"

"If you can leave the fifteen hundred for the bail hearing and a thousand for me to start working on her case, I'll have my paralegal put the wheels into motion today."

"Okay. I can do that," I told him, getting excited. "So, who do I give the money to?"

"You can pay me."

I reached in my signature Coco Chanel bag and pulled out a knot of crisp one-hundred-dollar bills. I counted twenty-five of them out, handed the stack to Mr. Shapiro and stuck the rest of them back into my bag. Judging from Mr. Shapiro's expression, he wished he would've asked me for more money. But, it was all good. He'd get the rest of it sooner or later. After he handed me a receipt for the cash I just gave him and one of his business cards, I shook his hand and made my exit from his office.

On my way to my car, I noticed Mr. Shapiro had written his cell phone number on the back of his card. I thought that was really nice of him, and what a good way to start off a lawyer-client relationship. Shit! If he kept this type of behavior up, I might just fuck him for G.P., being as though I ain't seen a wedding band on his finger.

The Bail Hearing

The courtroom was packed this morning. The judge hearing the cases was this black chick named Judge Jones. I heard she was nothing to play with and when it came to making examples out of people, she was the one to do it. I just hoped and prayed she showed a little mercy when Nikki went before her, 'cause, Nikki sho' nuff needed to get a bond. God knew she wasn't gonna be able to hold up in lockdown too much longer.

Now before her case was called, I met with Mr. Shapiro to get his view on what was to come. He told me Nikki had a good chance, considering she didn't have any prior criminal charges. When her case was finally called, I saw two female deputies pull Nikki from behind a closed door connected to the courtroom. She looked directly at me as they escorted her to the judge. I winked my eye and waved my hand at her the moment we made eye contact. She looked okay, considering her circumstances, but I knew her spirits weren't up. They couldn't be. Not at a time like this.

When she arrived at the designated area

where people who were being charged were to stand in front of the judge, Mr. Shapiro was right there beside her.

Judge Jones picked up a document from her desk and read it out loud before everybody in the courtroom. Then Mr. Shapiro made a few comments on behalf of Nikki and the fact that if she was not granted a bail, she could stand to lose a lot. Then this old-looking white chick, who was supposed to be the prosecutor, jumped in and made a couple of statements of her own which made Nikki look real bad. As a result, the judge just flat-out denied her a bail.

I just sat there, dumbfounded, because I couldn't believe these two women just railroaded my fucking cousin like that! I mean, she hadn't ever been in trouble a day in her life, but they just acted like she done killed somebody. I hopped up from my chair, gave Nikki some lip service and gestured for her to call me at two o'clock.

I assumed she got the message 'cause she nodded her head as both of the deputies took her back outta the courtroom.

Mr. Shapiro walked in the direction I was walking, which was outta the courtroom, too. I waited for him after I got in the hallway. "So, what's gon' happen now?" I rushed to ask him.

I could tell by his expression that he didn't want to answer me for fear that I was gonna hold him to whatever he told me. "Well, uh," he started saying, "we can either go before another judge and ask for a bail or we can request for a speedy trial."

"Is that all the options we have?"

"Yeah. Pretty much."

"So, if I go with another bond hearing, I'm gon' have to pay you fifteen hundred more dollars. Right?"

"Yeah."

"We'll request for a speedy trial 'cause Nikki is ready for this to be over wit'."

"Okay. Will do. But first, let me speak with the prosecutor. That way, I can find out what her plans are for this case. So, call me in a few days."

"Okay," I said and walked off.

It wouldn't have come as a surprise to me if Ricky had somebody watching my every move. The instant I stepped foot outta the court house, he called my cell phone.

The timing couldn't have been any better.

"Yeah," I answered.

"What happened? Did they give her a bond?"

"Nah. That lady judge denied it."

"So, what the lawyer gon' do now?"

"Well, he asked me if I wanted him to take Nikki in front of another judge to get a bond hearing. But, I told him nah."

"So, what he gon' do?"

"I told him to request for a speedy trial. So he said okay."

"Did you get to see Nikki?"

"Yeah. She looked like she was gon' cry. Especially after the judge denied her bond."

"Yo! She gon' be a'ight! Just stay on top of that lawyer dude. Keep her some dough on the books. Accept all her collect calls and everything gon' be love."

"Well, I told her to call me at two o'clock, so I could talk to her."

"Where you at now?"

"I just got in my car. And now I'm on my way to the crib."

"Well, hit me up on my cell later, 'cause I'ma be taking care of some shit all day."

"What else is new?" I commented and let out a long sigh.

Ricky babbled on a little more about all the stuff he had to take care of, and after he told me what time he was coming home, we ended the-conversation.

Nikki called at two o'clock on the nose. When the operator gave me the cue to accept the call, I pressed zero.

"Nikki," I called.

"Yeah," she replied in a very low tone.

"Speak up. I can hardly hear you."

Nikki cleared her throat and started rambling on about something, but I couldn't understand her. That's when I realized she was crying.

"Come on, Nikki, don't cry. You gotta be strong. I mean, this shit is gonna blow over."

"When? 'Cause, I can't see it happening. These people ain't gon' let me go."

"Stop talking like that! And listen to me, Nikki. 'Cause if it takes every dime I got, I'mma make sure you get outta there. So, just chill out wit' all that negative talk."

"But everybody I talk to in here is telling me I'm gon' do some time."

"Don't listen to them! Them hoes in there are

miserable and they ain't got nothing but time. So they want you to be in the same boat wit' them."

"Did you get to talk to Mr. Shapiro after court?"

"Yeah."

"What he say?"

"He said he's going to talk to the prosecutor first, to see what she wants to do. And then, after that, he said he gon' request for you to have a speedy trial. That way you can hurry up and get this shit behind you."

"How much he charging you for my case?"

"Don't worry 'bout that. That's being handled by Ricky."

"You saw Brian lately?"

"Nah. But I talked to him a couple times."

"Well, I still ain't been able to speak to him," Nikki told me in a disgusted manner.

"He probably got some other hoe out there to take my place."

"Girl, you know how it is. You ain't gotta be locked up for a nigga to fuck around on you. Shit, you could be living 'round the block from the hoe your man screwing and you wouldn't even know it, 'cause niggas these days ain't got no regard for nobody."

"Do me a favor," Nikki told me. And that's when I could tell she had stopped crying. "Call Brian on three-way for me."

"Hold on," I told her. I clicked over to my other line and dialed the number. When it started ringing, I clicked back over to Nikki.

"Hello," Brian answered after three rings.

"What's up with you?" Nikki didn't hesitate to ask.

"Yo! Who this?" he asked.

"Well, damn! I've only been gone for about a week and a half now, and already you don't recognize my voice?"

"This Nikki?" Brian asked, sounding unsure.

"Yeah," Nikki said and then she sucked her teeth.

"What's up, baby?" Brian continued as if he was happy to hear from her.

"You tell me. I mean, you know my situation."

"Did you ever get that bond hearing?"

"It was today."

"So, what happened? Did the judge give you a bond?"

"If you were there, then you would've known."

"Yo, I can't do that court scene. It be too many of them narcos running 'round that place."

"Well, why you ain't been accepting my phone calls?"

"When you tried to call me?"

"Brian, don't play games with me. You know damn well I've tried to call you a couple of times 'cause the last time I tried, you and your aunt Sarah answered the house phone at the same time. And when the automated system came on, both of ya'll hung up."

"Nah, that wasn't me."

"Look, Brian, please stop the lies. You busted. It's that simple. And the messed up part about this whole shit is that you ain't even have the audacity to send me some dough on my books. Or help Ricky pay for my lawyer."

"Yo, look, baby. Stop getting all worked up. Shit has been real crazy for me since you got bagged up. But I'mma handle it, though."

"And where do I fit in all that?"

"We'll talk about it."

"When?"

"Call me back in about an hour."

"Where?"

"At my crib."

"You sure you gon' be there?"

"Yeah, I'm on my way there now. But I gotta meet up wit' this kid first out at The Manor."

"Yeah, whatever," Nikki told him.

"A'ight," Brian replied and then he hung up.

I pressed the flash button to clear my line. After I hit the button, I heard the automated system letting me know Nikki only had five minutes left for her call.

"Damn, them people don't give ya' long to talk at all," I shouted out loud.

"I know. It sho' don't seem like we been on the phone for fifteen minutes already."

"Don't even worry 'bout it. Just call me back when it cuts off."

"Okay. But, did you hear Brian's lying ass?"

"Yep."

"Come on now, Kira. Who did he think he was talking to? Do I look like a sucker to him?"

"You should've asked him."

"Girl, he is so full of shit!" Nikki let out a long sigh.

"I could've told you that."

"You think he gon' wait for me?" Nikki asked me. I wanted so badly to tell her the real deal about Brian, but now wasn't a good time. She wouldn't be able to handle the truth. I brushed the question off and went at it from another angle.

"Girl, forget all that nonsense. Just focus on trying to get outta that jam. Shit, if you know like

I know, niggas come a dime a dozen. Especially the ones in the game."

"But, I don't want nobody else," Nikki cried.

"Look, if you keep thinking about Brian and what he's out there doing, then you gon' mess around and get sick. And speaking of which, have you been eating? 'Cause, you sho' looked like you lost a little bit of weight when I seen you today."

"Yeah. I've been eating a little bit."

"Girl, you better stop playing and eat."

"I eat."

"Okay. But don't let me see you again, and you look like you done lost some more weight."

"I'm straight."

"A' ight, then," I told her and left that subject alone. "Oh yeah, your daddy called and left you another message."

"When?"

"Last night. "

"What did he say?"

"He just said it would be nice if you'd return his phone calls. That's all."

"Well, when I call you back just put me on three-way with him."

"Are you gon' tell him where you at?"

"I'mma have to."

"Well, please don't tell him you on my three-way."

"I won't," Nikki told me. Then, about ten seconds later the jail system disconnected our call. Nikki called me right back, and that's when I called my uncle on three-way.

"The Simpson residence," he said when he answered.

"Dad. "

"Yes, Nikki," he replied in his stern voice.

"I just got all your messages."

"Where have you been? And why hasn't anybody heard from you?"

"Because, I been away."

"Away? Where, Nicole?"

Nikki was getting ready to answer her daddy, but her voice cracked up.

That's when I knew she was about to start crying all over again. "Nicole," my uncle called out in his nonchalant tone, "Where are you?"

"I'm in jail, Dad."

"For what? Are you alright?"

"Yeah."

"Why are you in jail?" he asked in a hysterical way.

"For drugs."

"What were you doing with drugs, baby?"

"Dad, it's a long story," she answered between sniffles.

"Well, tell me about it," he began to plead.

"I can't."

"And why not?"

Nikki sighed and said, "Look, Daddy, can you and Mama come see me?"

"Can we come see you today?"

"Yeah."

"Okay. Well, as soon as your mama gets home, we'll be right down there."

"Okay."

"Do we need to bring you anything?"

"I'm not allowed to have anything. The only thing this place will let me have is money. I can buy everything I need from their commissary."

"How much do you need?"

"Well, Kira dropped me off two hundred dollars a few days ago. So whatever you and mama can give will be fine."

"Okay, baby. I gotcha."

"Alright. Well, tell Mama I love her and that when ya'll come down here, I'm gonna tell ya'll everything that happened."

"I sure will."

"Okay, then. Well, I guess I'll see ya'll later."

"Okay. I love you."

"Love you, too," Nikki assured her dad.

Once everything was out on the table between Nikki and her dad and the goodbyes were signed and sealed, I cleared my uncle off the line. When I clicked back over to Nikki, I could hear her talking to one of the female C.O.s, about her getting some Tylenol for her headache. And after that conversation was over, me and Nikki talked some more until the time on the phone ran out.

I, on the other hand, fixed myself a sandwich and decided to go to the shop and hang out, just in case a few of my clients wanted to stop by.

Running Thangs

I set my alarm clock to wake me up at seven o'clock, so I could get to the shop for my eight o'clock appointment. After I got dressed, I headed downstairs to the kitchen for a glass of juice when I heard Ricky moving around in the den. Curiosity got the best of me so instead of going into the kitchen, I went straight into the den.

To my surprise, Ricky was sitting down on the couch, counting a table full of money placed in front of him.

"What you doing up so early?" I asked him.

"I gotta count this dough, so I can send it off."

"Are you almost finished?" I asked him as I walked closer.

"Yeah. Almost."

"Where you sending it to?"

"To Papi's people."

"Oh, so you fucking wit' them again?"

"Yeah. Just for right now, though."

"How much you gotta send them?"

"A hundred and fifty Gs," Ricky told me as he

wrapped a stack of one-hundred-dollar bills in four thick rubber bands.

"Did you ever find out who robbed your spot?"

"Nah. I didn't. But I got some people on it, though."

"You talk to Brian?"

"When?"

"I don't know. I mean, just in general."

"Yeah. Why?"

"He say anything about Nikki?"

"Nah. Not really."

"That's kind of fucked up, don't you think?"

"Well, what is he supposed to say?"

"Well damn, Ricky! Do I have to spell it out for you? I mean, come on. Nikki is locked up behind your shit! And Mr. Pretty Boy Brian was fucking her! So, don't you think he should be concerned about her, even if it's just a little bit?"

"He's concerned about her."

"He don't act like it."

"Well, it's just that he got a lot of shit on his plate right now."

"But, what about Nikki? I mean, he is her man, right?"

"Look, I don't know 'bout all that. All I know is that he's got some pretty big issues he's got to deal wit' and they can't wait."

"Well, Nikki ain't too happy about the way he's brushing her off. And it's gon' end up affecting her if he don't step up."

"What is she saying he's doing?"

"He don't accept her collect calls. He don't go and see her. And I know for a fact, he ain't sending her no cheese."

"Well, I'll talk to him 'bout that when I see him later."

"And what you think that's gon' do?"

"Look Kira, Brian listens to me, whether you know it or not."

"Well, what you gon' say to him?"

"I'mma tell 'em to get his shit together wit' Nikki."

"And you think he gon' do it?" I asked Ricky, as if I didn't believe a word he was telling me.

"Yeah."

"Okay. Whatever!" I threw my hand in the air. I knew he ain't going to do shit. All Ricky cared about right now was getting that money straight, so he could send it off to them Spanish cats he owes. But it's okay, 'cause if he don't do something it's gonna come back on his ass too, whether he knows it or not.

"I'm going to the shop," I told him as I turned around to leave.

"Wait," he said, scrambling to get up from the couch. "Let me get some pussy right quick."

I turned around and looked at Ricky with the most disgusted expression I could make. "Go get some pussy from that hoe you fucked wit' the night you stayed out. Remember . . . last week," I told him.

"What you talking 'bout? I wasn't out fucking nobody. Me and this nigga name Fleetwood took a ride to D.C. that night so we could straighten out some shit wit' a few of them cats out there."

"Yeah. Tell me anything," I said and walked straight out of the house to get into my car.

* * *

For the second surprise today, Ricky was still at home by the time I got back there from work. He was still in the then, sitting on the couch in his Calvin Klein boxer shorts and wife beater, playing a game of football on his PlayStation when I walked in the house. And like always, he was on his cell phone too, ripping somebody a new asshole.

"Look, I don't give a fuck what you do! Or how you do it! Just as long as my shit come back diesel!" I overheard him saying.

Now to my understanding, Ricky couldn't be talking about nothing else but his damn drugs. Every week around this time, he's flipping out on whomever he got cooking his coke up.

I remember back when Ricky used to cook his coke up himself, when we first got together. He wasn't big time back then. All he could afford to buy was a couple of ounces. If the price was right, every now and again he could jump up to 4 ½ oz. Ricky thought he was on top of the world when he graduated to that Big 8 status.

Those were the times when I used to sit back and watch him measure out the coke and the cut on the eyes. Ricky used to work it out by acting like he was a real chemist or something. He even taught me how to cook that shit up, but it was strictly for just-in-case purposes only.

When he finally ended his conversation, I was in the kitchen eating a slice of cake I baked about a week ago, and that's when he decided to call my name.

"Yo Kira, bring me one of them Red Stripes outta the refrigerator."

I wanted so badly to tell him to drop dead, but

I ain't go there with him. Like a nice wifey, I got him a cold beer and took it to him.

"You make some money today?" he asked me after I handed him the beer.

"A little. Why?"

"Just asked."

"What, you gon' give me some?"

Ricky didn't answer my question. All he did was laugh like I had said something funny. "You the one wit' all the dough," he finally replied.

"I can't tell. 'Cause I ain't the one 'round here driving an eighty-thousand-dollar whip."

"Oh, you can get one. Shit, I ain't stupid! I know you got some dough stashed."

"Yeah, in my bank account. And that ain't nuttin' to be calling a stash."

"Yeah. Tell me anything," Ricky said, trying to turn his comment into a joke. And like a good girl, I didn't feed into the game he was trying to play. I just brushed it right off my shoulders 'cause I knew right off the bat he was testing me. The truth was, he knew for a fact I'd been stealing his money. That's why he moved his shoebox somewhere else. But it was okay 'cause I knew this house like I knew every shoe I had in my closet. So, I will find it.

"Did you check the mail box yet?" I asked him.

"Yeah. But, wasn't nuttin' in there but a Victoria's Secret order book."

"You sure that was it?"

"Yeah. Why?"

"'Cause I'm waiting on a letter from Nikki."

"Well, it wasn't in the mailbox. Maybe it'll come tomorrow."

I fell down on the couch beside Ricky and let out a real loud sigh.

"Damn, what, ya tired or something?"

"Yeah. I am," I responded sarcastically.

Ricky didn't respond because he was getting his ass tore up playing the *GameDay 2004* game. I sat back and watched him play, like I always did. He loved the attention. Sometimes, when I was in the mood, I'd be his cheerleader since I looked better than them little tramps that cheer during halftime. After watching him play two more games, I became restless and demanded more space on the sofa. That way I could catch a quick nap.

Ricky moved over and I snuggled into the spot of the couch I was already sitting on. I tucked my legs behind Ricky's back and dozed off.

I woke up about thirty minutes later when I heard the doorbell ring. I just lay there and pretended to still be asleep so I wouldn't have to get up and answer it. Of course, my magic worked like a charm because after the second ring, Ricky got up to see who it was.

"What's up, nigga!" I heard a familiar voice say.

"Nuttin', son. Just getting ready to blaze up one of these dutches," Ricky replied.

"I'm just in time then," the familiar voice spoke again. That's when I realized it was Brian.

Now my first reaction was to straight flip out on him about how he was playing Nikki, but I layed low. I knew for a fact that if I said something out the way to him, Ricky was gonna jump in it and tell me to mind my business. So, I kept my mouth shut and lay there. They headed into the kitchen, probably 'cause I was in the den.

I heard Ricky offer Brian a Red Stripe, but Brian turned it down. "Nah. I can't mix that shit with this smoke. I'll be real fucked up, then," I overhead Brian say.

"Mo' fo' me then," Ricky responded. Then they started puffing and passing. Between puffing the smoke and sipping on the beer, Ricky went straight into conversation mode with Brian. By his tone, I could tell this conversation was getting ready to get serious. And since he left the TV on back here in the den, I eased up off the couch and turned it down a few notches just so I wouldn't miss a word they were about to say.

"I'mma need you to get wit' everybody today," I heard Ricky say, "'cause a lot of shit gon' change in about the next couple of days."

"What's up?" Brian asked him.

"Well, since that shit happened wit' Nikki, we gon' have to close down all the spots and put everybody in new ones."

"Where you gon' put them at?"

"I got a couple of places lined up. So, all you gotta do is get word to everybody that after they run out of work, to just let Pam come and scoop up the dough, 'cause she ain't gon' be carrying the re-up. And then let them know to take everything outta the houses and wait for you to call them wit' the new address."

"What about Pam?"

"What about her?"

"Are you gon' put her in a new spot too?"

"Yeah. Everybody's moving."

"You think this is a good idea?"

"Yeah. 'Cause we got a lot of money circulating right now, and I would hate for them narcos to intercept that, especially since we got the Spanish connect going strong again. They wouldn't be too happy about all that heat 'cause remember, most of the dough is going to them anyway. Ya feel me?"

"Yeah. I feel you. But let me ask you something . . ."

"What's up?"

"You think Nikki talking?"

"Nah. I don't. But, you can never be too sure 'cause like I just said, we can't stand no mix-ups."

"So what you want me to do about the work we just got today?"

"We gon' have to sit on it for a day or two. At least until after the move."

"But that's gon' hurt us, since it's the first of the month."

"I know. But, we gotta do it."

"What you think gon' happen wit' Nikki's case anyway? Do you still think the Feds gon' pick it up?"

"I don't know. It's kinda hard to say."

"Well, just say they done already picked it up. At any time they can tap every one of her conversations right from the jail. That way, they can find out who she's running for. And believe it or not, that's how a lot of niggas get jammed up. Running their fucking mouth over the phone. And I ain't gon' lie, that's one of the reasons why I don't accept her calls. I just feel like she might slip up and say something stupid. And then that's when I'mma be a statistic," Brian said, getting a little annoyed by the thought.

I, on the other hand, continued to lie back on

the couch and eavesdrop. And after hearing Brian trying to diss my cousin by putting a lot of crazy shit in Ricky's head, it really started to piss me the hell off. It took a lot outta me not to get up and go in the kitchen and straight flip out on the both of them. But I didn't. Instead, I remained quiet just so I could get some more information outta them clowns.

Ricky and Brian continued talking for about another hour, trying to iron out all the details about their plans to shift their business venture. Now what I didn't want to hear from their conversation was when Ricky stressed to Brian how that "if any mo' problems come up wit' any of the spots, then it's got to be eliminated."

Now the word "eliminate" could've meant anything. But I did know that when Ricky said eliminate, it meant to do something to somebody.

Now, I got the chills when he talked like that. Besides fucking around on me, knowing he was gonna do something to hurt somebody really bothered me. But, it did go along with the type of business he was in, which was why I tried to stay out of it as much as possible. Nikki was my only concern right now, since those two clowns couldn't care less.

Their main concern was how much money they could make and how many hoes they could fuck in the process.

After Brian left, I got up off the couch and headed to the bathroom. When I was coming out, Ricky was on his way back in the den, probably to finish getting his ass kicked playing that football game.

"You get enough sleep?" he asked me.

"No. Not really," I told him and went in the opposite direction.

I did this to get away from him as quickly as possible. As bad as I wanted to go back in the den to lie down, this was not the time. So instead, I went on up to my bedroom, where I knew I could get me some space.

Going Against Da' Grain

Everything seemed to be getting together since Nikki got into better spirits and Mr. Shapiro felt good about the outcome of the case. Until I got a call this morning on my cell phone. I recognized the number from my caller ID, so I answered it.

"How you doing, Mr. Shapiro?" I asked after placing the phone up to my ear.

"Where are you?" he wanted to know.

"En route to my shop. Why?"

"Because we need to talk."

"Do you need me to come to your office?"

"Well, I'm not going there any time soon. But. . . ." He tried to continue, but I cut him off.

"What's wrong?"

"I just got a call from the U.S. Attorney's office."

"Okay. And?"

"Well, I spoke with one of the attorneys there by the name of Karen Miller. And she just informed me that she's about to take over Nicole's case."

"So, what does that mean?"

"It means that after tomorrow, Nicole's case will be certified as a federal case."

"What!" I said in a way to let Mr. Shapiro know I was not happy about anything he had just told me. I knew right then and there shit was getting ready to get really ugly. Especially when Ricky got word about it. And since Brian put that crazy shit in his head about the Feds, I knew he was gonna want me to cut all ties wit' Nikki. But that wasn't gonna happen, at least not while I was living and breathing.

"Is there something you can do about it?" I asked Mr. Shapiro.

"No, there isn't. Nine times out of ten, when the U.S. attorney's office takes over a state case, then it's usually because they have some very strong evidence."

"So, what you think gon' happen now?"

"I can't say. But, I do know that the U.S. attorney wants Nicole to talk."

"Wait. You mean tell on who she was working for?"

"Yes. That's exactly what I mean. And the reason why they want her to talk is because they know, without a shadow of a doubt, that those drugs she was carrying belong to somebody they're probably investigating."

"What'll happen if she don't tell 'em?"

"Well, if she's convicted, she'll face a minimum of ten years in a federal prison."

"Ten years!" I shouted.

"Yes. I'm afraid that's the status of federal sentencing guidelines."

"Is there anyway she can beat this?"

"Right now, her chances are slim to none."

"So, you telling me my cousin is gon' do ten years in the Fed joint?"

"If she doesn't cooperate, she will."

Listening to Mr. Shapiro, I was beginning to believe everything was going downhill. I didn't feel any sound of hope in his voice. The reality of "the shit is about to hit the fan" began to sit in my mind. The thought of Nicole's case going federal gave me the chills. And to know the Feds wanted her to talk, wasn't gonna make a lot of people happy. But the sad part of all this was that I was gonna be put right in the middle of it.

"Does Nikki know about any of this?" I asked the attorney.

"No. But my secretary has scheduled an appointment for me to see her tomorrow."

"Well, she's supposed to call me later on tonight. So, I'mma tell her what's going on."

"Do you think that'll be a good idea?"

"Yeah. I think so."

"Well, let me ask you this."

"Go 'head."

"How would you classify the people Nikki was working for?"

"What you mean?"

"What I mean is, are they dangerous people?"

"Why you asking me that?"

"Because I need to know who we're dealing with."

"Well, I don't know what to tell you," I said sarcastically.

"Do you know the people Nikki's involved with?"

Before I answered Mr. Shapiro's question, I took a deep breath because I didn't know what to say. I figured that if I told him a lie, then it would probably hurt me somewhere down the line. And if I told him the truth, then that would probably hurt me, too.

Before I could make up mind, my cell phone started beeping. I told Mr. Shapiro to hold on and I took the phone away from my ear to see who was beeping in on the Caller ID. Come to find out, it was Ricky sending me a text message. It said, "Call the barbershop." I got back on the phone with Mr. Shapiro and told him I had to call him back.

"Okay. Call me back by seven o'clock."

"Alright, " I said and then I hung up.

Ricky rarely used his text message system with me, so I kinda figured something must've been wrong. Instead of calling him from my cell phone, I stopped off to this pay phone like a block up the road, since it was the first thing I seen.

Luckily I had some change in my car, 'cause normally I didn't. After I stood there and listened to the phone ring about five times the owner, Trey, finally answered it.

He was probably on the other end talking to his baby mama, 'cause he usually didn't let his phone ring too long before answering it.

"Ultimate Cutz!" he said.

"Hey, Trey," I said.

"Who this?" he asked, sounding all leery.

"It's me, Kira. Is Ricky still up there?"

"Yeah, Ma. Hold on," he told me.

Within two seconds Ricky was on the phone. "Yo, Kira," he said.

"Yeah. "

"Where you at?"

"I'm by the mall, why?"

"Which one?"

"Military Circle. Why?"

"'Cause, I need you to come scoop me up."

"What's wrong?"

"Look, please don't ask me any questions right now. Just hurry up and getcha ass down here to the barbershop."

"A'ight," I replied and sighed as I hung up the pay phone.

Once I was in my car and back on the road, I began to wonder what was going on and why Ricky wanted me to pick him up from the barbershop. My mind started racing about eighty miles a second. Then my heart started beating real fast. I couldn't help but wonder if Ricky had already known about the Feds picking up Nikki's case. Then it dawned on mc—that's probably what had him acting all crazy. As I began to pull up in front of the barbershop, Ricky made himself front and center and wasted no time by hopping in my car.

"Come on, let's go," he instructed.

"Where we going? And where is your car?" I snapped at him as I put my foot on the gas pedal.

"It's in the shop getting a new paint job."

"So, why you couldn't call me and tell me all this instead of sending me a text message?"

"Because I need you to do something for me. And instead of telling you what it was over the phone, I preferred telling you in person."

"So, what do you want me to do?"

"Well, first of all, I want you to take me and drop me off at the gambling spot. And then I need you to take this dough and put it in your safety deposit box." Ricky continued with his instructions as he pulled a very big manila envelope outta the inside of his jacket pocket.

"How much is in here?" I asked him after stuffing the envelope into my handbag.

"It's twenty grand in there. So, make sho' you put it up right after you drop me off."

"I will. But why you want me to put your money in my safe deposit box? I mean, why you ain't sticking it in one of the safes we got at the house?"

"Because, I'm getting ready to switch shit up! And from now on, once a week, I'mma give you some dough to put in the deposit box. And it's not gon' be for spending, either."

"I ain't gon' mess wit' your money."

"Good! 'Cause it's gon' be for a time when I can't get to my other money."

"What you mean, when you can't get to your other money? Is everything all right? I mean, do you know something I don't?"

"Look, all I'm saying is that I'm trying to stay out here on the streets as long as possible. And to do that, I gotta prepare for emergency situations 'cause one day, I might have to leave the country. And when I do, my dough gotta be straight." Ricky explained and then he exhaled deeply as he watched the cars that passed us.

I continued to drive in the direction of his favorite hangout spot. On the way, I couldn't get up the nerve to bring up Nikki's case. I just felt like now wasn't the time. Besides, I wanted to see where Nikki was gon' go wit' it first, which was another reason why I had to hold out just a little longer from telling Ricky.

After I let Ricky off, I pressed on to the bank and did what I had to do wit' Ricky's money. But, before I placed that big old envelope into the box, suspicion started killing me. I pulled all the money out and counted it. Just as I had suspected, there was more than twenty Gs in that envelope. Come to find out, he had double that amount in there, which threw me for a loop. I mean, he knew how nosey I was. So why would he lie and tell me one thing when it was another? He was probably testing me to see if I was gonna come back and tell him how much was really in there. I wasn't gonna fall for his games, though. I'mma play stupid wit' his ass like I always did, and let him think he got another one over my head.

Cut From A Different Cloth

My day was completely thrown off track. Everybody was pulling me in all different directions. I finally decided not to go into work at all today, since I had a lot of shit on my mind. I wasn't gonna be able to function, so I called my clients and rescheduled their appointments. Everybody was pretty understanding, which was good. I picked up a take-out order from Pargo's and headed on to the crib. It was around six something when Nikki called me. I was watching Judge Joe Brown when the phone started ringing.

"What's up, Kira?" Nikki greeted me.

"Hey, girl," I replied in an offbeat manner, which was why Nikki asked me, what was wrong.

"I'm just tired." I told her.

"Did you work today?"

"Nah."

"Well, why you so tired?"

"Because of all this shit that's going on."

"Don't tell me Ricky acting up again."

"Nah, it ain't him. It's about your case."

"What's wrong now!?" Nikki asked.

"Your lawyer called me today and told me the Feds is picking up your case."

"They what!" Nikki yelled through the phone, and then she got quiet.

I knew right then and there, she was about to break down because having the Feds pick up her case was what she was dreading. "But why?" she finally said.

"Because they want you to talk."

"Talk about what?"

"They want you to tell them who shit you was carrying."

"So, what happens if I don't?"

"They gon' try to give you ten years," I said in the calmest way I knew how. Even though, I knew Nikki wasn't ready to hear what I had just told her, I knew she needed to know. That was the least I could do.

"Did Mr. Shapiro say he could stop them from doing that?"

"Well, if you wanna know the truth, I don't think Mr. Shapiro can do anything. But he did tell me he was coming to see you tomorrow. So, ya'll can talk about this."

"If he can't do shit to help me, then why is he bringing his ass down here?"

"Nikki, please, calm down."

"I can't, Kira. I can't!"

"Well look, I'mma come see you tomorrow night, so, we can talk about this some more. A'ight?"

"Alright."

"Okay. Getcha some rest and do some praying, 'cause I think we can use some blessings right about now."

"I do that every night."

"Good. Now, wipe your tears away and hold your head up."

"I'll try." Nikki responded between her sniffles.

Before Nikki's time was up on the phone, I called Brian on three-way for her but as always, he wouldn't answer his phone. He knew it was Nikki using my three-way, 'cause I didn't have a reason to call him. And if Ricky wanted him, he'd use his cell phone or two-way to get in touch wit' him. But I thanked God that Nikki finally got the hint and stopped asking me to call Brian. It was the best move she could've ever made.

By the time I reached the jail to visit Nikki, I only had fifteen minutes left to sign in. I wasted no time by flashing to the deputy my ID and telling him who I was there to see.

Nikki was escorted down in about five minutes. I couldn't believe it but when I laid eyes on her, she smiled at me. I rushed up to the glass partition and picked up the phone. "What's up, girl?" I said smiling.

"Hey."

"You look like you picking up some weight."

"Trust me, I haven't."

"Your hair is cute. Who braided it?"

"This girl in here name Shelly."

"Is she gay?"

"I think so."

"Well, then, you better watch out," I advised Nikki as I smiled at her. "Because she's probably got plans to turn your ass out!"

"She can give me some head if she wants to. But trust me, I won't be doing her."

"Well, you better be careful then. 'Cause I heard a lot of chicks on lock throw their guns like niggaz!"

"Well, I guess I'm gonna have to keep that in mind, just in case she tries to come at me."

"I think that'll be a good idea." I began to giggle and then I said, "Did you get to talk to Mr. Shapiro today?"

"Yeah. "

"What did he say?" I wanted to know.

"Nothing but that the U.S. Marshals gon' be transferring me outta this jail real soon."

"Where he'd say they gon' take you?"

"He doesn't know. But he said it could be anywhere between Suffolk, Virginia Beach and Chesapeake, since all three of their city jails got government contracts to house federal prisoners."

"Did he say anything else about your case?"

"Nothing but that I needed to consider talking to the U.S. Attorney about what I know."

"And what did you say?"

"I told him I would let him know."

"And why would you tell him that?"

"Because, I'm not sure what I want to do. That's why."

"Well, I don't think telling on Ricky gon' get you a lesser sentence. And even if it did, I know once you open your mouth, shit gon' get real ugly."

"What you mean by that?"

"Look, Nikki I love you like you're my sister. But if and when Ricky finds out you snitched on him, he gon' have something done to you."

"Are you serious?"

"Yeah. I'm dead serious. And I can't let that happen."

Nikki laughed at me like I said something funny. "You gotta be kidding!" she asked me again.

"No, I'm not" I told her in the most sincere way I knew.

Instead of commenting, Nikki put her head down. I knew she was on the verge of crying. It was her nature. But what could I do? I had to be up front wit' her about what was gon' happen if she flipped the script on my husband. Besides, in this game, when you told on one person, you'd end up telling on someone else. That's when shit would get really ugly. So, to prevent all that nonsense from happening, I felt like I had to nip this shit in the bud right now. "Nikki," I said.

"What?" she replied as she lifted her head backup.

"I know I ain't telling you shit you wanna hear. But trust me, it's for your own good And not only that, but what am I going to do while Ricky's locked up?"

"When did you start caring about what happens to him?"

"That's not the point."

"Then what is it? 'Cause, I need some answers, being as though I'm the one on lock."

"But, it's not going to be like this for long." I started telling Nikki.

"Well, you tell that to the judge," Nikki replied, as the tears fell.

Before I could respond to Nikki's comment, the female deputy who escorted her down to see me, came back and told her visiting hours were over. "Call me later," I told Nikki, but she didn't respond. All she did was hang up the phone and walk away. This, of course, stunned the hell outta me. I went home and waited up almost all night for the phone to ring. But she never called.

Ricky came home about two o'clock in the morning and made a whole lot of noise trying to take his clothes off in his closet. By the time he got in the bed, I was fully awake and could smell at least ten bottles of Corona on his breath. And then he tried to get close to me. I moved my body a little in the opposite direction of him.

"You up?" he asked me.

"I am now."

"Well, can Daddy get some head?"

"Why didn't you get some from one of your hoes?"

"Now, why would I do that when I gotta wife at home?" Ricky replied, slurring his words.

"Yeah. Whatever!" I kept my back to him and didn't utter another word.

He must've caught the hint that shit wouldn't be jumping off in our bedroom tonight, 'cause he was sound asleep about three minutes later. Unfortunately I was unable to do the same and that was because Ricky's cell phone kept vibrating every other damn minute. I got really frustrated by it. I got outta bed to cut it off but when I looked for the power button, I noticed the word "duplicate" flashing on and off. I scrolled down to the menu option and found out what number was blowing up Ricky's phone.

The name keyed in below it was "Cinnamon." Now, she must have been a new one. Somebody Ricky done added to his harem, and probably another one of his hoes, which of course got me a little pissed off. Just when I was about to press the power button, her number started ringing his cell phone off the hook again.

Now it was three-thirty in the morning, so what could this trick have possibly wanted other than a late night fuck? To get the answer to my question, I answered the phone.

"Hello," I said, but didn't get a response. So, I said hello again. That time, she said something.

"Can I speak to Ricky?" she asked in a low and childlike tone. I guess that was supposed to be her sexy voice.

"He's sleep. Who is this?" I tried to be nice as I could 'cause, if I came off nasty, she'd probably hang up on me. And that's what I was trying to prevent

"His friend."

"Okay, friend. I know you gotta name."

"It's Cinnamon."

"Hi, Cinnamon. I'm Ricky's wife."

"I know who you are."

"Oh, you do?"

"Yeah. Ricky told me he was married."

"Well, what else did Ricky tell you?"

"That's it."

"Okay, since you know who I am, won't you tell me how close you and my husband is?"

"We're pretty close."

"Oh really?"

"Yeah."

"Is that why you're calling him this time of night?"

"I'm only returning his call from earlier."

"And when did he call you?"

"It was about an hour and a half ago."

Before I could say another word, my body got real warm. It felt like my blood was starting to boil. I took a deep breath and tried to hold my composure for dear life. "Look," I said to her in a bold way, "I'mma just cut to the chase. Are you fucking my husband, or what?'

"Are you?" Cinnamon asked sarcastically.

"He's my husband ain't he?" I snapped back.

"Look, I ain't trying to get in a fussing match wit' you. All I'm doing is trying to speak wit' Ricky. Now, since you say he's sleep, then I'll call him later."

"Wait, before you hang up. Are you gon' answer my question?"

"What question?"

"The 'are-you-fucking-my-husband' question!"

"Yeah! We're fucking! Why?"

Wait! Hold up! No this bitch didn't just tell me she's fucking my husband! What a low blow. And she hit me hard with that shit, too, 'cause, soon after she said what she said, a huge-assed knot appeared right in my stomach. I felt sick, just like that. So, what could I do? Nothing. Here I was, on the phone wit' a chick named Cinnamon, and I didn't know shit about her. I didn't even know how she looked. All I knew was that she was fucking Ricky. Boy, what a world we lived in.

"How long ya'll been fucking?" I finally asked her.

"We had been seeing each other for about a year and a half now."

"What!"

"Yeah."

"So, you don't care he gotta wife?"

"Why should I, when his money is long enough to take care of both of us?"

Here this chick went again, coming off at me with another low blow. I couldn't think of nothing else to do but go off on her ass. "You know what? You are one nasty bitch! And you got plenty of nerves, too. But, go 'head and keep fucking Ricky. I'm giving you permission."

"I don't need your permission, if I ain't got it all this time."

"Yeah. Keep it up, you smart-ass hoe! Just remember, I'm his wife! And when the shit boils down to it, everything's in my name."

"I already know that! That's why I'm gon' live the life wit' him as long as I can."

"You know what, bitch?" I tried to fire back but before I could get anything else outta my mouth, she hung up. So you know I was furious. But, why be mad at her? It was him. Ricky was the slimy bastard out there running around wit' his pants down, like his mind was going bad. And to think I defended his ass earlier when I was talking to Nikki. But it was all good 'cause, I was done with letting this nigga make a fool outta me. This shit had been going on long enough. After I took two deep breaths, I threw Ricky's cell phone down on the floor and took my ass to the guest room to get some sleep. Because if I would've stayed in the room with him another second, I probably would've tried to set his ass on fire.

Change of Heart

It was about eight o'clock in the morning. And I knew I had to hurry up and get to the shop in time for my nine o'clock appointment. But, I also knew I couldn't leave the house without screaming on Ricky first.

He crawled his slimy ass outta the bed around eight-thirty. And when he opened his eyes, I was the first thing he saw. "Why you looking at me like that?" he asked, as he rubbed and blinked both of his eyelids.

"I talked to your bitch last night!" I told him, as I stood at the foot of the bed wit' my arms folded.

"What bitch?"

"Cinnamon, nigga!"

"Cinnamon?" Ricky said, as if he didn't know whom I was talking about.

"Don't play stupid! You know who the hell I'm talking about."

"Baby, I swear I don't know no Cinnamon." Ricky started pleading.

"Well, she sho' know you. And she told me ya'll been fucking for over a year now."

"That bitch lying! I am not fucking her. Don't believe that shit!"

"Don't believe that shit?" I yelled out loud. "But, I thought you ain't know who the hell she was?"

Ricky jumped outta bed and stood up in front of me wit' nothing on except his boxer shorts. He grabbed me by my arms and put on the most sincerest expression he could come up wit'. "Ma," he said, "you know how bitches are! Don't feed into that shit she told you."

"Why you lie?" I asked him.

"Lie about what?" he replied looking dumbfounded.

"About know who she was."

"Because, I knew you was gon' act like you doing now."

"Get off me!" I said to Ricky and snatched my arms away from him. "'Cause, you ain't shit! Always lying about all them hoes you done fucked around on me wit'!"

"Kira, she is lying!"

"That damn girl ain't lying! So, shut up! Trust me, I already know ya'll been screwing about for over a year and a half now. And just the thought of it makes me sick to my stomach," I yelled and swung my right fist at Ricky at the same time. "What you trying to get her pregnant too?"

"Nah, baby!"

"Fuck you! I ain't cha' baby! But, that's all right! Payback gon' be a mutha! You bastard!"

Once I aired out all my anger and frustrations at Ricky, I left the house. I knew I wasn't in no mood to do anybody's hair today. But, I also knew I needed something to take my mind off of what I was going through wit' Ricky. My shop was the place to do it.

My stylist Sunshine was already there when I came. She was curling one of her clients when I walked through the door.

"Anybody called me?" I asked.

"Nope. But, your nine o'clock just came and left. She did say she was coming back though."

"A'ight," I said and walked straight back to my office, which is in the back of the salon. The instant I closed the door and sat down in my chair, I bawled my eyes out like a baby. 'Cause after all these years of being married to Ricky, I finally realized the burdens that come along wit' being his wife have become too heavy to carry. And this was strange behavior for me. Because when Ricky does his dirt, I'll normally let it roll off my back. But meanwhile I was wallowing in my drama, Sunshine came barging in my office. "Girl, you alright?" she asked me the moment she saw me.

"Yeah. I'm fine," I replied as I began to wipe away my tears.

"You sure? 'Cause, I heard you crying from the washbowl area."

"Yeah. I'm sure," I told Sunshine, trying to convince her. Because on the flip side, she'll be the last chick I tell my damn business to. Quiet as it's been kept, I know she wants to fuck wit' Ricky. And I know this because, she done told another one of my stylist here that shit, which of course got back to my favorite stylist Rhonda. And if something is said 'round here about me or my man and Rhonda knows about it, oh trust me, I'm gon' know about it too.

So you see, Sunshine's ass ain't to be trusted. That's why hell would have to freeze over before I tell her, I'm going through problems wit' my man. And boy, I know she would love to hear that.

"Well, you don't look like you're alright." She pressed the issue.

"It's just my cousin's situation is weighing me down. That's all." I lied and told her.

"Oh, girl. I thought you were having man problems."

"Nah. I don't get those problems very often," I replied attempting to confuse her and throw the skank bitch some disappointment.

Sunshine rubbed my back and threw on a fake smile. "Well, pull it together! 'Cause your nine o'clock appointment is back."

"Okay. Tell her I'll be wit' her in a few minutes."

"A'ight," she said and then left my office.

It took me about ten minutes to get myself together and fix my make-up. I had to make sure I was up to par before I made my appearance. I couldn't risk none of these chicks up in here trying to get into my business. It would ruin the business relationships I had with my stylists. Plus, the shop was doing too well to have something like this ruin it. No way. I couldn't let it happen. So, I picked myself up, dusted myself off and then I walked outta my office with the biggest smile I could muster.

Halfway through the day, I started feeling a little better. One of my Christian customers, by the name of Janet, came through for a roller set. She was a very gifted and spiritual woman. Every time she came by, she made it her business to say something uplifting to me while I rolled her hair at my station. For some reason or another, this visit with her was different. She had no intentions of getting her hair done because the minute she walked through the doors of my salon, she grabbed my right arm and quietly asked if she could speak to me privately. I obliged and escorted her into my back office.

"What's wrong Ms. Janet?" I immediately asked her after I closed and locked the door behind us.

She proceeded to take a seat in the chair right before me and I took a seat on the corner of my desk facing her. That's when she placed both of her hands in mine and looked intensely into my eyes. She began saying, "The Lord has laid you heavily on my heart. And just so you know, I'm not here to dig into your personal life. But, I am here to deliver God's message."

I braced myself to fully retain everything Ms. Janet was about to spill into my lap; my heart started racing really fast. I knew right off the bat what she was about to tell me. I used to go to church faithfully when I was growing up, so I was familiar with how God could talk through people. And for her to come at me the way she did, I knew it couldn't be nobody else but the Man upstairs. So, I gave her my undivided attention.

Ms. Janet started reciting different scriptures and telling me how much love God has for me. Then she said, "Kira, it has also been revealed to me that there's a huge cloud looming above you. And because of it, you've been put in a compromising position. So, God wants to help you." She smiled at me. I kinda smiled back at her, but at the same time my eyes got a little watery. Ms. Janet noticed it that instant. That's why she stood up and hugged me, even as she assured me that God had my back. Even though I already knew this, having someone who knew so little about me to say the same thing seems to always give a person a tad bit more hope.

Immediately after she helped me wipe a few of my tears away, Ms. Janet grabbed my hands again. This time she instructed me to bow my head as she bowed hers.

From the moment she began to pray, I began to feel tons of weight lifting off me. I mean, it was like God was literally relieving me of all of the drama I had in my immediate circle. What made matters so much better was that I wasn't afraid of crying.

After the prayer was over, Ms. Janet sat with me for about fifteen minutes in an effort to pull me back together. The last thing I wanted to do was stir up a whole lot of suspicion about why my eyes were puffy. With Ms. Janet's help, we eliminated all of that. But, in the end, there was always one person in every group who'd find a way to poke their nose in your business. When I returned to the shop after walking Ms. Janet out to her car, I overheard Sunshine whispering to her client, "I wonder what that was all about?"

I stopped in my tracks and said sarcastically, "Does it even matter?"

"No, not really!" Sunshine snapped back and then she mumbled something under her breath.

"Are you sure?" I pressed. At this point, I was seriously tired of her mess.

Sunshine retorted, "Look, it ain't all that serious!"

She pulled off a pair of latex gloves and she instructed her client to follow her to the washbowl. For the rest of the day, she and I managed not to pass any more words and business continued as usual.

Now while I was unlocking the front door to let my last client out, I noticed a couple of crackers sitting in a dark blue undercover car. They were parked on the other side of the street, looking right in my direction.

The shit scared the hell outta me, too; but I knew exactly what they were out there for. I played it off like I didn't see them and gradually began to pull the door's miniblinds down, then turned the "open" sign around to the "closed" side.

Once I had done that, I became a nervous wreck. I believe I was probably feeling the same way Nikki felt when they were getting ready to arrest her.

What puzzled me was why they were outside watching my shop? Were they out there for me? Or were they out there waiting for Ricky to show up?

I did not know the answers to any of those questions, and I wasn't in too much of a hurry to find out, either. I gathered my things and walked out to my car. I avoided eye contact the whole time. Once I was in my car, I exited the parking lot with caution. I also tried getting a quick look at the license plates to see if it was a government vehicle, but it was too dark to see.

I headed up Virginia Beach Blvd. to catch highway I-264, off Witch Duck Road. It didn't surprise me that those two white men were still behind me, which was why I wanted to call Ricky bad as hell. However, I was too afraid to use my cell phone. I felt like if they knew where I worked, then they either had my car bugged or all my phones tapped. Instead of making the phone call, I put my foot down harder on the gas pedal to pick up the speed.

I was driving up Virginia Beach Blvd. doing sixty miles per hour. I believed it was enough speed to try and maneuver my car out the sight of them crackers following me. When my exit was about to come up, I waited until the last minute to make my turn.

My sudden move was to throw them off. And to my surprise, it did, 'cause when I looked in my rearview mirror, I noticed that the white men were causing traffic to slow down, so they could cross lanes and make the right turn behind me. Now, when I saw this, I sped up some more and then I jumped onto the highway.

I also kept my eyes glued to the rearview mirror, to see if I was still being followed. But, the further I got ahead, the harder it was for me to see. This was because it was dark and all the headlights seemed to look the same. I decided to get off on the next exit, which was South Military Highway, going in the direction of downtown Norfolk.

A couple of other cars were trying to make the exit too, so I sped up a little bit just so I could get off in front of them. I continued driving up Military Highway until I decided to make a turn onto Indian River Road. I drove about two more miles until I noticed there wasn't a car following in my direction, which made me feel not as scared. I drove a few more blocks and made a couple more left and right turns. That's when I noticed I was in the Berkeley section of Norfolk.

I pulled over at a BP gas station to use their pay phone, but somebody was already using it. I sat in my car and waited until he was done.

Now it took this idiot about ten minutes to get his ass off the phone after he saw me sitting in my car, waiting to use it. He must've figured I should've had a cell phone or two-way, being as though I was driving a 2003 whip. This, of course, was true, but I was having a dilemma.

I scrambled at the pay phone trying to figure out what I was gon' say to Ricky. If the Feds had all our phones tapped, I didn't want to let them know that I knew they were following me. So, instead of calling him directly, I called the one-eight-hundred number for his two-way and had one of the reps to send him a text message to call me at the pay phone. But, after sitting there for almost an hour, I realized the pay phone didn't even allow incoming calls. So, what was I to do? that's when I decided to call the one-eight-hundred number back. This time, I sent a message that told Ricky to meet me at the Waffle House in downtown Norfolk, because we needed to talk.

It probably took me about five minutes to get downtown. When I pulled up to the restaurant, I noticed there were only two people being waited on. That was enough for me, so I decided to sit in my car once I found a parking space. My other reason for staying in my car was so that I could watch my surroundings.

While I sat and waited, my cell phone began to ring. I looked at the Caller ID, but whoever was calling me had their number blocked out. Now, who would block out their number? I mean, it's not like a whole bunch of people had my number. So, who in the hell could it be? That's when I realized that it could be one of them crackers, trying to find my whereabouts. But I wasn't stupid. As far as I was concerned, they didn't have to ever worry about me using this phone again.

My phone finally stopped ringing after about twenty rings. I turned it off immediately after it stopped. That's when my mind started racing. I wondered if it could've been Ricky. Or, it could've been Brian, trying to get a message to me from Ricky. But it was too late. The phone had already stopped ringing. I laid my head back against my headrest and continued to wait for Ricky to show up.

After the first hour went by, I started getting worried again. It wasn't like Ricky to ignore any of his text messages. I mean, that thing was like his lifeline. There was never a time where he didn't have it with him, or had it turned off. So, why was he not responding to my messages?

I waited another hour for him and then I decided to leave. But, where was I going to go? I was too scared to go home, 'cause them crackers might be there waiting for me.

There was nowhere else I could go but to a hotel. So, that's what I decided to do.

Drug Money

I finally found a hotel I felt comfortable staying in. It was in the ritzy part of Chesapeake. I knew I would be fine after I got myself together mentally.

I kept my cell phone off in my pocketbook since I had no use for it. Besides, who could I call? Not Ricky, being as though he was missing in action. And not only that, but if I did manage to speak to him, who knew who would be listening in on our conversation? I couldn't risk them crackers finding out where I was. Luckily, I'd made a few hundred bucks at the shop, 'cause, I couldn't risk using my credit cards, either.

After another hour of me forcing myself not to pace the floor another step, I sat down on the bed and turned on the TV. The eleven o'clock news was on, so there was no question what time it was. Before I knew it, I was off to sleep.

The shit that went on earlier with them crackers must've weighed heavily on my mind, 'cause

I didn't sleep very long. I woke up about three o'clock in the morning and wondered what was going on out there in those streets. My thoughts began to turn in fast motion. I couldn't help but think about what was gon' happen next. I mean, it wasn't like I had a choice, like normal people. I lost my right to make choices once I got involved with Ricky. I didn't care about the "what ifs." All I cared about was what his dough could buy me. The expensive clothes and jewelry were all that mattered to me.

And being as though he was handsome, with a big dick, only made things better. Especially since I was just coming outta the beauty academy and needed some fringe benefits. Ricky offered me a helluva bonus package. I remember the first day we met. We were both at the Roger Brown's Sports Club in P-town, watching the NBA playoffs with our friends. Me and my girlfriends were at our table, sipping on some margaritas, when our waitress came over to tell us that a few guys, who she noticed was spending a lot of money, wanted to know if they could sit with us. I told her to tell them, yeah. About two minutes later, Ricky and three of his boys walked up. Brian was one of the cats with Ricky, and the other two were two cats that went by the name of Sam and Black. Both of them were on lock right now for drugs, but they were doing their bid up north in New Jersey.

After the initial hook-up through our waitress, phone numbers were passed and history was made. And, of course, I let Ricky take me out to dinner. Plus, I fucked him that same night. I thought I had played myself by doing that but, being as though I whipped this pussy on him, he didn't seem to mind it at all. Once the wheels started spinning, I got a big-assed diamond ring, money to open a beauty salon, and a nice wedding at my grandmother's church. Now, here we were! Well, here I was, sitting in my hotel room, hiding out from the fuckin' white man. Not knowing what was gonna happen the second I stepped foot outside this building was the part that would torture you. I hated the feeling. I thought of nothing else to do but close my eyes in hopes of falling back to sleep. It worked, because when I opened my eyes again, it was light outside. It was seventhirty in the morning, according to the clock on the TV. Without thinking twice, I jumped on the hotel phone and dialed Glen Shapiro's cell phone number. I felt like he would be the only person who could help me at this moment.

"This is Mr. Shapiro," he answered.

"Hey. This is Kira," I said anxiously.

"Hi, Kira. How you doing this morning?"

"Not too good." I sighed heavily.

"What's going on?"

"I'm not sure. But right now, I'm staying at a hotel because I was too scared to go home last night."

"Why?"

"Because, I saw two white men sitting outside my salon. And then, when I got in my car to leave, they started following me. So, I started driving real fast and got away."

"Who were the men following you?"

"I think it was a couple of Feds."

"And why do you think that?"

"Because you're the one who told me they

wanted Nikki to give them information about who she was working for."

"Well, are you in any way connected to her case?"

"No."

"So, why would federal agents be following you?"

"I was hoping you could tell me that."

"I'm sorry, but I don't have the answer."

"Well, could you find out what's going on?"

"I don't see why I can't."

"Well, I'm at the Wesleyan Hotel out in Chesapeake. So, call me when you hear something."

"What's your room number?"

"Room 312."

"Alright."

"Thanks for doing this for me."

"Don't mention it," Glen replied and then we both hung up.

I was still kind of puzzled as to why Ricky never answered any of my messages. I called his lawyer to make sure he wasn't locked up. I figured if anybody should know where Ricky was, it would be Mr. Robinson. He answered his cell phone on the second ring. "Hello," he said.

"Hi, Mr. Robinson. This is Kira, Ricky's wife."

"Hey. How you doing?"

"Not too good."

"What's wrong?"

"Well, first of all, I'm looking for my husband. So, I was wondering if you've heard from him?"

"No, I haven't."

"Okay. This is not good."

"What's going on?"

"Well, last night I noticed two white men, who I ain't never seen before, sitting outside watching my salon. And when I got in my car to leave, they started following me. But somehow, I got away."

"How were they dressed?"

"I couldn't tell. But they were driving a dark blue or black colored Ford."

"Did they look like detectives?"

"Kind of. That's why I tried calling Ricky to let him know what was going on. But, he never got back wit' me."

"Where are you now?"

"I was too scared to go home last night. So, I checked into the Wesleyan Hotel."

"Okay. Sit tight and let me make a few phone calls. What room are you in?"

"Three-twelve."

"Alright. Stay by the phone."

"Okay," I told him and then we hung up too.

As I sat and waited for both phone calls, I picked up the menu from the table and ordered me some room service. I wasn't all that hungry, but I knew I needed to put something on my stomach. I decided to try the seafood omelette with a cold glass of orange juice. It sounded good to me. And within fifteen minutes, that bad boy was there. After I tipped the room service guy, I sat down to eat. But before I could get into it real good, the telephone began to ring. My heart started beating real fast, but I didn't let that stop me from answering it. "Hello," I said.

"Hi, Kira. This is Mr. Shapiro."

"What you find out?"

"Well I just got off the phone with one of my contacts over at the Federal Building. And I was informed that there are only three major drug investigations going on in this immediate area. Your salon was not listed as one of their hot spots."

"So, who in the hell were those men sitting outside my shop watching me?"

"It could've been some local cops, or a couple DEA agents."

"But why?"

"Can't say."

"Well, what you think I should do?"

"Are you doing anything illegal?"

"No. I mean, all I do is go to work every day and come home."

"You say you're married, right?"

"Yes."

"Well, what does your husband do for a living?" Mr. Shapiro asked me.

Now, how in the hell was I going to answer this question? Was I supposed to lie, or what? I mean, if I lied, then how was Glen going to help me and my problem? But, if I told the truth, then I could also be making matters worse. So, I elected not to answer his question altogether. "What does my husband have to do wit' this?" I asked.

"Well, I'm only trying to help you figure out why these people are watching you. Because if you're not doing anything illegal, then someone very close to you is. So, if this is the case, then that gives them leverage to investigate those around the person they're trying to build a case against."

"Do you think I should go home?"

"I don't see what's stopping you."

"But, what if they arrest me?"

"They shouldn't. Unless you're doing something you're not telling me."

"Oh, trust me! I ain't doing nothing!"

"Okay. Well, you got my number. Call me if something comes up."

"Alright. Thanks."

"Don't mention it."

I got off the phone with Mr. Shapiro, sat back on the bed and began to wonder all over again who those men were. Even though I was told it wasn't the Feds, it still didn't make me feel any better. As far as I knew, it could be anybody with a badge trying to lock my ass up, too. So, I still needed some answers.

Mr. Robinson called me back about an hour later. I damn near had a heart attack waiting for him to call. "So, what you hear?" I anxiously asked.

"I got some good news and some bad news. Now which one do you want to hear first?"

"Give me the bad news first."

"Well, I haven't been able to find out who was following you. But, I have spoken with your husband."

My heart almost jumped outta my chest when Mr. Robinson told me he spoke to Ricky. I got happy as hell. "When?" I asked him.

"Just a few minutes ago."

"Where is he? And what did he say?"

"Well, he said he's out of the area. But, he'll be back later on tonight."

"How did you get in touch wit' him?"

"I called his cellular phone."

"I did, too, but, he didn't answer any of my calls."

"Well, he said he's going to call you after he gets to where he's going."

"Did you tell him about what happened to me last night?"

"Yes, I did."

"And what did he say?"

"He told me to tell you that those people are harmless, so there's nothing to worry about. And he'll be home later tonight to explain everything to you."

"That's it?" I asked in a sarcastic manner.

"I'm afraid so."

"Okay. Thanks, Mr. Robinson."

"The pleasure is all mine."

After I got off the phone with Mr. Robinson, I started dialing Ricky's cell number, because I was furious. I could not believe that I was around here about to have a panic attack, and this bastard was outta town, having himself a fuckin' ball. And then, on top of that, he refused to answer all my damn calls. As the phone started ringing, I got really eager to curse his ass out. But again, this bastard refused to answer his phone.

I slammed the phone down, 'cause I was mad. I mean, really to a point where I could cut his throat if he came walking through my hotel door right now.

I thought of nothing else to do but gather my things and go home. So, home was where I went.

Married To Da' Game

Driving up the street to my house felt kind of weird. I was somewhat scared that somebody might be watching me. But I didn't see any unfamiliar cars parked near my house, so I felt kind of relieved. Ricky came home about eleven o'clock. And boy, was I in a foul mood. He must've sensed it, because he started explaining the minute he saw me watching TV in the den.

"I know you mad," he started running off at the mouth. "But, I can explain everything."

"I'm listening." I said in a very low tone and giving him the nastiest grit I could come up with.

"Well, first of all, them guys that was watching you was just a couple of dudes who work for this Russian cat I be fucking wit' from time to time."

"Why were they watching my shop?"

"Because, it's just something they do when I get fronted a big load of they shit. They just making sho' they're protecting their investment."

"But, what the fuck I got to do wit' it?"

"Look, Kira, they just making sure I ain't gon' run off wit' they shit. That's all."

"That's all?!" I screamed. "Ric ,, do you know how petrified them muthafuckas made me? And then, when I tried to call you about it, you don't even answer your fucking phone. Now, what kind of shit you on? I mean, you're carrying me like you do them niggas in the street."

"Nah, baby it ain't like that."

"Then, how is it?" I asked as I stood up in front of him. "Tell me, 'cause I need to know."

"Look, a lot of shit is about to change. So, just bear wit' me and I promise I'll take you anywhere you wanna go when all this is over."

"I don't wanna go on a trip!"

"Then, what do you want?"

"I want outta this fuckin' marriage. I want outta all this bullshit you keep dragging me through."

"So, you telling me you want a divorce?"

"Yeah. That's actually what I'm saying, 'cause, you don't give a damn about me. All you care about is what's in them damn streets."

Hearing me expressing myself and almost crying, Ricky grabbed me into his arms and held me really tight. "Get off me!" I yelled.

"I ain't gon' let you go until you stop talking crazy."

"I ain't talking crazy. Everything I'm saying is real."

"Look Kira, I'm not divorcing you. So, you can let that idea go back where it came from. But, if you want me to give you some space, then I'll leave for a few days."

"And go where? To be wit' that bitch, Cinnamon!"

"Let's not go there again."

"Why not? I mean, she was probably who you

was wit' last night. That's why you ain't answer none of my fuckin' pages."

"I didn't even get your pages."

"You're a fuckin' lie!" I snapped at him and broke away from his grip.

"I ain't lying. My battery went dead last night. That's why I ain't get none of your text messages."

"How fucking convenient!" I said and left him standing in the den, while I headed up to our bedroom.

As I began to walk up the steps, Ricky came running behind me. "Don't come behind me!" I yelled.

But he refused to listen. He was on my heels. And the minute I tried closing our bedroom door, he pushed it back open. "Stop tripping, will ya?" he yelled back.

"Could you just leave me alone?" I screamed once again.

"I'm not. So, you might as well deal wit' it."

"Don't you think I'm tired of dealing wit' your shit?"

"Look, Ma, I know shit ain't been going the way you want it. But, I promise you, it's gon' get better."

"Yeah. Yeah. Yeah. You been singing this same ole song since we been together."

"But now, shit is changing."

"Yeah, for you it is." I told Ricky and took a few steps backwards.

"Okay, I tell you what. Give me a week to handle everything that's going on. And then, I want us to go somewhere in the mountains, so we can try to work this thing out."

"But, I'm not in the mood for that! Don't you get it?"

"So, what you in the mood for?"

"Right now, I just want you to leave me alone."

"A'ight. I'mma leave you alone. But, don't go to sleep, 'cause, I'm coming right back."

After hearing this jackass tell me he was about to leave, I wanted so badly to ask him where was he about to go. But, I refused to let down my guard. I acted as if I didn't care, even though I did. And on his way out, Ricky tried to kiss me on my forehead, but I moved my head away from him. He caught the hint and left.

I ain't gon' lie, because the moment he left, I wanted to cry my heart out. But I couldn't. I felt like I had to make myself be strong 'cause, it was becoming clearer by the day that this nigga wasn't concerned about nobody but himself, his money and his hoes. Those were the main reasons why our marriage wreaked so much havoc. And the fact that Ms. Janet came out of the blue and advised me to rid myself of the demons that controlled Ricky, was confirmation that I had to make some severe changes in my life. So, that's what I was going to do.

The next day I went down to the jail to see Nikki. She was surprised to see me after what had happened on the last visit. She made the comment, "I can't believe you came all the way down here to see me."

"Is that why you ain't been calling me?"

"Did you honestly think I was going to call you after that performance you put on the last time you came to see me?"

"Look, never mind that! I was on some 'protect my man' type of shit that day. But today, I'm going to set the record straight."

"What's up?"

"I came down here to tell you to do whatever you gotta do to get yourself up outta here."

"What brought this on?" Nikki asked me, giving me a puzzled look.

"I'm just tired, Nikki, that's all."

"So, what done happened now?"

"Girl, just a whole bunch of mess. I don't know where to begin."

"I hope it ain't behind another chickenhead this time."

"Well, yeah, you know there's always gotta be one of them in the picture. But, it's something deeper than that. That's why it's time for me to start doing me. And since you gotcha self tied up in all this bullshit behind my husband, I want you to start doing you, too."

"But, do you realize when I tell them who stuff I had, they gon' wanna know everything: from down to how I met him and who he's working for?"

"I know that. But, you can't tell them what you don't know."

"Yeah, you're right. But, I know everything else, like where his spots are and whose running them."

"Too late. He done already closed them down."

"When did he do that?"

"He met up wit' Brian right after you got locked up and told him to shut them down. And all I know is that they moved every last one of his spots somewhere else."

"So, Brian is still his flunky, huh?"

"You know that ain't gon' change."

"Well, he gon' get some of this shit I'm getting ready to dish out, too. Since he wanna do for everybody else except me."

Nikki and I continued talking about what was about to pop off. We knew shit was 'bout to get ugly, and a lot of people wasn't gonna be too happy about it, either. It wouldn't surprise me if Ricky got some of his henchmen to show their faces after the word got out. So, what I'd have to do was get a plan into motion for myself. According to Rule #5 in the *Hustler's Manual*, whoever got caught dirty and had to do some time, no matter how much time it was, was forbidden to rat out anybody in the crew. Niggas got killed behind shit like that. And if the person snitching didn't get dealt with, then somebody close to them would. That's just how the game was. People say, if you live by the gun, you die by the gun!

A couple of days later, I got up with Glen Shapiro to work out some last-minute details before he headed out of his office to meet with the U.S. Attorney.

"Are you sure about this?" he asked me.

"Yeah. I'm sure," I replied after hesitating a little.

"I sense a bit of hesitation on your part."

"Well, to be honest, I am having second thoughts. But that's only because I'm afraid Ricky gon' do something really stupid."

"Like what?"

"Let's just say that whatever he do ain't gon' be pretty."

"Are you gon' need some protection?"

"Damn right!"

"Well, if the federal government assists you

with twenty-four-hour protection, you're gonna
have to move outta your house."

"I know that."

"So, do you have any money put away?"

"Yeah. A little."

"Good. Because you might need it."

"So, am I gonna have to give up my hair salon?"

"Yes, you are."

"Well, how am I going to do that? I mean,
that's my life."

"I'm sorry, Kira. But if you decide to help Nicole
bring your husband and his organization down,
you're going to have to leave everything you've
established behind."

"Everything!"

"Yes. Everything," Mr. Shapiro repeated.

I sat back in the chair and looked out Mr.
Shapiro's office window, which overlooked downtown Norfolk. I could see the entire city, almost.
I began to wonder whether or not I was ready to
give up everything I had built up, just like that.
Then reality sunk in and that's when I realized
how miserable I was living with the very man who
gave me anything I wanted. It wasn't nothing for
him to buy my home, my car and over a hundred
thousand dollars in jewels. Now, tell me, how I
could walk away from that?

Then again no one knew I had over three hundred thousand dollars stashed away in my safe deposit box. Plus, the money Ricky gave me to put in
there a couple weeks ago would put me over the
four-hundred-and-fifty-thousand-dollar mark. So,
I'd be straight when I did my disappearing act. But,
there's one thing I had to do, and that was move all
the dough outta that deposit box. Because if push

came to shove, Ricky would probably tell the Feds about the money he gave me, just to keep me from keeping it. I'd have to get on the move if I was trying to prevent that.

"It ain't nothing but material things. I'll be able to get it again," I finally said.

"So, are you ready?"

"Yeah. Let's do this."

"Okay, then. I need you to sign these documents, which state that you have consented to an interview, but only if immunity is granted."

"Did the U.S. Attorney tell you what day the meeting is gonna be?"

"No. Not yet. But I expect to get that after I visit with her today."

"Well, call me when you find out."

"I definitely will."

After I signed the papers, I headed back to my house. On the way there I began to think about what I had just committed myself to doing. Not to mention, there was no way I could reverse it. I was officially about to become a snitch, just so my cousin wouldn't have to do a ten-year bid in the Fed joint. How was I going to face Ricky, knowing in the back of my mind I was about to help Nikki set him up. Was I being grimy, or what?

I couldn't think of any answers to my questions. So I thought about how much Ricky had hurt and disrespected me throughout our seven-year marriage. This was the only way I could feel justified for what I was about to do. And it worked, too.

As I pulled up to the house I noticed Ricky wasn't home, which relieved me for a bit. I rushed inside and began to take inventory of the things I would be taking with me when it was time for me to make my exit.

I started off in my bedroom first, and discovered that I might have to do some re-evaluating. I mean, truth be told, I had some nice shit. Which made me realize that I wasn't about to leave any of my minks, furs or shoes behind. A lot of my shoes I probably wouldn't even be able to replace, being as though only a few of their kind was made. And after I began to pull items out of my jewelry box, I also realized that I had some hot-assed pieces. So, you know that shit was going with me. I wasn't about to see any other way.

My living room was my next stop, but the only thing I wanted outta there was my photo album collection. There was no way I would be able to replace them, either. By the time I had made my rounds around my whole entire house and sat down in the den with a bag of Lay's potato chips and some French onion dip, Ricky made his appearance.

"Baby," he yelled as he opened the front door, "where you at?"

"I'm in the den." I answered him with a mouth full of food.

Ricky came running. When he got good enough in my view, he whipped out two airline tickets. "Look, baby, see! I told you I was gon' make shit right!" he said trying to catch his breath.

"What are you talking about? And what is that?" I asked him, even though I already knew what it was.

"It's two tickets to Europe."

"Europe!"

"Yeah, baby. We going to Amsterdam. Everything is already paid for. And look, here's a picture of the hotel we gon' be staying in." Ricky pulled out a brochure.

I took a look at it, and then I looked back at Ricky. "The hotel is nice. But, why did you pick Amsterdam outta all places in the world?"

"Because, we've already been to Cancun and Puerto Rico. So, I just thought we should go somewhere different this time. And not only that, I heard weed over there is legal," Ricky continued with a smile.

"Yeah. I betcha did. That's probably the only reason why you wanna go there."

"Nah, it ain't."

"Yeah. Whatever!" I replied and handed him the brochure back.

"So, we gon' do this, right?"

"When is it?"

"I scheduled it for Valentine's Day, which is only two-and-a-half weeks away. So, you down?"

"I don't care," I said nonchalantly, trying to make it seem that I was still mad with him. But in all honesty, I was feeling real bad. I had my husband standing right in front of me with some airline tickets he just got for us to go outta the country with and I was about to play a major role in getting him locked up. Damn, that was real grimy!

"That's what's up!" Ricky said. "I'mma give you some dough a few days before we leave, so you can go to the mall and getcha self a few things. Okay?"

"A'ight."

"Well, here, hold on to the tickets. Put 'em up so they won't get lost. I gotta run back out for a minute."

"A'ight."

"You cooking tonight?"

"What you want?"

"Anything but chicken."

"A'ight."

"Well, I'mma call you when I'm on my way back."

"A'ight."

The minute Ricky walked out that front door, I felt the pressure lift from me instantly. But at the same time, knowing he was gonna be coming back in a couple hours kinda made me feel a little edgy. Pretending like everything was gonna be alright wasn't blending too well with my conscience. I had to convince myself that if I took this thing one step at a time, it would be over before I knew it, which was all I wanted.

Ricky called me like he said he would, which was right after Judge Joe Brown went off. I got up and went into the kitchen and once I decided to cook him a couple of salmon fillets on the George Foreman grill, it took me no time to do it.

I also threw on a pot of hot water, so I could boil a few cobs of corn; being as though that was one of Ricky's favorite vegetables. And it went real well with the salmon.

He came home about thirty minutes after he called me, which was perfect timing 'cause dinner was hot and ready. "Hmmm, it smells good!" I heard him say as he came into the kitchen.

But I didn't say anything. All I did was continue doing what I was doing, and that was fixing him a plate.

"Give me two of them corn on the cobs," he continued after he reached over and looked in the pot.

"Well, get the tub of butter outta the refrigerator," I told him as I pulled the corn outta the pot.

Ricky went into the refrigerator and got the butter. Then he took a seat at the kitchen table and waited for me to bring him his plate. I took a fork outta the dishwasher, placed it on the plate and handed it to him.

"Damn this shit looks good!" he commented.

"Thanks," I replied as I fixed my own plate.

"You talked to Nikki lately?" he asked with a mouthful of food.

"Yeah. Why?"

"What's going on wit' her case?" It pretty much sounded like a trick question, but I played it off and told him what he wanted to hear.

"She still might have a chance to get out of it," I finally said.

"How much is this costing me?"

"Ten large."

"Well, it's not that bad." He continued trying his best to make conversation. But before he could come up with something else to say, his cell phone started ringing.

"Yo, wuz up, son?" he said to the caller. "I'm in the crib. So, go 'head and park your whip."

He folded his phone back up and set it on the table.

"Any more salmon over there? 'Cause my man Russ is outside and he might want something to eat."

"Nah. I only cooked two filets."

"Well, make him a sandwich or something."

"He ain't come here to see me. So, you do it!"

"Oh, Ma, don't be like that. Russ is good peoples."

"I don't care!"

"Well, at least get him one of them Red Stripes in the refrigerator."

Not even a minute later, Russ came knocking on the front door. Ricky rushed to the foyer to open it.

"What's up nigga!" I heard Ricky say.

"Not too much," Russ responded.

"Come on in the den," Ricky told him.

As Ricky walked past the entrance to the kitchen, I got a quick look at this unfamiliar guy he called Russ. Russ was kind of tall and real ugly from a quick glance. But that NBA leather coat he had on was hot to death. I also noticed that he was carrying something in a Footlocker bag. It must have been some money he probably owed Ricky.

I hurried and got a cold Red Stripe from outta the freezer so I could be nosey.

"You wanna beer?" I asked when I approached Russ.

He looked up at me like he was mesmerized or something. And then I realized I was looking kinda sexy in the suede pants I was wearing. They made my hips sit out a couple more inches and made my ass look three times bigger than it was.

"Nah. I'm straight," he said.

"Yo, Russ. This my wife, Kira." Ricky introduced us. "Kira, this is my new business partner, Russ. He just got in from D.C."

"Hi, how you doing?" Russ said.

"I'm fine. Nice to meet you," I told him and then I made my exit.

On my way out of the den, I noticed Russ trying to get a look at my ass on the sneak tip, but Ricky was watching him like a hawk. Doing shit like that wasn't cool when you were doing business with the chick's man. I continued walking back into the kitchen, but, I wasn't too far that I couldn't hear what they were talking about.

Back in the kitchen, I sat in my chair to finish my meal. What was so crazy about it all, was that I couldn't think about nothing else but this Russ guy. I mean, it wasn't like he was cute or anything, because he wasn't. I thought it was his accent 'cause, he did sound like he was from South America, or the Caribbean, or something. And not only that, but he did dress nice and he smelled good, too. Stuff like that turned me the hell on. And since it was killing me to find out what he was doing in my house, I got really quiet so I could hear what him and Ricky were talking about.

"That shit you gave me was tight! Those niggas back in D.C. love it!" I heard Russ tell Ricky.

"I know. Them Russian niggas I fuck wit', they stuff is always on point. That's why I'm gon' need you keep doing what you doing. And before long, we gon' have the whole East coast on lock!" Ricky replied.

"Sounds good to me." Russ said, as I heard him rattle the bag. "Here's your dough."

It got quiet for a few seconds and then Ricky spoke. "Well, it looks like it's all here," he finally commented.

"Everyt'ing!" Russ told him in his accented voice.

Both Ricky and Russ continued talking for about fifteen more minutes, which was enough time for me to straighten up the kitchen and change into a pair of booty shorts. Ricky hated me wearing them around his company. I did it anyway, 'cause I knew it pissed him off. Now, before Russ got up to leave, I made it my business to be standing by the front door like I was trying to fix the lock on the doorknob. As Russ walked toward me; I made sure my back was facing him.

"What's wrong wit' the door?" Ricky asked me.

"The lock from the door knob is acting up," I told him.

"Wait, let me take a look at it," he volunteered.

"Oh, wait a minute. I got it. I think," I said quickly.

I twisted the doorknob a couple of times and then I pressed down on the lock really hard.

"Okay. Now, I got it." I moved outta the way of Ricky and Russ.

"Nice meeting you," Russ said to me on his way out.

"It was nice meeting you, too," I said.

"I'mma call you in a couple of days," Ricky told him.

"A'ight. Do that," Russ replied.

As Ricky stood in the doorway to watch Russ get in his car, I got a quick look at him from the living room window. The car he was driving was old and dented up. I could tell that it was something he drove around in when he was carrying food.

Driving old-looking cars like that was another way to prevent the narcos from pulling you over.

After Russ pulled off, Ricky closed the front door, which was my cue to get the hell outta the window. I would've been dead wrong to let Ricky catch me sweating that nigga, especially after I showed Russ a little bit of Ricky's property.

Nevertheless, Ricky never mentioned anything about what I was wearing. All he was concerned about was that money was rolling in and to keep it rolling, he knew he had to get more product out there. After he closed and locked the front door, he rushed right back into the den. And like his shadow, I was on his tail with twenty questions on my mind.

As I walked into the den, Ricky was shoving a Nike shoebox back into the Footlocker bag.

"Who is this guy, Russ?" I asked in a somewhat sassy way.

"He's just another hookup of mine. That's all."

"You sho'he ain't the police?"

"Nah. That cat is far from being a narco," Ricky began to explain. "Papi introduced me to him at the Christmas party that cat Bishop had a month ago."

"I don't care where you met him. You just better stop letting all these niggas know where you lay your head at!"

"Oh, nah. It ain't like that wit' that cat Russ. I mean, this nigga is large. I been to his crib and everything," Ricky told me. "His house is about the same size as ours. And he got this ole Spanish lady to come and clean his house three times a week!"

"Who cares?" I said in a tone like I wasn't interested. But truth be told, I did care. I wanted to know everything about this Russ cat, but I knew I wouldn't be able get any more information outta Ricky. Ricky was too smart for that. So, I figured I'mma have to do a little investigating on my own. I also knew it wouldn't be too hard to see Russ again, being as though Ricky was now dealing with him. So, I'll have my day.

Ricky ended up leaving the house after he threw the whole Footlocker bag into his big safe hidden under our bed and grabbed his car keys. It didn't take a rocket scientist to figure out he was on his way to this small apartment he's renting, since he kept saying "Time to make the donuts."

He used that apartment to cook and stash his coke. The only three people who knew where it was were me, Ricky and his aunt Sharon. And that's because the lease was in Sharon's name and she helped him cook and bag up his stuff.

Come to think about it, Ricky done had that hideout spot for about a year and a half now. Since then, they ain't had no problems with niggas breaking into it. Which was kinda good for him, considering all the other problems he has had with the local stick-up kids.

I, on the other hand, settled down in my bedroom and watched some TV until I fell asleep.

Game Time

Around ten o'clock the very next morning, Mr. Shapiro called me on my cell phone to give me the heads up about when me and Nikki were supposed to be meeting the Feds. When the call came through, me and Ricky were sitting at the kitchen table eating a plate of eggs and corned beef hash I had just picked up from the Denny's restaurant up the street. "Hello." I said.

"Good morning Kira. This is Mr. Shapiro."

"Good morning."

"I've got some information for you. So, is this a good time for you?"

"No, not really," I told him.

"Is your husband around?"

"Yeah." I answered, trying not to change the tone of my voice.

"Okay. Well, I'll tell you what. I'm about to go to court, because I have a case scheduled at eleven o'clock. So if you like, I could either call you back when I get to the office, or you can call me after five."

"It doesn't matter. Either way is alright with me."

"Okay, then. I guess I'll be calling you back after I get out of court."

"That's fine."

"Okay. Talk to you then."

"Alright. Bye."

"Bye."

After I pressed the end button on my phone and looked up, Ricky was looking straight in my face. "Who was that?" he asked in a serious tone.

"Oh, that wasn't nobody but Nikki's lawyer."

"What he talking 'bout?" Ricky pressed the issue.

"Nothing but that things wit' Nikki's case is looking up. And that he sent me a copy of her motion. So, he wanted to know if I had gotten it yet, and I told him, no."

"When is her next court date?"

"He hasn't set one yet."

"Why not?"

"Because he said he wants Nikki to go in front of a certain judge."

"Well, when you find out when her court date is, let me know so I can send one of my peoples down there witcha."

"And what they gon' do?" I asked.

"They ain't gon' do nothing."

"So, why you gon' send one of your flunkies wit' me? I mean, I've been doing fine all time."

"Well, damn! All I want them to do is find out what's going on, so I can be two steps ahead of them."

"What you think I been doing? Just sitting around, not saying nothing to you? 'Cause, if I recall, I've told you everything Nikki's lawyer done told me," I replied sarcastically.

"Well, okay. You gotta point! So, don't bite my head off."

Instead of making a comment I got up from the table to throw the rest of my food in the trashcan, since I suddenly lost my appetite. After that, I put my plate in the sink and turned to leave the kitchen.

"Now, I know you ain't mad over that?" Ricky said.

"Boy, leave me alone," I replied and headed on into the den. I just knew Ricky was gon' get outta his chair and follow me, but this time, he didn't. I guess things do get old. Which made me wonder whether or not he was onto what was about to go down.

But then again, if he did know, then why was he acting so calm about it? It just didn't make sense. And since I didn't wanna press the issue, I didn't say anything else about it.

Later on, around one p.m., was when I decided to leave the house for work. Ricky had already been gone for at least an hour or more. He hopped in the shower around eleven, got dressed, grabbed some dough outta his safe under our bed and left. He didn't even mention to me where he was going, which was kinda unusual. It was all good, though. Trust me, I wasn't gon' sweat it.

Now when I got to the shop, it was as packed as I'd expected. Everybody said their normal greetings to me when I came through the door, which always lifted me up, especially if my mornings start off bad, which has been kinda often lately. It seemed like everybody I came into contact with thought I had it going on, because of everything I had. And since I didn't discuss my personal life with them, they automatically assumed everything was good. But, I am trying to tell them about how everything that glitters ain't gold. They don't hear me, though.

So after I placed my coat and handbag in my back office, Rhonda popped in to have a chat.

"What took you so long to come to work?" She began to question me. "Oh, don't tell me. I know what it was." She started smiling. "You gotcha self a hot plate of dick this morning, huh?"

"Nope," I replied and smiled.

"Why you lying? I see it all over your face."

"Girl, trust me, I wasn't in no mood for dick this morning."

"So, what's up? You a'ight?

"Yeah. I'm fine."

"You sho'? I mean, you know you can talk to me."

"Yeah. I know. But, right now ain't the time. I'll keep that in mind, though."

"A'ight," Rhonda said and then we both hugged each other. "Oh yeah, let me tell you what happened early this morning?" Rhonda continued.

"What happened?"

"Gurrrl. . . ." Rhonda started, but I cut her off.

"Wait. Close the door first," I told her.

After Rhonda closed my office door, she went on to tell me what had happened. Come to find out, Sunshine almost got her tail kicked by the baby mama of this cat she was messing with named Kenny. Kenny was a known hustler from the Berkeley section of Norfolk. Hoes were on him like flies on shit, but Sunshine couldn't care less about them. Her main objective was to get whatever she could and go.

That's probably why Kenny's baby mama wanted to slap Sunshine around a little bit. Luckily somebody called the police and nobody got hurt.

"Well, what was Sunshine saying while all this was going on?" I asked.

"You know she was talking shit! But, she not once carried her ass outside them doors when the girl invited her out there."

"So, how did the baby mama look?"

"She was real cute. She was a little bit on the chunky side, though. It looked like she just had a baby."

"Oh, so I see why Sunshine didn't carry her ass outside. Shit, she probably would've gotten her ass kicked."

"I think so, too."

"So, what did the police say?"

"He just told that chick to leave and if she came back, she could get a trespassing charge."

"Anything else happen 'round here?"

"Nope. Not really."

"Well, let me get to my clients, then. 'Cause I know they are tired of waiting for my ass."

Both Rhonda and I got up from the chairs in my office. But before she opened the door to leave, she stopped and turned around to look at me. "Don't tell Sunshine I told you what happened today."

"You know I ain't gon' say nothing!" I assured Rhonda.

So as I walked over to my booth, I noticed Sunshine gritting at me from the corner of my eye.

I brushed it off 'cause, I knew she was trying to feel me out and see if Rhonda done already told me what happened to her. But, I was gon' be cool and act like ain't nothing been said because, whether she knew it or not, I had better things to be worrying about. And Sunshine wasn't on that list.

"Kira you got some of them white strips?" she so boldly asked me.

"Yeah. Why? You need some?" I replied just as nice as I knew how.

"Yeah." Sunshine started walking into my direction. I reached in my drawer and pulled out a handful of them strips and handed them to her. Sunshine came closer and leaned her head over to mine.

"I know Rhonda done told you about that episode of drama I had earlier," she mumbled into my ears.

Instead of putting Rhonda in the spotlight, I acted like I didn't know what Sunshine was talking about. "Drama!" I said, dumbfounded. "What was Rhonda supposed to tell me?"

"It was about this nigga I be getting wit' from time to time. But, I'm just so surprised that she ain't told you about it, since she was in your office for quite a bit of time."

"Nah. She ain't told me nothing."

"Well, I'll get witcha later and let you know what went down."

"A'ight," I said in my most sincere tone.

Sunshine walked back over to her booth. From time to time I noticed that she would glance over in my direction like she was searching for something. And quiet as kept, she wasn't stupid. She knew dag-gon' well that Rhonda had already done ran everything down to me. If she was to ever find out that was really the case, I believed Sunshine would run up on Rhonda and try to whip her ass, too. So, knowing that, I was gon' try my best to keep that on the hush-hush!

The crowd started dying out around seven o'clock that evening. Rhonda and two other of my stylists got outta Dodge about six. So, it was just me and Sunshine left. She had two people under the dryer and I only had one sitting in my chair. So, it was kind of quiet, even though we had the radio playing and the TV going strong.

Still and all, I was ready to get outta there but by the same token, I was not ready to go home. And since I had not talked to Mr. Shapiro yet, that only made things worse. Especially when I felt like I was in the dark about something and it was concerning my husband. After I finished styling my last client's hair, I got my things and headed outside behind her. As soon as I got on the road, I pulled out my cell phone and dialed up Mr. Shapiro.

He finally answered his cell phone after I let it ring about ten times.

"Hello," he said.

"Mr. Shapiro, this is Kira. I thought you were gon' call me?"

"Oh, I'm sorry. But, I've been really busy working on this other case I have."

"So, did you speak to the lady prosecutor yet?"

"Yes, as a matter of fact, I have."

"So, what did she say?"

"Well, first of all, I got her to give you and Nicole immunity. But, she wants to know everything you know."

"So, when is this meeting supposed to take place?"

"Early Friday morning, at nine thirty."

"But, that's the day after tomorrow!"

"Yes. I know that. So, you know what you need to do is get yourself together mentally. Because they are going to have a lot of questions for you. Do you understand?"

"Yeah. I understand."

"So, will you be ready?"

"Yeah. I guess."

"No. You can't be guessing. I need you to be sure."

"Don't worry. I'll be ready."

"Okay. So, I'll see you on Friday."

"Yep." I pressed the end button on my phone. Thinking about meeting with the federal prosecutor on Friday gave me the chills. Then I realized I was doing all of this for family. Plus, it was a way for me to finally get away from the selfish bastard I was married to.

When I pulled up to the house, Ricky's Benz was parked in the driveway, along with a very small rental car. I had to end up parking my whip on the street.

"Ricky, whose car is that, taking up my space in the driveway?" I yelled as I walked through the front door.

Before Ricky answered me, I heard footsteps walking from the kitchen in my direction.

"It's my rental car," he replied once we were face to face.

"What you need a rental car for?" I wanted to know.

"Because, I'm getting ready to make a trip."

"Where you going now?" I snapped.

"Me and Russ getting ready to run up to D.C."

"You just love riding to D.C., don't you?"

"Look, it's only a business trip. And not only that, if these niggas bite on this bait we 'bout to throw at them, we gon' be some rich muthafuckas real soon."

"When you leaving?"

"As soon as Russ gets here."

"So, he supposed to be leaving his car here?"

"Nah, he said he was gon' catch a cab over here."

"Well, how long ya'll gon' be?"

"We'll be back tomorrow."

Instead of commenting, I looked Ricky up and down, then shook my head in disgust as I walked away from him.

"What was that for?" he asked me.

As I began to answer him, the doorbell rang. "Who is it?" Ricky yelled.

"It's Russ," I clearly heard Ricky's friend say.

Ricky opened the door and greeted him. "What's up?!" Ricky said happily.

"Nuthin'. Just trying to maintain," Russ replied in his thick accent.

I was in the kitchen getting some juice outta the refrigerator by the time Russ came in. Ricky escorted him into the den and told him to chill until he was ready to leave. On his way, Russ peeped his head into the kitchen and said hello. I spoke back as he walked by. Then I just stood there with my back up against the kitchen sink, waiting patiently for Ricky to go upstairs and finish getting dressed; that way, I could slide on into the den and get more acquainted with this Russ cat.

I noticed the minute I walked into the den that Ricky had him watching the sports channel. It was obvious Russ wasn't that tuned in because the second I walked into the room, all eyes were on me. And all he could do was smile.

"Are you okay? I mean, can I get you something?"

"Nah. I'm good."

"Are you sure?"

"Yeah. I'm sure."

After he gave me the okay that he was fine, I took a seat on the other sofa, which was only a few feet away from him. "Are you watching this?" I asked him.

"Nah. Not really. You can turn it."

"Your accent is really thick. Where are you from?"

"I'm from Trinidad."

"How long you been living in the states?"

"For about five years now."

"Do you like it?"

"Yeah. It's cool."

"Do you go back home to visit sometime?"

"Yeah. Sometimes."

"Do you travel a lot?"

"Sometimes."

"So, who's going to do the driving today?" I asked as I tried desperately to make conversation.

"Both of us."

"Well, what does your woman have to say about you leaving her to go outta town?"

"Nothing."

"Why?"

"Because, I don't have a woman to question me about things like that."

"And why not?"

"I don't know."

"You got any kids?"

"Nah. But, I would love to have some," he replied. Which, of course, shocked the hell outta me. I mean, I couldn't believe a nigga like Russ didn't have any children. It was too good to be true. And not only that, I knew he had a lot of dough, so where was the wifey?

"How many kids do you want?"

"About four or five is good."

"Damn, you want a little league basketball team, huh?"

Russ started smiling. "Something like that. Do you and Ricky got kids?"

"He has some wit' former girlfriends. But I don't."

"Do you wanna have kids?"

"Maybe some day."

"Do you work?" His questions kept coming.

"I own a beauty salon."

"Ahh, that's nice."

"Yeah. But it can be a pain in the neck sometimes, though."

"Do you do hair yourself?"

"Yeah."

"Do you have a person there to do manicures?"

"Why, you gon' come by and support us?"

"I might."

"Well, here's my card just in case you decide to

come by." I took one of my business cards out of my handbag and handed it to him.

Russ and I talked a little bit more until Ricky came back downstairs and broke up the party. He gave Russ the cue that it was time to leave. Before Ricky walked outta the house, he kissed me on my forehead and promised he would call the minute he got to D.C. I knew it was a lie, 'cause he hated it when I knew his every move. I think it was a controlling issue with him. But, who cares? One way or another I'm gon' come out on top.

The very next morning I got a call from Nikki. She was real excited when she heard my voice. "I just got a visit from Mr. Shapiro," she told me.

"What he say?"

"He told me about the meeting we supposed to have tomorrow morning wit' the Feds and the prosecutor."

"Yeah. He told me about it, too."

"Are you ready for it?"

"If I ain't, I might as well be."

"Is Ricky home?"

"Nah. Him and this cat named Russ went to D.C. last night. He said he'd be back home today."

"Is he still fucking up?"

"You know he is. He ain't gon' change."

"Are you going to work today?"

"Yeah. I got about five or six clients coming in."

"Do I still have my job as your assistant when I get outta this place?"

"You can work there, but I ain't gon' be there."

"What you mean?"

"Didn't Mr. Shapiro tell you?"

"Nah. What?"

"Once we give them Feds all that info about Ricky and his crew, we gon' have to leave."

"Leave and go where?"

"Wherever they send us."

"So, we gon' be in a witness protection type of thing?"

"Yep."

"I can't leave my family!" Nikki said, getting all hyped.

"Please turn down your volume before one of them chicks in there hear you."

"So, what about my family?"

"What about them?"

"Are you telling me I ain't gon' be able to see them?"

"Nikki, this is some serious shit we about to do," I began to explain. "In these days and time, you can't snitch on somebody and expect to come outta jail and live like ain't nothing happen. People get killed behind shit like this."

"So, what you think we should do?"

"Listen, it's up to you. I'm doing everything because of you."

After I said what I had to say, Nikki got quiet. The statement I just made sent her into thinking mode. I sat back and waited for her to break the ice.

"Will I be able to visit them?"

"I don't know. You gon' have to take that up wit' those people."

Nikki sighed and then she said, "Look, I just wanna get outta here. So, as far as me wanting to be able to visit my family . . . well, I guess, I'mma have to cross that bridge when I get to it."

"Well, I guess I'll be seeing you tomorrow, then."

"I guess so."

"Well, call me later 'cause I need to get to the shop."

"Alright," Nikki said and then we both hung up.

Underground

"Who has my bumpers?" I yelled aloud for the whole shop to hear me.

"I got them over here," Rhonda said.

"Bring 'em here. I need 'em," I told her.

"You would think she'd have her own bumpers by now, wit' all that money she makes," Sunshine commented nastily.

"Won't you mind your business and worry about if somebody else's girlfriend gon' come up here to beat your ass for messing wit' they man!" Rhonda told Sunshine.

"Whatever!" Sunshine replied.

"Look, ya'll need to chill out! We are running a business here," I told them both.

Rhonda handed me my bumpers and went back to her station, while Sunshine took a smoke break. I continued perming my client's hair and after I was done, I took a break too. Instead of going out front with Sunshine, where I knew I would hear a lot of drama, I went into my back office and closed the door behind me.

I knew getting some quiet time to myself was

too good to be true because as soon as I sat down at my desk I heard a knock on my door.

"Who is it?" I asked.

"It's me, Rhonda."

I sighed because I really didn't feel like being bothered, but instead I told her to come on in.

"Close the door behind you," I told her as she entered into my office.

"Kira, I know you don't like when we be screaming on each other when clients are here, but, I couldn't help it. Sunshine has been fucking wit' me ever since I walked in here today."

"What's going on?"

"I don't know."

"So, you're telling me you haven't done nothing to her?"

"Yeah. I haven't done anything."

"Well, let me talk to her. I'll find out what's going on."

"Nah. Don't say nothing." Rhonda sounded all paranoid.

"So, what do you want me to do?"

"Nothing. I just wanted you to know what was going on."

"Are you sure?"

"Yeah."

"Okay. Well, I ain't gon' say nothing this time. But, if ya'll start up again, I'm gon' say something."

"Alright," Rhonda replied as she sat there in the chair across from me. Then she looked down to the floor.

"Is that all you wanted to talk about?" I asked.

Rhonda looked back up at me and that's when I noticed her eyes were watery.

"What's wrong?" I asked with concern, but Rhonda didn't say anything. I got up outta my chair to console her. As soon as I wrapped my arms around her, she broke down and cried. "Tony moved out last night," she finally said, between the sniffing.

"Why?" I wanted to know.

"Because, I found out he was screwing this other chick named Brandy. And when I asked him about it, he had the nerve to blow up about it, talking about if I don't trust him then ain't no need for him to be here. And that's when he packed up his shit and left."

"Did he say where he was going?"

"Nah." Rhonda continued to cry.

"Please stop crying," I told Rhonda as I continued to hold on to her.

"Kira, girl, I'm all messed up." Rhonda began to speak. "I was up all night crying wit' a big-ass knot in my stomach. And not only that, I ain't even had no appetite all day."

"Girl, I sho' know what you going through."

"Well, what you think I should do?"

"First, tell me how you found out he was messing wit' this chick Brandy."

"Because, my sister's best friend Avonne seen both of them going into one of them hotel rooms at the Holiday Inn in Hampton."

"Well, do you love Tony?"

"Yeah. Sometimes."

"Well, listen, I can't tell you what you need to do. But, I will say this out of love for you and your kids. And that is, no man ain't worth you getting all sick behind. Because if they screwed around on you once and you didn't put your foot down, then trust me his ass gon' do it again and again. You know I know!"

"But, I love him."

"I know you do. But ask yourself, who do you love more? Him or yourself?"

Rhonda went on and on about her problems with her man. And not once did I hear her tell me she was ready to leave him. She was my girl and all, but something had to give. After I decided that I had sat in her pity party long enough, I made up an excuse to get her ass outta my office.

"Look, wipe your tears 'cause, we gon' have to cut this short. I've got to use the bathroom," I lied.

"Alright." Rhonda started wiping her nose.

I got up and left first. About two minutes later she came out and walked back over to her station. I stayed in the bathroom, I know, for about twenty minutes, being as though that was the only place I wouldn't be disturbed. When I finally came out, I noticed I had a surprise visitor sitting in the waiting room.

My heart began to beat really fast but, I couldn't let my emotions show it. So, I took a deep breath and strutted my stuff to the front of the salon. As my appearance became more visible to my guest, he began to smile.

"What are you doing here?" I asked Russ.

"I'm here to patronize your salon," he said. "That is why you gave me your card. Right?"

"But, I give my cards out to everybody," I said with a humongous smile.

"Well, I'm using mine. So, can I get some service?"

"What do you need done?"

"I need everything," Russ said with a gorgeous smile.

"Please be more specific." I tried not to smile back.

"Okay," he said, as he cleared his throat, "I want my hair conditioned and my hands done."

"Well, I do have a nail tech on duty. But, what hair are you trying to condition?"

"I have a little bit." He continued to smile.

"You just want to give me a hard time, huh?"

"No. I just want you to massage my scalp, if that's alright."

I stepped back and thought to myself for a minute. If I didn't know any better, I could've sworn this Russ guy was trying to flirt with me. And the way he was talking to me, kind of turned me on. Then I realized I couldn't let loose. Not here. 'Cause these tramps were waiting to find out the dirt on me so they could go back and tell Ricky. I decided to be good just this time.

"I hope you know it's gon' cost you an arm and a leg for my services."

"Well, I just wanna let you know that I brought two arms and two legs wit' me, just in case."

I smiled and said, "Come on to the washbowl, witcha smart mouth!"

While I was prepping Russ for a wash and condition treatment, I noticed every eye in the shop was on me. I even saw Sunshine whispering to her client as she watched me from the corner of her eye. I didn't care, though. Sometimes it felt good to know you were always the topic of somebody's conversation. And to have them playing the guessing game, made it all the better.

"Lean your head back," I told Russ as I adjusted the water temperature.

"What is that you're wearing?"

"What you mean? My shirt?"

"Nah. I'm talking about your perfume. It smells good."

"Oh, that's Romance by Ralph Lauren."

"I like that."

"Yeah? Well, I like it too," I replied with a smile. "So, how long you and my husband been back from ya'll trip?"

"Umm," Russ started thinking, "We got back about two hours ago."

I looked over at the clock on my wall and it read three-thirty. "How did you get up here?" I wondered aloud.

"I drove myself."

"What you driving?"

"Does it matter?"

"No, not really," I explained, "but I just don't want Ricky to catch you up here."

"Why not? I mean, I'm only here to patronize your business. And anyway, I done already told him I was coming."

After hearing Russ's comment, I looked him dead in his eyes. In doing so, I felt kind of weird. It was like he was trying to hypnotize me with his eyes. Then it felt like he was casting a spell on me because the only way I was able to break his trance was when Sunshine called my name. "Yeah," I answered and looked into her direction.

"Can I use your spritz?" she asked.

"Yeah. It's in my top drawer," I told her and then put my focus back on Russ.

"Your hands feel good massaging my head, " he commented.

I didn't reply. But I did smile for him.

"How long you and Ricky been married?"

"He didn't tell you?"

"I didn't ask him."

"Seven years."

"Well, why don't ya'll have children?"

"I don't think I can have any."

"Who says?"

"Nobody. But it seems like every time me and Ricky tried, it never happened."

"It probably wasn't meant to be."

"Probably." I instructed him to lift his head up so I could dry his hair with a towel. "What about you?" I asked.

"What? Kids?"

"Yeah. "

"Remember when I was back at your house, I told you I ain't have none."

"Oh yeah, I remember!"

"Yeah, I bet you do."

"And what is that supposed to mean?"

"Nuttin'. I'm just messing wit' you."

"Okay. But, I know you gotta have a girl-friend."

"No, I don't."

"Yeah right!" I said, as I ruffled his head with the towel.

"No, I'm serious."

"Yeah. That's what they all say," I commented and then I instructed him to follow me to my station. After he sat down I said, "Do you want me to edge you up a li'l bit?"

"Yeah. And then I want you to spray some of that

good-smelling oil sheen right there in my head."
Russ pointed to the products on my stand.

I quickly conditioned and treated what little
bit of hair Russ had on his itty-bitty head. Once
I was done with trimming him up with the clip-
pers, I brushed him off and then I handed him
a hand mirror so he could get a better look at my
finishing touches. He began to form a cute little
smile, so I knew he must've liked it.

"Man if you can keep my head looking this,
I'mma have to trade my barber in for you."

I smiled back and said. "Yeah, I know I got
skills!" I removed the cape from around his neck.

"How much I owe you?" He asked as he
reached into his right pants pocket.

I grabbed his left hand. "Stop! Don't do that!"
I told him.

"Do what?" He answered as he pulled out a
phat roll of C-notes.

I tried desperately not to stare but since everybody else was watching him, I couldn't dare pass
up the opportunity.

"Here you go," he finally said as he handed me
two one-hundred-dollar bills.

"What you doing? It doesn't cost two hundred
dollars for a treatment and an edge up."

"I know that."

"So, what's up, then?"

"It's just a tip for good, quality service."

"Are you sure?"

"Yep. So, go on and buy yourself something
sexy to wear for your husband tonight."

"Are you being sarcastic?" I asked him with a
smile.

"You figure it out," he said in gangsta-type slang. And believe it or not, I got a kick out of it.

"How much time you giving me to do this?" I replied in a sassy tone.

"For you, Ma, I'mma let you take as much time as you want. But, don't keep me waiting for too long." He just gave me one of them looks like, *"Yeah, I want you! And I know you want me too!"* I mean, I was catching feelings for this nigga already.

Now here I was standing in the middle of my salon with a nigga I knew everybody in here would kill to have. But he wasn't interested in them. He wanted me. And the crazy thing was that I wanted him too. But, I couldn't act like I did, especially around these talking hoes. Half of them would have loved to run back to Ricky with some drama. So, I'd have to play this thing right. But first, I had to get Russ outside so I could keep everybody outta my conversation. "Come on, let me walk you to your whip," I told him.

On our way out the door, I caught Sunshine and her client out of the corner of my eye, whispering to each other as me and Russ walked by them. I wasn't gon' pay her ass no mind 'cause she wasn't doing nothing but hating on me. That bitch would have killed to be in my shoes. So, when Russ grabbed the doorknob and opened the front door for me, I walked ahead of him.

"Where's your car?" I asked, trying to get his attention off my ass.

Even though I didn't have eyes in the back of my head, I could read men's body language. The moment I walked by Russ, he got quiet. That's because he only had a couple seconds to concentrate on either how I looked underneath my jeans, or how his dick would feel by hitting my ass from the back. I just hoped that if I did ever decide to screw him, he didn't have no li'l dick.

"It's right there," Russ finally said.

I looked in the direction he was pointing and saw a small, beat-up car. I looked back at Russ and said with a smile, "That's cute, if you ain't trying to leave outta this parking lot."

Russ laughed. "I ain't as fortunate to ride in a Benz like your hubby."

"I ain't as fortunate, either." I replied as we walked toward his car.

"Look who's talking."

"What you mean?"

"I peeped out your whip while it was sitting up in your driveway. You ain't doing bad at all."

"What else you done peeped out?"

"It's too soon to say. But I'm sure you'll find out, if you want to."

"And what does that mean?" I threw him one of my sexy smiles.

"Just be patient. Time will reveal it."

"Is it good or bad?"

"Look, all I'm gon' say is that when I present it to you, I promise you ain't gon' look back."

"A'ight!" I told him as he hopped in the car and drove off.

Catching Feelings

From the moment Russ left, that's when I began to think of nothing else but him. I mean, the last time I felt like this was when I first got with Ricky. I knew from jump I was gonna have to put my creeping skills into overtime. Luckily, Ricky wasn't at home when I got in. I wasn't in the mood to see him right now. After I took me a hot, long shower, I hopped in bed and flicked on the TV. I laid back and started watching a good movie on the Lifetime Channel until my cell phone started ringing.

I didn't recognize the number, so under normal circumstances, I wouldn't answer it. But somehow, I felt I needed to answer this call.

"Hello," I said, putting on my sexiest voice.

"Was you sleep?" the caller asked me. After hearing the voice it kind of threw me for a loop. At first, it sounded like Russ. Then again, it sounded like Ricky.

Now, there was one thing I couldn't do and that was say the wrong name. Ricky would have flipped the script if I mentioned another nigga's name, especially the name of somebody who did business with him. So instead of answering the question, I threw a question back at him.

"Does it matter?" I said.

"Yeah it does."

"For who?" I asked, trying to play hard to get after sensing who it was.

"For me."

"Okay. But do you know what time it is?" I asked Russ.

"Yeah. I know. But, I figured this would be the best time to talk to you since your hubby ain't lying beside you."

"And how do you know that?"

"Because he's in the middle of a dice game."

"How you know that?"

"'Cause, I just left him."

"So, you be out there throwing away money too?"

"Every now and then."

"So, to what do I owe the pleasure of this phone call?"

"I just wanted to say good night."

"That's it?"

"Yep."

"Okay. Well, say it."

Russ must've thought my comment was funny, 'cause he broke out laughing.

"What's so funny?" I asked him.

"You," he told me.

"Well, I didn't mean to be."

"It's all love."

"Okay. But I'm still waiting for you to say good night."

Russ took a deep breath and then he said, "Sweet dreams."

"Good night," I replied.

As I was about to end the call Russ said, "Can I call you tomorrow?"

"Did you ask me could you call me tonight?"

"No."

"Well, there's your answer. And anyway, don't you think Ricky would have flipped the script if he knew you were chatting on the phone this time of the night wit' his wife?"

"Yeah, he would. But, if his wife wasn't in the talking mood, she would've hung up the phone a long time ago."

"Is that so?"

"I think so."

"Well, look, I'll tell you what, since this conversation is going in the other direction, I'm gon' have to call it a night. So, I guess that's a good enough reason for you to call me tomorrow."

"Sounds good to me."

"Okay, then. Night-night."

I turned my cell phone off the moment I hung up with Russ. And when I turned over on my side to go to sleep, I couldn't because once again, Russ was on my mind. All I could think about was how he tried to flirt with me at the salon earlier and how he looked at me. Truth be told, I was enjoying the hell out of it. And with Ricky acting up the way he's been doing all these years, I was starting to believe that I might be able to play a game of get-back. After an hour of reminiscing about Russ, I finally fell asleep.

* * *

When I got up the next day, I heard voices downstairs in the kitchen. One of the voices was Ricky's. I gave myself a chance to tune in to the other voice; that's when I realized it was Russ. Without thinking, I jumped out of bed and threw on my robe. Now, I knew I was about to piss Ricky off by coming downstairs in my night-wear, but who cared about how he felt? It's about me. As I walked down the stairs, my heart started pumping really fast. I knew it wasn't because of what Ricky was gon' say when he saw me; it was because I couldn't wait to see the reaction I was gon' get from Russ. And to make it look like an accident, I had to put on a front like I didn't hear another voice. So, when I got ready to go through the doorway of the kitchen, I called out Ricky's name.

"Ricky," I said.

"Yeah," he answered.

I walked through the doorway with a surprised expression "Oh damn!" I forced my act to work. "I ain't know somebody else was here." I began to walk backwards. I did it slowly so Russ could get a good look at me.

"Well, now that cha know it, you know what to do," Ricky replied sarcastically.

Before I was completely out of sight, I noticed Russ getting a quick look at me. He couldn't look at me too long, because he knew that it would be a straight-up case of disrespect for Ricky. To do it in Ricky's face ain't how the game was supposed to be played. On the other hand, my agenda for that morning was complete, so there was nothing else for me to do but to slip on some clothes and head out to work.

On my way out of the house, Russ decided it was time for him to leave too. I had already started driving up the street when I noticed Russ coming up behind me. It was no coincidence he had to leave not even a minute after me. I just hoped Ricky wasn't too bright that morning to figure it out. I guess Russ had the same thought in mind because instead of trying to get me to pull over, he turned off on another street. I was kind of disappointed that he didn't follow me. Then I realized that it was probably for the best, so, I continued on my daily path to work.

When I drove into the parking lot of my business, I noticed that there were not that many cars parked out front. In fact, I only recognized two of the four cars parked. Before I got outta my car to see what the deal was, my cell phone started ringing. Whoever was calling me blocked out their number but, this time it didn't bother me, so I answered it.

"Hello," I said.

"Kira, this is Shapiro."

"Hey. What's up?"

"Will you be available later today for a meeting with the agents and the U.S. Attorney?"

"Do I have a choice?" I asked and then sighed.

"Well yeah, but . . ."

"But what?" I asked in frustration.

"Look, Kira, these people are willing to give you immunity. And, of course, let your cousin get off scot-free. But in order for this to happen, you have to meet them on their terms."

"Yeah, I know. People can't go a day without throwing shit in the game!"

"What are you saying?" Mr. Shapiro asked.

I sighed again. "It wasn't important. What time are they talking about?"

"Three o'clock."

"But, that's just three hours from now!"

"I know I'm giving short notice, but, this meeting is very important."

"So, where do I have to be?"

"At the new federal building on Granby Street."

"I can't go there!" I snapped. "What if somebody see me?"

"Okay, I'll tell you what. Meet me at my office by two-thirty and that way, I could get you in the back entrance with me."

"A'ight," I said nonchalantly.

"So, this means you'll be there?"

Before I could answer, my cell phone beeped, letting me know somebody was trying to get through on my other line. I told Mr. Shapiro what he wanted to hear and pressed the flash button.

"Hello," I anxiously said after recognizing the number.

"You hungry?" Russ asked me.

"Why? You bringing me some something to eat?" I replied in one of my most notorious, sexy voices.

"Nah. But I can have it delivered to you."

"Where you at?" I so desperately wanted to know.

"Why?"

"Because I want to know."

"Well, it's a secret. So, just tell me what some of your favorite foods are."

Before I answered Russ's question, I thought

to myself a minute. I mean, it wasn't like I didn't know what to say. But knowing whether or not he was playing some type of game was kind of eating away at me.

"So, are you gon' tell me? Or am I gon' have to play the guessing game?"

I smiled at Russ's comment, which of course changed my mood from my last call from Mr. Shapiro.

"Hello. Are you there?" Russ continued.

"Yeah. I'm still here."

"So, what you working wit'?"

"Well, I love salads."

"What else?"

"And seafood."

"What kind of seafood?"

"Crab legs, fried oysters and shrimp."

"Is that it?"

"Well, I could go on but if I did, we'll be on the phone for I know, at least a couple more hours."

"Are you at the shop yet?"

"Yeah. I just pulled up."

"A'ight."

"So, what you saying?!"

"Just sit back and do what you do. You'll see."

"Okay. Whatever you say."

"A'ight."

I headed into the shop and immediately found out why there were only four cars parked out front. Rhonda approached me at the door.

"Where's everybody?" I asked her, as I looked around the shop.

"I thought you knew," Rhonda said.

"Knew what?"

"Sunshine moved into her own shop this morning."

"She didn't tell me anything."

"She didn't say nothing to you?"

"Nah."

"Well, everybody else knew."

"So, when did you find out?"

"Last night," Rhonda said. "She sho' acted like it wasn't a secret."

"Well, it sho' went over my head 'cause I didn't know anything." I walked over to my station.

Rhonda walked behind me and said, "I'm glad she gone if you wanna know the truth."

"Did she leave her booth rent?"

"Nope. But Penny and Tabitha did."

"Oh, so they went too?"

"Yep."

"What about Trina?"

"She called about thirty minutes ago and said she was gon' be a little late."

"Any of my clients called?"

"Nah."

"Has the mailman been here yet?"

"Yeah," Rhonda replied as she walked back over to continue rolling her client's hair.

"Where is it?"

"I put it in your office."

I closed the door to my office the minute I walked in. Then I started sorting out the mail. There were only three legal-size envelopes in the stack. All of them were pieces of junk mail and advertisement schemes, so I threw them all into the trashcan.

Meanwhile, the salon telephone started to ring. Rhonda answered it and about a second later, she yelled back to my office to let me know the call was for me.

"This is Kira. How can I help you?" I said the moment Rhonda hung up her line.

"Why you ain't answering your damn cell phone?" Ricky shouted very loudly.

"Because, I ain't hear it ring."

"How long you gon' be at the shop?"

"Why?"

"'Cause, I need you to do something for me."

"What is it?"

"I'll be by there later. So be ready."

"What is later?"

"I don't know. Just be ready."

"What if I'm in the middle of doing a client's hair?"

"Well, I'll call you when I'm getting on the road."

"A'ight," I said nonchalantly and hung up the phone.

By the time I came outta my office, Rhonda was giving her client some money so she could run an errand for her.

"What you getting ready to do?" I asked.

"I'm sending Paulette over to Alice Mae's to pick up my order."

"What you order?"

"I'm getting the barbecue chicken with potato salad and collard greens," Rhonda replied.

"Do you wanna get something too?" Paulette asked me.

"Nah. I'm alright."

"You sure? 'Cause, I ain't gon' be in the sharing mood when my food get here," Rhonda continued.

I smiled and said. "Rhonda, I ain't thinking 'bout you or your food."

"Good! 'Cause I am real hungry!" she commented.

After Paulette left to pick up the food, it was only me and Rhonda standing around like chickens with our heads cut off. Rhonda threw me a question outta left field. "Who was that guy that came in here yesterday?"

"Who? Russ?"

"Is that his name?"

"Yeah."

"So, what's up wit' him?"

"What you mean?" I said in a dumbfounded manner.

"Don't play stupid! I saw how he was looking at you yesterday."

"Girl, you was seeing things, 'cause, it ain't even like that wit' me and him."

"How ya'll know each other?"

"He's one of Ricky's friends."

"Well, Ricky better look out 'cause if he don't watch it, that Russ gon' snatch you right on up."

I sucked my teeth and said, "Me and Russ are only friends. That's it!"

"Well, it must be nice to have friends to come by and shell out hundreds of dollars for a conditioner treatment."

"Damn! You saw all that?"

"Girl, I try not to miss shit 'round here."

I laughed and said, "I see."

Rhonda was about to crack another one of her jokes about Russ, but her attention drifted to the front door. I looked too and saw this short guy coming through the front door, carrying a huge brown paper bag. "Can I help you?" I asked him.

"I've got a delivery for Kira."

"That's me," I told him and that's when he started walking toward me.

"What's in the bag?" I wanted to know.

"Some very hot food," he replied and smiled.

"Where is it from?" I asked as he handed me the bag.

"From the Light House."

"You mean to tell me ya'll deliver food from way down on the oceanfront to here?"

"I don't work there," the guy explained. "My man Russ ordered the food and told me to go pick it up and bring it to you."

I smiled. "Tell him I said thanks."

"A'ight," the guy replied and left.

I knew once the guy closed the door behind him, Rhonda was gon' start poking at me for some answers. I turned my back to her and started opening the bag.

"Oh don't try to turn your back now!" she laughed. "I knew I wasn't crazy!"

"What you talking about?" I asked, trying to sound dumbfounded.

But Rhonda wasn't buying it. She knew something was going on with me and Russ and she was gon' make it her business to find out. "Come on, now, Kira," Rhonda pleaded as she walked up behind me, trying to see what was in the paper bag.

"Stop holding out on me. I know you got some skeletons in your closet. Shit, we all do, if you want to know the truth."

I turned toward Rhonda and watched her take a seat in the salon chair right next to me.

"Well, I'm waiting!"

"You promise you ain't gon' say nothing?"

"Girl, spill it! You know I ain't gon' say nothing!"

"Damn, I don't even know where to start." I set the bag down on the plastic container that stored my hair products.

"Just start from when you first met him."

Before I started giving Rhonda all the details about Russ and me, I took a seat in the other salon chair. "Well," I began, then sighed. "I met him about a week ago when be came by my house to talk to Ricky."

"Okay! And?"

"And when we saw each other and talked while Ricky was upstairs, I guess we just kinda clicked."

"Do you like him?"

"I think so."

"Is he loaded?"

"I think go."

"What kind of car does he have?"

"I don't know."

"What you mean, 'you don't know?'"

"Because the couple of times I've seen him, he was driving this little dust buster."

"Well, that don't mean nothing. Niggaz drive shit like that all the time," Rhonda explained. "It keeps the police off them."

"Yeah, I remember when Ricky use to play that role."

"Yeah, me too! But, now you probably can't catch him in one," Rhonda said as she laughed.

"You're probably right," I replied before I reached for the paper bag.

"So, what did he get you?"

I pulled out and opened the aluminum containers that were packed neatly in the bag.

"Well, I've got a whole bunch of fried shrimp, with a salad. And he ordered me some big-ass Alaskan crab legs."

"Damn! They are big too," Rhonda commented as I pulled them out of the bag.

"I know!"

"Did they put a container of melted butter in your bag?"

"Yeah. They put two of them in here."

"Are you gon' be able to eat all that?"

"Nah."

"Good! 'Cause I sho' want some."

"Well, go in the supply room and get a paper plate."

As Rhonda got up to go to the supply room, Ricky walked through the front door of the salon. "Where is everybody?" he asked.

"Why?" I asked sarcastically.

"Because, I ain't never seen it so empty in here."

"Well, let me just say change is good."

"Is that so?" Ricky replied. He took a seat in the chair Rhonda had gotten out of.

"Yeah." I grabbed one of the shrimp and bit it.

"What you got there?"

"Why?"

"Because it smells good. That's why!"

"What does it look like?"

"I couldn't tell from the way you threw it in your mouth."

"Well, it's fried shrimps."

Ricky was getting ready to make another comment but when he saw Rhonda coming out from the back of the shop, he looked in her direction and said, "So, Rhonda, tell me how's life treating you?"

"Nuttin'. Just trying to maintain," she replied.

"Well, you sho' doing a good job of it."

Rhonda smiled at Ricky's comment. He looked back at me and said, "Come on. Let's go in your office."

I set my food back on the plastic container and followed Ricky into my office. I gave Rhonda the okay to help herself to the crab legs before I closed the door to my office.

The second after I closed the door, Ricky started blabbing off at the mouth about him getting ready to make a run out of town, and that he needed me to make a couple of trips to his aunt's house to pick up his dough and stick it in the safe deposit box.

"When am I supposed to do this?"

"What is today?"

"It's Friday."

"Okay," Ricky said and sighed. "You gon' have to make a pick up tomorrow night and Monday evening."

"How much money I gotta pick up?" I asked as I sat down on the end of my desk.

"Well, it's supposed to be fifty Gs each time. So, make sure you count it before you stash it."

"So, how long you gon' be gone?"

"Until Tuesday night."

"Where you going?"

"Me and Brian taking a trip down to North Carolina."

"For what?"

"For business. And that's all you need to know."

"You sho' you ain't going to see one of your hoes down there?"

Ricky got up from the chair and said, "Look, I ain't trying to hear all that."

"You never do," I snapped back.

Ricky reached for the doorknob.

"If you need some emergency money while I'm gone, take it from the dough you picking up from my aunt."

"Yeah. Whatever," I said with a sigh.

I followed Ricky out of my office and outside to his car. He attempted to say goodbye to Rhonda but she was in the middle of a conversation with her client, so she didn't hear him.

Outside at Ricky's car, I just stood there and watched him put the key in the ignition. He made no other comment to me, besides telling me he was gon' call me once he checked in a hotel. He and I both knew he wasn't gon' do jack! He knew he never called me. But I guess he keeps telling me that because it sounded good.

After he pulled off, I went back into the shop. "Girl, them damn crab legs are good as hell!" Rhonda commented the minute I closed the front door behind me.

"Well, did you save me some?"

"Yeah. But I ain't want to," she laughed.

I sat back down on the chair in my station and started eating my food. While I was tearing my crab legs apart, I couldn't help but think about Russ. I mean, the bottom line was that I was starting to like him a lot. What ate at me was not knowing whether or not he liked me back. For all I knew, Ricky could have been using Russ to set me up. Then again, I could be wrong. Since my heart said yes, I was gon' jump on the band-wagon to see where it was gon' take me.

"What you over there thinking about?" Rhonda asked me.

"Nothing really," I replied with a smile.

"Wait! Hold up! I know that look," Rhonda said as she walked back over to where I was sitting.

"What look?" I tried to camouflage my expression.

"You know what I'm talking about."

I smiled some more "No, I don't!"

Rhonda sat back down in the seat beside me and looked me directly in my face. "I know you thinking about the guy that sent you this food."

"No, I'm not."

"Kira, I ain't stupid. And anyway, you done already told me you like him."

"No, I didn't!" I said, getting excited. "Now, what I said was that I think I like him."

"What's the difference?"

"There's a lot of difference."

"Well, have you called and thanked him for the food?"

"Nah. Not yet. But, I will," I assured Rhonda.

It seemed like time was flying when I looked down at my watch and noticed it was two o'clock already. Luckily, I only had one client left and she was under the dryer. With thirty minutes left to burn, I decided to go ahead and call Russ.

And before he answered, I cleared my throat so I could put my sexy voice into overdrive.

"Hello," he answered.

"Thanks for the food."

"How was it?"

"It was real good."

"Did you save me some?"

"Yeah, if you want some crab legs."

"Nah. I'm straight." Then it got really quiet. I blurted out, "Are you going down south wit' Ricky?"

"Nah. He ain't said nothing to me about it."

"Have you met Brian yet?"

"Nah. Why?"

"It's nothing, really. I mean, that's who he said he was going outta town with."

"Well, he didn't say anything to me about it."

"Are you going back home this weekend?"

"No. Why?"

"I was just asking."

"So, what you gon' be doing while Ricky's gone?"

"I don't know."

"Well, can I take you out to dinner or a movie this weekend?"

Right before I answered Russ's question, I stopped to think about what would happen if I accepted his invitation. Not to mention, how Ricky would feel he if found out. Then I realized he ain't never thought about how I felt when he took all his women out. So, I agreed to going out wit' Russ tomorrow night.

"So, where you wanna go?" he asked me.

"I really don't know. But, wherever we do

decide to go, it's gon' have to be somewhere far, like Williamsburg or Lightfoot."

"A'ight! That's cool!"

"It better be. 'Cause I can't be having none of Ricky's boys seeing me with you. Shit would get real ugly!"

I let out a long sigh. "Okay! If that's the way you wanna do it, I'm witcha!"

"Alright. So, I guess it's a date, huh?"

"I guess so."

"Well, let me get back to my client, since I've got a three o'clock appointment today."

"A'ight. So, can I call you later?"

"Yeah. You can do that."

"A'ight. Talk to you later."

"A'ight."

On my way out of the shop I told Rhonda to tell anybody that came to see me that I was gone for the rest of the day. I also gave her permission to feel free to render service to any of my clients who were desperately in need of getting their hair done. She gave me the okay that she would handle it.

Mr. Shapiro was on his way out of his office building when I drove up. After I parked my car and got out of it, I hopped right into his car.

"Are you ready?" he asked me without hesitation.

I took a deep breath and sighed. "I think so."

"Well, just remember that I will be by your side the whole entire time. So there will be no need for you to get nervous."

"Okay. If you say so."

It didn't take no time for me and Mr. Shapiro to get to the federal building. After we were let in through the back entrance, three U.S. Marshals escorted us to a conference room on the fifth

floor. There were two white men and a black
woman sitting down and talking when we opened
the door. I automatically assumed that these were
the people I was coming to talk to.

Mr. Shapiro pulled out a chair for me to sit in.
He sat in the chair next to mine. "Are you comfortable?" he asked me.

"Yeah. I'm fine," I replied.

The black lady introduced herself to me first,
saying her name was Mrs. Blake. Then she went
into a spiel about her being the U.S. Attorney
working to bring indictments to any and everybody involved with Ricky.

"So, I'm gathering you've already talked to my
cousin."

"Yes, we have. As a matter of fact, she was just
escorted back over to the jail about an hour ago.
And. . . . if you're ready to get down to it, you'll
be able to get out of here, too." she said.

"Well, I'm ready," I told her.

"Okay. Now, before we get down to business,
let me introduce you to Special Agent Burke and
Special Agent Carter. These men are heading
the investigation on this case."

I looked over at both of them crackers and
nodded my head at them. I mean, was I suppose
to go over to them and shake their hands? Hell
nah! It was bad enough that I was ratting out my
husband and his flunkies. To make myself not
look so bad, I was gon' play the game of not to
volunteer information; if they didn't ask, then I
wouldn't tell.

But what I didn't think about until now was
that Russ was now one of Ricky's partners. So,
when these people started questioning me about

who was connected with Ricky, I was gonna have to give them Russ's name. And I couldn't do that. I mean, I was liking this cat already. Plus, if I let these people hook him on the stick, I'd never know whether or not me and him were meant to be together. And I didn't want that to happen.

"How long have you and your husband been together?" Mrs. Blake started off with the questions.

"For a little over seven years," I told her.

"Was he dealing drugs when you met him? Or did it start after you and he decided to continue on with the relationship?"

I took a deep breath and said, "He was doing it before I came into his life."

"Well, would you be able to put a number on the quantity of drugs your husband has possessed and distributed from the time you and he met?"

"Nah. I mean, that would be impossible to do."

"How is that complicated?"

"Because, I'm not always around him when he conducts his business."

"So, who is around him when he does?"

"I don't know," I answered in a nonchalant manner.

"Well, what do you know?" Burke asked.

"What do you want to know?" I snapped back at him.

Mrs. Blake cleared her throat and said, "We want to know all the names of everyone who's involved. And if you can remember dates of conversations or drug transactions your husband has been involved in up until today that would very helpful as well."

"I don't know everybody's name."

"Well, tell us what you know," Burke said.

I looked away from everybody and stared out of the window. I figured this would be a good way for me to gather my thoughts. And it worked, because when I turned back around, I started talking until their ears came off. I gave them almost everybody who worked for Ricky. I even told them about the times he done had meetings in the back of our house, just to discuss who was gon' be making the deliveries this day or the next. I told them where the drugs were stashed at and that Ricky's aunt had full control of that spot, because the apartment was in her name and plus, he trusted her. He ain't never had one ounce of his drugs come up short. And that how he said he was gon' keep it.

"Have you ever played a part in his everyday adventures?" Mrs. Blake asked me.

"If you're talking about me selling or transporting them, then nah, I ain't never did that."

"What kind of role did you play?" Special Agent Carter asked.

"Well, being as though I'm his wife, I have handled some of his money."

"Who financed your business?" Mrs. Blake asked.

"I did."

"How?" she continued.

"When my mother died, I was her beneficiary. So, I took the money that the insurance company gave me and invested in my shop."

"Would you be able to provide us with that information?" Mrs. Blake wanted to know.

"Yeah. "

"Okay. Now, what can you tell us about the men who your husband buys his drugs from?" Mrs. Blake continued.

"Nothing. I mean, I've never met them before."

"Not once?"

"No, I haven't." I tried to stress this to them, but I don't think they believed me 'cause after I couldn't give them the names of the people Ricky was getting his shit from, both of the agents and the lady prosecutor turned and looked at each other like I was lying or something. But I didn't say nothing. I just let it ride.

"Do you and Ricky have a joint bank account?" Mrs. Blake asked.

"Not anymore."

"What happened?"

"I closed it."

"Why?" Carter asked.

"Because, we used to fuss about what money was his and what money was mine."

"Where does he keep his money now?" Burke asked.

"I don't know. I mean, he would never tell me that."

"Why?" Mrs. Blake asked.

"Because, he used to accuse me of stealing his money."

"Were you?" Carter jumped in and asked.

"No, I wasn't."

"So, you're telling us that you don't have any knowledge whatsoever about where your husband keeps his money?" Carter continued.

"Yes. The big money, I don't know where it is. But, every now and again, I see him putting pocket change up in his safe."

"What is considered pocket change?" Mrs. Blake wanted to know.

"Like maybe six or seven thousand."

"Does he have any illegal guns stored away at your residence?" Carter asked.

"Not that I know of."

"What about drugs?" Agent Burke asked.

"What about it?"

"Has he ever stored his drugs there?"

"No way," I began to explain. "He has always lived by the code."

"What code is that?" Agent Burke wondered.

"It is, never keep drugs where you rest at!"

"Well, throughout my career as a federal agent, I have found that a lot of drug dealers don't adhere to that code," Burke commented.

"Yeah, I know. I see it on almost every episode of *Cops.*"

"Do you know where your husband is now?" Mrs. Blake asked.

"Yeah, I do."

"So, tell us."

"He came by the salon a couple hours ago and said he was going down south to North Carolina."

"Did he say why he was going?" Carter asked.

"All he said was that he and Brian had to go down there to take care of some business."

"What part of North Carolina?" Mrs. Blake asked.

"He didn't say," I replied as I looked straight into Mrs. Blake's eyes. That's when she let out a long sigh. She also placed the pencil she had been using down on the legal pad.

"Can you think of anything else we haven't covered?" she asked.

"Not right now."

"Well, if you do, have Mr. Shapiro get in touch with either me or Special Agents Burke and Carter."

"Okay. I can do that," I assured her.

"Oh yeah," Mrs. Blake continued, "would you be willing to wear a wire one time or another?"

"I don't know. I gotta think about it."

"Well, think about it. Because it might come to the point where it's needed."

"I'll let you know," I replied with hesitation. "So, what's gon' happen now?"

"Well, first of all, I've got to compile all the information I have. Then I've got to run it by my boss to have him sign off on it. And then I've got to present it to a federal judge, to get indictments," she replied.

"So, how long does that take?" I asked her.

"Anywhere from three to six weeks."

"So, what am I supposed to be doing while you're doing that?"

"Just go on with your life and act like this meeting never took place," she advised me.

"But, that's gonna be really hard to do."

"I know that. But, just try. And I mean, try very hard. Because if someone finds out you've been talking with us, your life could be in danger."

"No shit!" I commented as I jumped up from the chair.

When the meeting was finally over, Mr. Shapiro told me how impressed he was about the way I handled myself. He also told me he was gon' get in touch with me after he spoke with Mrs. Blake, being as though it was appropriate to give her enough time to go over the information she had gathered. I told him that was fine and hopped out of his car the minute we arrived back at his office.

Collect Calls

It wouldn't have surprised me if Nikki had psychic powers, 'cause the second I stepped foot in the house, she was ringing my phone off the hook.

"I accept the charges," I told the operator as I sat down on the sofa and tried to take my shoes off at the same time.

"Did you see those people today?" she didn't hesitate to ask.

"Yeah. I just left them."

"So, what they say?"

"Nothing, really. I mean, I was the one doing all the talking."

"Well, did they say when I was gon' be getting out?"

"Nah."

"Why didn't you ask them?"

"Because, I didn't think about it."

"Damn!" Nikki said in frustration.

"Look, don't start getting all stressed out. Your time is coming. And when it does, you gon' be back on the streets wit' me," I told her.

"Well, tell me this."

"What's up?"

"Did they say how long it's gon' take for them to start arresting everybody?"

"Yeah. The lady told me it's gon' take about three to six weeks."

"So, you mean to tell me, I'm gon' have to stay in jail for another month?" Nikki asked me, irritated.

"I guess so," I replied, but with uncertainty. Then I got quiet.

It took Nikki about ninety seconds to break the ice. When she did, she said, "Look, I know I'm a big girl and nobody twisted my arm to do what I did. So, I wanna thank you for everything you've done for me."

"You ain't gotta thank me. Shit, we family! And plus, I know you would've done the same thing for me."

"Yep. I sure would."

We talked about everything we was gon' do when she got outta jail. What we didn't talk about was where we was gon' go and how much money I been stashing away. I did that because most likely, the Feds had my phone tapped. So, when Nikki's time was up on the phone, I told her how much I loved her and that her troubles would be over very soon.

"I love you too, girl. So, be careful out there," she replied.

"I will," I assured her.

The number of cars parked out in front of my shop kind of looked better, being as though it was a Saturday. Rhonda and Trina were busy curling their clients' hair, when I walked in.

"Hey everybody!" I greeted them after I walked in. That's when I saw that I had five clients waiting patiently. I walked on over to my station to put down my handbag and then called my client Ms. Jean, because she was scheduled to be my first appointment for today.

"How you doing, Ms. Jean?" I asked her.

"I'm doing fine, baby."

"So, what you getting done today?"

"Well, I'm gon' need a perm first."

"Okay. But what kind of style you want?"

"Just give some kind of up-do."

"Okay. Sit over in that chair, so I can base your scalp."

Without hesitating, I relaxed and conditioned Ms. Jean's hair in less than fifteen minutes, then I stuck her under the dryer. My other clients fell into my schedule like a set of dominoes. Before I knew it, everybody who was in my appointment book was in and out like clockwork.

Rhonda and Trina were still doing their clients when I began to clean up my area. Trina and her client were gossiping about somebody. I couldn't make out what they were saying but when two women were together, they could do nothing else but gossip.

Trina was talking on the phone while she was styling her client. And the bad part about it was that I knew who she was talking to. When she started cussing and saying, "Nigga, you know you ain't shit!" she couldn't be talking to nobody else but her baby daddy. When I felt I'd had enough of what was going on in the salon, I said goodbye and jetted to my car.

On the way home, I couldn't think about

nothing else but Russ. I kept reminiscing about every incident me and him had encountered, which got me more excited about our little date tonight.

As soon as I got in the house, I checked my messages and then I took off all my clothes so I could get comfortable. To my surprise, I didn't have any messages stored on the answering machine. I grabbed me a couple of Oreo cookies from the cookie jar and I headed on upstairs to my bedroom.

In my bedroom was where I was having troubles with figuring out what to wear tonight. I also began to feel kind of odd, being as though I was going out with one of my husband's peoples. Then it took me no time at all to get over the feeling.

All I had to do was think about how Ricky has fucked around on me all these many years. By doing what I was about to do tonight, it made me feel justified. After two hours of digging through all three of my closets, I finally found the perfect get-up.

I couldn't imagine wearing nothing else but this new Christian Dior dress that Ricky got me for Christmas, along with the boots to match. Then I pulled out all of my jewels so that trying to find the right diamond ring and bracelet to wear with my dress wouldn't be so hard.

Now that everything was laid out, there was nothing else for me to do but take a shower and get dressed. Doing that took about an hour. I always had to make sure that everything was right. Nothing could be out of place and that included make-up, hair, and all. Once that was taken care of, I hopped on my cell phone and called Russ.

"What's up?" he asked me the second he answered.

"I was calling to see where you wanted me to meet you."

"Where you at?"

"At home."

"Are you ready?"

"Yep."

"Are we still driving out to Williamsburg?"

"Yeah. I mean, that was the plan."

"What time is it?"

"It's six-thirty five."

"A'ight then, meet me in Newport News."

"Where?"

"Take the second Jefferson Avenue exit and meet me at Patrick Henry Mall."

"Which side you gon' be parked at?"

"Come over by the food court and I'll be waiting."

"Okay. But just keep your phone on just in case."

"A'ight." We both cut off our lines.

Sitting On 22s

Everybody and they mamas was out shopping, as far as I could see, because the parking lot was filled up with all kinds of vehicles. I had to call Russ back on his cell, so he could direct me in his direction.

"Are you driving your Lex?" he asked me.

"Yeah."

"Okay. I see you now."

"Where are you?" I asked with much curiosity.

"I'm over here on your right, parked beside this red Maxima."

Following Russ's instructions, I looked over to my right and then I looked for the Maxima he said he was parked beside. Then I finally saw him.

Big as day, this nigga was sitting on twenty-twos, driving a pearl white Escalade. It was pretty as hell, but I wasn't gon' tell him it was. I would hate for him to get the wrong idea, like I ain't used to nice shit.

So, when I parked my whip and got in his, I just told him it was nice and left it at that, even though he lied to me about not being able to afford expensive vehicles. And to have personalized license plates that said "Russ 3" only put the icing on the cake.

"What kind of music you listen to?" he asked me after I buckled my seat belt.

"I like anything from the group Floetry. And I also like Alicia Keys."

"Well, good, because I got both of them."

Russ put on Alicia Keys' CD first. We listened to the entire CD until we got to Lightfoot, which was only ten minutes outside of Williamsburg. When we started driving down the strip, where the outlets were, we decided to eat at this Japanese restaurant. After Russ parked his truck, he came around to my side and opened the door. Truth be told, Ricky ain't never did no shit like that for me. It felt good, but kind of funny. The way I carried on, Russ didn't even notice it.

"Have you been here before?" Russ wanted to know.

"Nah. But, I've been to some other ones," I explained as we were escorted to our seats.

I talked Russ into sitting around the hibachi grill; that way our food would be cooked in front of us.

"You smell good!" he commented.

"Thanks," I said and then smiled.

"And before I forget, your dress is hot!"

I smiled again and said, "You are full of compliments tonight."

"I just tell it, like I see it."

The Japanese chef was really funny and the food was banging. I could really tell that Russ was enjoying himself.

And like him, I was enjoying myself, too. I almost slipped up and told him that I didn't want the night to end.

We got back on the road to head back to Newport News around nine-fifteen. So to me, the night was still young. That's why I asked Russ if he wanted to hang out for another hour or so.

"Damn right!" was his answer. So instead of taking me right to my car, he drove out to Buckroe Beach. It was too cold to get out and walk, so we sat in his truck and talked.

"Are you happy?" he asked me.

"What kind of question is that?" I replied.

"It's a question that only needs a yes or a no answer."

"Well, the answer is no."

"So, why stay in a situation when you're not happy?"

"Because, I can't control other people."

"Well, are you happy hanging out wit' me?"

Before I answered Russ, I looked him straight in his eyes and said, "What is this, another one of your trick questions?"

He smiled and said, "It's whatever you want it to be."

"I bet it is," I replied. I started looking through his CD collection, in the hope of finding something from the old school. After going through every CD Russ had stored away in the arm rest compartment, I pulled out the greatest hits from Teena Marie, "'Dear Lover.' This is the jam! I can't believe you got it," I said in a cheerful way.

"You don't know nuttin 'bout Teena Marie!" Russ said jokingly.

"You crazy! I love her. I mean, this is one singing sista!"

"Yeah. She can blow," Russ agreed.

Now, here we were, sitting in his truck parked in front of the beach, listening to my girl Teena, as we watched the stars in the sky. We were honestly acting like we was a couple. The fact that Russ was talking a good game, set the mood on an even keel. If I wasn't married to that dog-assed husband of mine, I would probably be laid up in a nice-assed hotel suite, fucking the hell outta this nigga.

But, since I was married, I wasn't gon' play myself. I mean, come on! I didn't know if Russ was on that kiss and tell shit! So, I had to play it straight because niggas these days and age loved fucking the next man's girl! They could go back and laugh at them and tell the dude how much of a hoe their woman was. No sir, I wasn't about to be another statistic of that Faith Evans & Tupac shit! No way, it wasn't gon' happen!

As the music continued to play, I drifted back out my window and watched the moon shine on the waves in the ocean. That's when Russ grabbed my left hand.

"How many carats is that?" he asked me.

"Seven. Why?"

"Nuttin', just curious."

"What? You don't think I deserve it?"

"I don't know. Do you?"

"I might!" I said and then I smiled at him again.

"Can I ask you something personal?" Russ said, sounding so serious.

"Yeah. Go 'head."

"Are you gon' ever leave Ricky?"

"I've thought about it."

"What makes you think about it?"

"Because of the things he continues to take me through."

"Has he ever hit you?"

"No. I mean, I've never had a problem wit' that. It's just that when he leaves the house to hang in the streets, it's like, Kira who?"

"Do you think he's gon' ever change?"

"I know he ain't!"

"So, what's your plan?"

"I haven't put one together. But when I do, it's gon' be official," I said with much authority.

"Do you love him?"

"Of course I do. Now, can we talk about something else?" I insisted.

"What's on your mind?" he asked.

"Well, remember when you stopped by my salon and told me you was there to patronize my shop?"

"Yeah."

"Okay, well, do you have a business that I could patronize?"

Russ started laughing and then he said, "You think you gotta lot of sense. Don't you, Ms. Kira?"

"I would like to think so." I watched him clear his throat as he was about to say something.

"But, to answer your question," he continued, "nah, I ain't got no business."

"Why not?"

"That's a good question."

"Well, answer it."

"I don't know what to say."

"Just tell me why you don't own a business.

I mean, come on. If you can drive around in a Cadillac truck, then you can go into business for yourself."

"You know what? You sound just like my mother."

"That must be a sign, then."

"It might be," Russ replied and looked down at his watch.

"What time is it?" I asked.

"Twenty minutes to eleven."

"It's getting late, huh?"

"You think so?"

"Well, for me it is."

"You ready for me to take you to your car?"

"I would like that."

I got another smile from Russ and then he started the truck back up. I laid my head back against the headrest to enjoy the ride. But through the whole drive back to my car, Russ turned on the silent mode. I mean, he didn't say anything to me. All he did was look straight ahead at the oncoming traffic. I just assumed he was in deep thought. And that was cool, because I got like that sometimes too.

When Russ pulled up beside my car, he snapped out of it and words started coming out of left field. He was acting like he didn't want me to get outta his truck. Every one of his questions had something to do with me getting up with him, in the near future. He was asking me questions like: Can we do this again? Can I call you at the shop? Would you like to take a trip to D.C. with me? When can I see you again?

So, I smiled nicely and said, "I can't promise you. But, I'll let you know."

"A'ight. That's cool."

"Oh, and thanks for dinner."

"You're welcome, anytime."

I got out and closed the door behind me.

He waited for me to drive off before he would move. I put my foot on the pedal and jetted outta there.

It didn't take me long at all to get home. I noticed my next-door neighbor, Mr. Harvey, peeping out the window at me when I pulled up. Ricky probably had him on his payroll to watch me. I threw my hand up and waved at him. I guess he thought I didn't see him 'cause when I waved my hand, he jumped back and hurried up to close his bedroom curtains.

I, on the other hand, went on into my house so I could get outta my clothes and into something comfortable. And after that mission was accomplished, I cut my light off and jumped headfirst into my bed. For some odd reason, I couldn't get myself to fall asleep even though I was dead tired; then it came to me. I smiled as I started reminiscing about my first night out with Mr. Russ himself.

And when that was over, I was able to fall asleep.

Niggaz On Da' Prowl

The next morning I got a call from Ricky's Aunt Sharon. It sounded like she was pretty upset. "What happened to you last night?" she asked in a sarcastic way.

"What you mean, what happened to me?" I snapped back.

"You were supposed to make a pick up from me last night."

"Ahh, shit! I forgot!"

"Well, I'mma need you to come get it now."

"What time is it?"

"It's seven-thirty."

"A'ight. Give me thirty minutes and I'll be there."

"Okay. But, we can't let this happen again, 'cause you know Ricky would go off on both of us."

"Yeah. A'ight! Whatever." I gave her the dial tone. But she was right. Ricky would go the hell off on us. But, who cared? I mean, the world wasn't gon' stop turning because of it.

I got up, brushed my teeth, washed my face and then I was out the door. I didn't have time to put on some clothes, so I threw on a pair of old jeans, a sweatshirt, my Sixers ball cap, and my G-Unit sneakers. Wasn't nuttin' wrong with looking gully every now and then. Since I had to go out to meet Aunt Sharon, I had to play the part, being as though she was the ghetto queen.

Now when I got to the area where I had to meet her, I had always been instructed to make a lot of detours, just to make sure wasn't anybody following me. When I was about to do that, it dawned on me that I might run into the Feds, being as though I'd already told them about every spot Ricky had. Then I thought to myself about the possibilities of my house phone being tapped. If it was, then it wouldn't be a secret to the Feds that I was about to make a pickup. So, the thing for me to do now was think about what I was gon' tell 'em, when they asked.

But anyway, Sharon was at her post, which was expected. There was nothing left for me to do but go around the back of the house and pick up a black plastic trash bag out of the garbage can while Sharon watched me from the upstairs window, just to make sure the pick-up was done.

Since I got what I came for, I had to hide it on my body before I walked back around to the front of the house. That way I didn't stir up any suspicion about what I was carrying. When I did that, I was in my car and outta there in less than two minutes flat. That was a new record for me, which was good. And not only that, but on my way back outta the neighborhood, I didn't notice any undercover po-pos lingering around, trying to bust somebody. That made my day go by a little easier.

* * *

I drove straight to my bank and was escorted to my safe deposit box the minute I set foot in the lobby. I got quick service like that 'cause I'd been a member of that bank for a long time. And because of the way I was treated, I would continue to be a member for as long as I could.

After the bank manager closed the door to the private room he placed me in, I pulled out the plastic bag of money and started counting it. By the time I was done counting it, I came up with ten Gs short of fifty. Now I knew what Ricky told me I was supposed to be picking up. So, to have dough in my hand and coming up with a number that was not what it was supposed to be, would be a problem. The thing for me to do right now was to call up Sharon and find out what the hell was going on.

Once Ricky's dough was stashed in my deposit box, I got outta there and went to the nearest payphone.

"Sharon," I said, as soon as she answered her cell phone.

"Yeah. Who is this?" she asked.

"It's Kira."

"What's up, baby girl?"

"The count for that bag was off ten Gs."

"No, it wasn't!" Sharon said, in an irritating way.

"Yes, it was. I counted it twice."

"Well, maybe somebody took it after I stashed it out back."

"Well, maybe somebody did! 'Cause it's not in that bag." I snapped at her.

"Well, I don't know why you got an attitude!" Sharon snapped back at me. "Because if you would've came by here when you was supposed to, then everything would be on point."

"Oh, please don't start pointing the fingers!"

"I ain't pointing no fingers. But, the truth is the truth!"

"Ain't no damn truth in nothing you just said."

"So, what you trying to say?"

"I ain't saying shit! I'mma let Ricky do all the talking when he comes back."

"And what is he supposed to do to me?" Sharon started loud talking me. "Remember, I'm family, bitch! His favorite aunt! And he knows I wouldn't do nothing to hurt him. You the tramp that needs to be worrying about what he gon' do to you."

"Oh, so Ricky supposed to be doing something to me?"

"Why don't you ask him?"

"Nah. I'm asking you."

"But, I thought you said you was gon' let Ricky do all the talking?"

"Whatever Sharon!" I said in frustration. Then I gave her the dial tone.

The second I hung up the phone, I jumped back into my car. I couldn't help but think about the comments Sharon just made to me over the phone. I mean, she ain't never talked to me like that before. And then, hearing her call me a bitch and saying I needed to be worrying about what Ricky gon' do to me, really threw me for a loop. Then I thought about what I had in store for him and his crew, so there was nothing between us except for "an eye for an eye."

* * *

I noticed I needed to get some gas for my car, so I pulled over to a Citgo gas station just two blocks away from the pay phone I used. To my surprise, I ran into Ricky's daughter Fredrica and her mama. There was also another young chick with them, so I assumed she must've been a girlfriend of Frances. Especially from the way she was dressed. Knockoff clothing from the Koreans had them looking cheap from head to toe. But, I wasn't gon' be nasty, so, I spoke.

"Hey, Fredrica."

When Frances heard her daughter's name being called, all three of them turned and looked in my direction as I walked into the convenience store. Fredrica spoke back to me, but I could hear the gritting of her teeth while she was doing it.

"Where my daddy at?" she asked me in a grown and sassy way.

"He's outta town, baby," I replied to her as I approached them.

Frances looked me up and down and said, "His ass is always outta town! He ain't never got no time for his daughter! But, that's alright!

"Because, when his ass go to jail, he gon' be begging me to bring her down there to see him. But it ain't gon' happen. So, you make sure you tell him."

I put on a fake smile and said, "Okay. Will do."

I got in line to pay for my gas.

On my way back out to my car, I saw Frances and her girlfriend whispering to each other and giggling as they walked by me. They hopped in this old-looking car and left as soon as I started up mine.

It wasn't too long after I got back on the road when my cell phone started ringing. "Hello," I said, after looking down at my Caller ID and finding out it was Ricky.

"What's going on wit' you and my aunt Sharon?" he asked as if he was really pissed off.

"Ain't nothing going on!" I snapped back.

"Well, why is ten Gs missing out that pack?"

"You should've asked your aunt Sharon while you had her on the phone."

"I did. But I want you to tell me why you ain't pick that pack up last night when I asked you to?"

"Because I forgot!"

"But, that's not good enough, Kira!"

"Okay, then. What you want me to say?"

"It ain't about that! It's about you having my back when I ask you to."

"Oh, so you don't think I got your back?"

"Now, what kind of question is that?"

"A question you need to answer!"

"Look, I ain't got time for your bullshit, Kira! Just pick up the other two bags and I'll see you when I get back."

"Well, did you tell your favorite aunt not to take anymore of your dough?"

"Look, I ain't trying to hear that shit you talking. Just do like I asked you. And for tonight and tomorrow, Sharon gon' give you the bag in your hand instead of ya'll doing it the other way.

"Yeah, whatever!" I replied sarcastically and hung up on him.

* * *

Two weeks went by and I didn't hear nothing from Mr. Shapiro or the Feds, which made me feel a little uneasy. I hated being in the dark about things involving me. It put a real big knot in my stomach and I couldn't control it.

Ricky had come back from North Carolina and left home again to go to D.C., to see his other child he had behind my back. He didn't even ask me to go, which was another slap in the face. Just so he could get his baby mama to give him some ass. Shit, I knew what time it was. Niggaz always wanted to go back and screw they baby mamas every now and then. They figured it was a mandatory thing! That's why baby mamas caused all the drama.

Thugging It Out

Me and Ricky's trip to Amsterdam was coming up pretty fast. We only had four days left until we left; which was the day before Valentine's Day. But I was having second thoughts about going, because of everything that was going on.

Ricky, on the other hand, was real excited about it. He couldn't talk about nothing else but that trip. "Baby, I can't wait 'til we hop on the plane to get outta here!" he commented. *"Boy! Boy! Boy!* We gon' have a ball!"

I was sitting at the kitchen table, sorting out the bills and writing checks for them while Ricky was running off at the mouth. Before I could say anything to him his cell phone starting ringing.

"Yo, son what's up?" he didn't hesitate to say.

"Look man, everything gon' be a'ight. She'll be done wit' it before it gets dark. So, I'mma call you," Ricky told the caller and hung up.

"These niggaz act like the world gon' end if they can't get they re-up on time!" Ricky said out loud as he put his cell phone on the kitchen table.

"Who was that?" I wanted to know.

"It was Mike. But I heard Remo in the background, talking about they done missed a whole lot of dough that came through there."

Instead of commenting on what Ricky was saying, I continued on writing the checks for the bills. But, Ricky continued talking. He got a big kick outta playing the role of the head nigga in charge. It made him feel like all his flunkies couldn't do nothing without him. And to have the type of dough he had, gave him the power he loved.

"Did you move my box of Black & Milds from off the counter?" he asked me.

"Yeah. I put 'em on top of the sugar canister."

"Well, what you do wit' my lighter?"

"I didn't see no lighter."

"But, they were together."

"Look, Ricky, don't worry me about no damn lighter! Get a pack of matches outta the kitchen drawer."

"Damn! Don't bite my head off!"

"Well, leave me alone! You see me over here trying to write these checks and balance my checkbook."

"A'ight, then. I'mma leave you alone," Ricky assured me and walked outta the kitchen in the direction of the den. He turned around when he heard his two-way radio beeping back in the kitchen with me.

"Aaaayy, yooo!" the familiar voice yelled through the radio.

Ricky grabbed the radio from the table, pressed down on the talk button and said, "What's up, B?!"

Ricky don't call nobody else 'B' but Brian, so that had to be who he was talking to.

"Have you talked to Mike yet?" I heard Brian say when Ricky released the button for Brian to respond.

"Yeah. Why?" Ricky replied.

"'Cause shit is getting busy 'round here, son! And niggaz ain't got nuttin' to work wit'," Brian explained, like he was stressed.

"Yo, B, I understand that. But, I can't do nuttin' about that now. I done already told Mike my peoples was working on it!"

"Well, when you think shit gon' be popping?"

"Look, everybody gon' be straight before it gets dark. A'ight?"

"Yeah! That's what's up!" Brian replied with excitement.

"So, we straight on that?" Ricky asked him.

"Yeah. We straight. Just hit me up when you got the word!"

"A'ight!" Ricky turned off his two-way after their conversation was over.

I turned myself around in the chair and said, "Why is it that your cell phone bills get higher every month?"

"How much is it?" He walked toward me.

"It's two hundred and eighty-nine dollars."

"Well, pay it."

"I will. But, you still didn't answer my question."

"What you want me to say?"

"I want you to answer my question."

"Well, I guess it's because I'm using my phone more and more by the day," he replied sarcastically.

"Stop being a smart ass!"

"You the one wanted an answer. So, I gave you one." Ricky walked back out the kitchen.

"Oh, whatever!" I shouted back at him before I went back to what I was doing.

I was still sitting at the kitchen table, writing out checks, when the house phone started ringing. I tried to answer it, but Ricky beat me to it and then he yelled, "Kira, get the phone."

"Who is it?" I asked.

"It's Nicole."

"A'ight. I got it!" I yelled back to him and waited for him to hang up his line. And when he did, I said, "What's up?"

"Nothing," Nikki replied.

"Have you heard from Mr. Shapiro?"

"Nope."

"Me either."

"What you thinks going on?"

"I don't know. But, now is not the time to be talking about that."

"What, you think Ricky gon' hear us?"

"Not you. But me."

Nikki sighed real loud and said, "You seen Brian lately?"

"Nah. But him and Ricky was just talking each other on their two-way radios about ten minutes ago."

"Did they say something about me?"

"Nope."

"That's messed up!" Nikki replied. "I hope his ass gets picked up first."

"Look, you need to chill out wit' that."

"I know, I know. But, I'm just so frustrated!"

"I know you are. But, everything's gon' be alright."

"Yeah. I know." Nikki she sighed a little.

"Did your mom and dad come visit you yesterday?"

"Yeah, they came."

"How is your money?"

"I'm good for another two to three weeks."

"Are you holding shit down?"

"Yeah. I'm cool!" Nikki told me and then she asked, "What you doing?"

"Sitting at the kitchen table, going through my bills."

"Yo, I appreciate you holding shit down at my crib!"

"Don't sweat that! 'Cause, that's what family supposed to do." After my little spiel, Nikki gave me the rundown about her life there on lockdown which, of course, took up the rest of her phone time. But before the system disconnected us, she was able to tell me when she would be able to call me again. So, it was settled.

For What It's Worth

Right after Nikki hung up, I got up from the table to hang the phone up when I heard footsteps walking toward me. It wasn't anybody but Ricky.

And the funny thing about it was that I already knew why he was coming back into the kitchen. It was killing him to know what me and Nikki was talking about, with his paranoid self.

"What's going on wit' your cousin?" Ricky asked the instant he stepped foot in the kitchen.

"What you mean, what's going wit' her?"

"I mean, is she a'ight?"

"Yeah. She's fine."

"So have the po-pos been on her about who stuff she had?"

Now where did that question come from? I mean, did he know? But, if he didn't, now wouldn't be a good time to look him straight in the face. That would have been a dead giveaway. Me and him done been together long enough for him to know when I was lying or telling the truth. I had to force myself to answer him, but with my back facing him.

"Not to my knowledge," I finally said.

"What you mean, not to your knowledge? You either know or you don't."

"Well, let's just say that she ain't been talking to nobody but her lawyer," I snapped back. I took a sip from my can of soda that was right beside my checkbook.

"I hope so." Ricky let out a long sigh of relief and walked over to the refrigerator. "You ain't gotta go to work today, do you?" he asked as he grabbed himself a bottle of Corona.

"Nope. Not on a Monday." I hurried up and answered because I was glad we was off the subject about the police.

"Well, what you gon' be doing?"

"I don't know. Why?"

"Because, I was thinking about going down to the Benz dealership."

"For what?"

"So I can see what they got."

"Look, I am not about to put another one of your cars in my name, so you and your bitches can ride around thinking ya'll on top of the world."

"What bitches? And anyway, how you know it's for me?"

"I know it ain't for me!"

"How you know that?"

"Look Ricky, stop wit' the drama please. I mean, can't you see I'm trying to take care of business here?"

"You ain't finish wit' that yet?"

"No, because you keep bothering me."

"A'ight. I'mma leave you alone. So, let me

know when you're done." He walked right back outta the kitchen.

The second Ricky left, I got right back into what I was doing. After about another thirty minutes, I was finally done. So, I got up from the table and went on upstairs to my bedroom. Ricky must've had his ears glued to the walls 'cause he was right on my heels.

"So, you gon' go wit' me or not?" he asked as soon as he seen me at the top of the stairwell.

"I ain't thought about it."

"Come on, let's go. And then after we leave there we can run by Alice Mae's and get some food."

Ricky thought he was so slick. He knew I loved me some soul food, and especially at Alice Mae's. They be having some good fried chicken and macaroni and cheese. And the candy yams and collard greens be on point, too. That's why I couldn't resist Ricky when he threw that into plan. We both got dressed, hopped in his Benz and headed out.

Of course, Ricky had me chauffeur him around. He always did that when we were together. He never liked to drive, which was why we hardly ever went out together.

While we were on the road Ricky's cell phone started ringing. Ricky looked down at the Caller ID and whoever it was, Ricky didn't wanna talk to 'em. Or shall I say, he didn't wanna talk to 'em while I was with him because when it stopped ringing, it got quiet for a second or two and then started ringing again. But instead of looking back at the Caller ID, Ricky turned up the volume on the radio so I wouldn't hear it ring over and over.

He knew he didn't wanna hear me go off on

his ass, but, it was too late. My wheels were already spinning and he knew it, too, when he saw my facial expression.

"You think you so damn slick!" I snapped at him as I grabbed the volume button and turned it off.

"Yo, why you tripping?" He gave me the dumbest look ever.

"Why you ain't answering your cell?"

"Because I didn't wanna talk."

"Who was it?" I shouted.

"It was Shampoo."

"You a damn lie!" I tried to snatch his cell phone outta his hand. "Let me see it!" I demanded.

But Ricky wasn't trying to let it go. "Why you tripping?" he asked me.

I refused to answer him. I said, "Just give me the phone, Ricky."

"Why?"

"You must got something to hide," I commented sarcastically.

"I ain't got shit to hide!" He got defensive.

"Gimme the phone, Ricky." My tone got lower but a little more serious.

"For what?" he continued as he kept his guard up.

I slapped him right up against his head as hard as I could.

"Keep it up, Ricky! Just keep right on playing wit' me!"

"I ain't playing. So, you better keep your hand to yourself."

"I ain't playing either!" I started yelling again and then I tried to swing at him again, but he blocked my blow with his arm. "I'm just so tired of your slick ass!"

"Would you stop hitting me! And keep your eyes on the road, before we get in an accident."

"Fuck you! I got this!"

By the time we made it to the Benz dealership, I was not in nobody's mood to get out and see nothing. I sat in the car and waited for Ricky to do what he came there to do. The guy Ricky normally dealt with was this Arab cat name Nick, which was short for Nickolas.

Nick wasn't around, so Ricky had to settle for this fat, white dude named Paul. Now, Paul wasn't your average, savvy-looking, white-collar cat. He put you in the mind of an insurance salesman. I could tell by Ricky's body language that this guy wasn't giving him the prices he was looking for. "When is Nick coming in?" I heard Ricky ask the guy.

"I'm not sure," Paul told Ricky.

"A'ight," Ricky replied and threw his hand up in the air. "Well, can you tell him that I need him to call me?"

Paul nodded his head and said, "Yeah, I can do that."

"A' ight." Ricky walked back to the car. "Yo, that fat dude is crazy!" he commented as if he was frustrated.

I didn't respond. I wasn't in the mood to say anything. So, I just listened to him.

"That cracker trying to peck my head!" Ricky said. "Talking about, he can't let that red convertible SL 500 go for nothing less than 85 Gs."

"What year is it?" I was curious enough to ask.

"It's a 2004 model."

"How much they want for it?"

"The ticket on the window say $91 Gs. But I

know if I talk to Nick, he'll be able to take off at least ten or fifteen grand."

"So, what you gon' do wit' this car?"

"I'mma keep it."

"But, I thought you didn't like two-door cars."

"I don't."

"So, why you trying to get it?"

"Because, I'mma give it to you."

Wait! Hold up! Did this no-good-assed nigga just tell me he was trying to get that joint for me? Yeah, he done did something wrong. They said you can tell when your man done did something wrong, 'cause gifts would start coming from outta nowhere.

Yeah, he probably got somebody else pregnant, wit' his nasty ass! I wouldn't find out about that until the baby is born. So, yeah, he could go right ahead and cop that joint for me because sooner or later, the truth was gon' come out. And when it did, I wasn't even gon' worry about it 'cause I was gon' be in the wind. And I wasn't gon' look back.

"Oh, so you ain't got nothing to say?" Ricky said, trying to get me to comment.

"What you want me to say?" I threw the question right back at him.

"Well, damn! I mean, you can at least say thanks!"

"For what?" I said, sarcastically. "You ain't bought it yet!"

"But I am."

"Okay! Well, I'll say thanks when you give me the keys," I replied and sucked my teeth in a sassy type of way.

"You are a trip! You know that?" Ricky commented as he shook his head. "I done created a monster!"

Yep! He sure did! He just didn't know he done created a whole lot of other shit, too. But, he was gonna find out soon enough. Sitting over in the passenger seat like he the man, wearing a hundred-thousand-dollar, iced-out Chopard wrist watch with the ring to match.

"Come on. Let's go and get something to eat." He picked up a CD and stuck it in the CD player.

I drove outta the parking lot of the dealership and jumped back on the highway, taking the Downtown Norfolk exit. We got to Alice Mae's in about fifteen minutes. The guy for the valet parking was standing at the curb ready to park our car when we pulled up. I gave him the keys when we got outta the car. Ricky reached in his pants pocket and gave him a twenty-dollar bill.

There was a band playing jazz when we walked through the door. It sounded good as hell, too. Ricky must've liked them too, because he kept nodding his head.

"What will you be drinking this evening?" our waitress asked us.

Ricky ordered a shot of Rèmy Martin. I ordered a peach daiquiri with whipped cream and a strawberry on top.

"Let me know when you two are ready to order," our waitress told us.

"Oh, we're ready," Ricky assured her.

"Yeah. We're gonna eat from the buffet," I told her.

"Okay. Then help yourself," she replied.

"Okay. Thanks." Me and Ricky got up from our chairs.

The food on the buffet looked so good. I picked up two pieces of fried chicken, a spoonful of macaroni and cheese, some cabbage and candied yams. Ricky got a plateful of beef spareribs, some cabbage and a little bit of the macaroni and cheese. When we got back to our table, hot buttery rolls were sitting in a bowl, waiting for us to tear 'em apart.

Now while we was eating, I caught our waitress staring at Ricky from across the other side of the restaurant. She was all in his face. His jewelry probably had her star struck. But, I was gonna nip that in the bud! When she brought her ass back over here, I was gonna blind her with the rock on my finger. Then I was gonna let her know that I was *wifey!*

I wasn't gon' flip out on her, though. I was gonna be just as nice and nasty as I could. I couldn't let her see my ghetto side. But most of all, I had to let her know that I was the bigger woman and I was not insecure by a long shot. Those days were long gone. I was truly numb when it came to Ricky screwing around.

"Would you like to have another peach daiquiri?" she asked me.

"Yes. Please," I replied, using my left hand to give her my used cocktail glass. And just like I knew she would, she got hypnotized when she saw my jewels.

"Your ring is nice," she complimented me.

I threw on my fake smile and said, "Thank you. I just hope it gets bigger on our tenth-year anniversary."

"Ya'll married?" she asked, like she was surprised.

"Yep. It's going on eight years now," I continued as I poured more and more salt on her phony ass.

"Dag. That's a long time. I mean, I ain't never been wit' nobody that long. How do ya'll do it?"

"Trust me it ain't been that easy." I commented as I looked Ricky dead in his face.

The waitress must've caught the hint, so she said, "Well, whatever ya'll been doing, it's been working."

"Thank you." I put another forkful of my macaroni and cheese in my mouth.

"Well, I'mma let ya'll get back to your food. But, just let me know if you need something."

"Okay." I kept on eating.

When she walked away from our table, I made sure I kept my eyes on Ricky because sometimes his eyes tend to get away from him. "You know you wanna look at her ass!" I said.

"What you talking 'bout?" He sounded so surprised.

"Don't play games wit' me! I saw you staring at her ass when she walked away from us the first time. But, I ain't say nothing."

"You seeing things, 'cause I ain't do shit!"

"Whatever! Because I know I ain't seeing things!"

"Look, Kira, can we just go somewhere without all the drama? I'm trying to enjoy myself and you sitting over there looking for shit to fuss about!"

"You sho' know how to shift the blame, don't you!" I responded sarcastically.

"Look! Can you just please let me eat in peace?"

I didn't reply to Ricky's plea to eat in peace. I just rolled my eyes and continued on eating myself. He did have a point. And by him making it seem like I was the one starting up an argument, it kinda worked. So, I just sat there with a stupid expression and tried not to let it seem like what he said bothered me.

What really helped me out was that my cell phone started ringing. That kinda cut real deep into the tension at our table, which was what we needed. I looked down at my Caller ID and saw it was my stylist, Rhonda, trying to get through.

"Hello," I said.

"Hey girl!" Rhonda said to me.

"Hey! What's up?"

"Guess who I saw a few minutes ago?"

"Who?"

"Tabitha."

"Where you see her at?"

"She was at the beauty supply store. And you will not believe what she told me."

"What she say?"

"Is Ricky near you?" Rhonda wanted to know.

"Yeah. Why?"

"Well, I'mma have to get wit' you when he ain't around you."

"Why?"

"Because, when I tell you what Tab told me, you gon' go the hell off."

"No, I'm not." I tried to convince Rhonda to tell me what was going on.

"You at home?"

"Nah. I'm at Alice Mae's."

"Well, can you call me back?"

"No."

"Why?"

"Because, I'm talking to you now."

"Look, Kira, what I'm about to tell you is going to be really ugly, And since Ricky is sitting there right next to you, you might haul off and smack the shit outta him."

"Okay. Hold that thought!" I looked over at Ricky and said to him, "I'll be right back, 'cause I can't hear from the music."

I walked completely outta the restaurant so I could get every drop of information Rhonda was trying to give me. I didn't wander off too far because where I was standing was the perfect spot for me to see all movement around our table.

"Go head and tell me. I'm outside the restaurant now," I told Rhonda.

Rhonda took a deep breath and then she said, "Look, you gotta promise me that you won't tell Ricky you got this information from me."

"Okay, I promise."

"Well, Tab told me she heard Sunshine talking to Ricky on the shop phone yesterday."

"She was talking to my Ricky?"

"Yeah. And, she said she heard Sunshine telling him how much fun she had wit' him in Myrtle Beach two weeks ago."

"Wait! Hold up! Slow down!" I instructed Rhonda, because my heart started racing real fast. But my mind wasn't registering everything I just heard.

"Are you alright?" Rhonda wanted to know.

Before I answered her I looked through the window of the restaurant to see what Ricky was doing. I watched him stare at every chick's ass that walked by him while he was eating; my stomach began to turn.

"Kira!" Rhonda said.

"Yeah," I finally said.

"What you doing?"

"I'm just standing here looking at that piece of shit-ass husband of mine. And trying to think of what I'm gon' say to him when I walk back in this restaurant."

"Wait! Don't say nothing!"

"Come on, now. You know I ain't gon' be able to be quiet about this! I mean, how low can you go? It's bad enough that he done screwed every hoe in the Tidewater area. But, to sneak around and go behind my back and fuck a trick I work wit' everyday is real grimy."

"Well, if you think that's grimy, Tab also told me that Sunshine is over at her shop bragging to everybody about all the jewelry and clothes Ricky bought her. And that he peeled off twenty grand for that shop she got and all the accessories in it."

"You sure she talking about my Ricky?"

"Yeah, I'm sure. Because, she said she seen him come by the shop this past Saturday. She said Sunshine got in his car and left wit' him and then he dropped her back off about two hours later."

"So, Sunshine fucking my husband! And laughing about it behind my back, huh?"

"That's what it sounds like."

"Well, I'mma have the last laugh!"

"So, what you gon' do?"

"I don't know. But right now, I feel like putting a gun up to both of their heads and emptying out the whole magazine on their asses!"

"Well, it's natural to feel like that. But, please don't do it. Ain't neither one of them worth you spending the rest of your life in jail."

"I know. But when will it stop? I mean, I've been going through shit wit' Ricky for almost eight years now. And he says he gon' change, but he never does."

Rhonda sucked her teeth and said, "Girl, they all say that, sounding like broken records. That's why you gon' have to handle this another way."

"Like how?"

"I don't know. But, we'll come up wit' something. So, try not to let Ricky know his cover is blown until after you set his ass on blaze!"

"Now that's gon' be real hard."

"I know it is but try. So, before you got back in the restaurant, take a deep breath and count to ten."

"Yeah, like that's gon' work."

"Just try it," Rhonda instructed me. "And I'll call you later on this evening after I get wit' Tab."

"A'ight," I said and then we both hung up.

Before I walked back into the restaurant I did exactly what Rhonda told me to do. But it seemed like the closer I got to Ricky, everything Rhonda advised me to do was slowly going right back outta the window. That's when I got struck by a reality check. It was revealed to me that all the pain and agony Ricky done took me through was slowly riding on him. And since I was seeking a plan of revenge, all the information I done gave to the Feds was gon' take care of everything.

That's when I was able to put a smile on my face. Figuring out what I was gon' do to Sunshine, though, was another story.

"What you smiling for?" Ricky asked me the minute I got back to the table.

"Because of a joke I just heard," I replied, as I continued to smile.

"Who was that you were talking to?"

"One of my clients," I lied.

"Well, can you hurry up and eat? Because, I'm gon' need to make a quick run."

"To where?"

"The barbershop. I told Brian to meet me there."

"What time did you tell 'em you was gon' be there?"

"In about thirty minutes."

I sat down at the table to finish eating what I had started before I got my phone call from Rhonda. It was not as warm as I wanted it to be, but it was okay. And once I was down to the last little bite on my plate, Ricky asked our waitress for the check.

"Keep the change," he told the waitress after he handed her two twenty-dollar bills.

"Thanks!" she replied, as giddily as she knew how.

"Wit' a tip like that, she might slide you her phone number before we leave," I commented after the waitress walked off.

"Please, Kira, don't start it up again!" Ricky begged me.

And I didn't. Because I had another plan for his no good ass.

Brian hopped in the back seat of Ricky's car the second we pulled up. He looked like he had something really important to tell Ricky. And since I was sitting there, I was about to hear what he had to say.

"What's up, peoples," Brian said to me and Ricky as he sat down in the seat.

"Hey," I spoke to him without even looking in

his direction and the way I said it was quick and very short. Brian could sense that he was on my shit list, because of the way he carried my cousin. So, instead of pressing the issue with me, he turned to Ricky and said, "Yo, I know who ran up in your spot and robbed Mike and Remo."

Ricky turned around in the passenger seat in the blink of an eye and said anxiously, "Who was it?"

"Some young niggas from outta Norview."

"Do I know 'em?"

"Nah. But, this chick who braid my hair said she overheard them niggas bragging about it. Saying, those D.C. cats is weak! And that one of our own had us set up! And from the way shit was going, we gon' get hit up again."

Hearing Brian tell him what the Norview niggas said, Ricky got really hyped and said, "Yo, who is these niggas? I mean, they coming off like they gangstas or something!"

"She said it was a nigga named June. Another nigga named Dez. And some fat nigga named Buck."

"Well, did they tell her which nigga on my squad helped them take my shit?"

"Yeah. She said it was Remo," Brian explained. "And come to find out, Remo's baby mama is the nigga June's sister."

"Oh, so these niggas trying to play me for soft, huh?" Ricky commented with frustration. "Yeah. A'ight! We gon' see who's weak!"

"So, what you want me to do?" Brian wanted to know.

"I want you to two-way Mike, Shampoo and Monty. Tell them niggaz to meet me at the spot out

Campostella at seven o'clock. And not a minute later."

"A'ight."

"Oh yeah, get back wit' that girl and find out where them niggaz live at. And try to get all that information before we meet back up."

"So what you gon' do about the deliveries for later? I mean, you know niggas is waiting to go to work."

"Well, tell 'em the shit ain't right yet!"

"A'ight. But, you know we gon' lose out on a lot of dough!"

"Yeah. I know. But if we don't correct this situation right now, we gon' lose out on a lot more."

Brian put on a stupid expression and said, "Yeah, dog, you right."

"A'ight. So, it's settled." Ricky turned back around in his seat and Brian opened the door to get out of the car. "Oh yeah," Ricky began to speak again, "If Mike and them start asking questions about what the meeting is for, just tell 'em you don't know."

"A' ight," Brian replied and then he closed the back door behind him.

Ricky instructed me to drive back to the house, so I did. When we pulled up, I was the only one who got outta the car.

"Please don't do nuttin' stupid!" I warned him.

He didn't respond.

I went on in the house and he left.

Doing Me

I wasted no time hoppmg my ass on the cell phone after Ricky left. I only had one objective and that was getting Mr. Shapiro on the phone.

"This is Shapiro," he answered.

"Hey, this is Kira," I replied.

"How you doing?"

"I'm alright."

"So, what can I do for you?" he asked.

I went into detail about the conversation I heard between Ricky and Brian. Then I told him what I thought would happen once Ricky got with everybody at seven o'clock tonight

"Where is this meeting supposed to take place?"

"Somewhere m the Campostella area."

"And you don't know exactly where?"

"Nope."

"So, where is Ricky now?"

"He just left."

"Well, right now, there's really nothing we can do but wait. However, I am truly glad that you called me with this information. This would really help Nicole if something happens to that guy Remo."

"So, what you think I should do?"

"Just sit back and let this whole thing play out."

"Well, have you heard from the U.S. Attorney?"

"Yes. I spoke with her a few days ago."

"So, what did she say?"

"Well, let's just say she's working very hard to get the indictments. And after that happens, then everybody will be picked up."

"I already know that! I mean, she needs to get on the ball! Because I'm ready for this whole thing to be over wit'!"

"I know you are. And so is Nicole. But, these things take time."

"Well, how much more time does she need? Shit, me and Ricky getting ready to leave and go to Amsterdam in the next couple of days."

"For how long?"

"Seven days. So, if somebody is arrested while we're gone, word is going to get back to Ricky. And trust me, when it does, he will do everything in his power not to come back."

"Well, let me make a couple calls and see what I can do to speed the process up."

"Please."

"I will. Let me get back with you tomorrow."

"Okay."

"Alright. So, I guess I'll be talking to you then."

"Okay." I said again and then we hung up.

I laid my cell phone down on the coffee table in my den and took a seat on the sofa. But before I could sit down good, I heard a couple of knocks on my front door. I had to get right back up, just to see who it was.

"Who is it?" I asked abruptly, because I didn't want to be bothered.

"It's me, Russ," I heard the familiar voice say. Without even thinking, I opened the door.

"What are you doing here?" I asked as my heartbeats began to pick up speed.

"I came to see you," he boldly told me.

"Russ, you must be crazy!"

He smiled at me and said, "Nah, I ain't crazy by a long shot. But I am infatuated."

"Look," I said to him to try and get his attention, "do you know that if Ricky catches you here, shit gon' hit the fan?"

"I just got off the phone wit' Ricky. And he's not gon' be home for at least another hour or two."

"Well, if you just talked to him, then where did he say he was going?"

"He didn't say where he was going. But he did say he had to be somewhere by seven."

I looked Russ up and down after he convinced me that he'd talked to Ricky. I knew that I couldn't let my guard down, even though my heart was telling me different.

"So, what, you just gon' let me stand here?"

Before I answered Russ, I looked across the street at my neighbor's house. I had to make sure he wasn't peeping out of any of his windows. When I realized that he wasn't, I stepped back outta the doorway, just enough for Russ to step inside. He closed the door behind him.

"So, why ain't you been returning my calls?" Russ asked me the moment the door was shut.

"Was I supposed to?" I replied sarcastically.

Instead of responding to my sarcasm, Russ

leaned over and tongue-kissed me. Even though I was caught off guard, I couldn't make myself stop him. I honestly enjoyed every bit of it. I mean, Russ's kiss was like magic. It seemed like every time we rotated our lips, feelings crept into motion. So I pulled back and said, "Wait. What are we doing?"

"Why did you stop?"

"Because, this ain't right! And especially here."

"So, when?"

"What do you mean, when?"

"Stop fighting it. You know I can make you happy."

"Maybe you can. But, I am a married woman."

"Yeah, I know. But, does your husband know that?" Russ replied sarcastically.

After hearing Russ's comments, I couldn't say anything. He was right, Ricky didn't care. And everybody knew it. They been knowing it for a long time now. This, of course, made me look like the biggest fool walking. So, I just stood there in front of Russ as my eyes began to water.

"Damn! I'm sorry," he said, and then he took me into his arms. As he cradled me in his arms, it was obvious that I had let my guard down. I felt really weak as I began to replay every incident Ricky had crushed my heart with. And then, to just find out that Ricky was sleeping with Sunshine really broke me down. Tears started falling everywhere. Having Russ there to hold me was what I truly needed.

"Go 'head. Let it out," he told me. That's when I held him tighter. "Come on, so you can sit down."

He led me into the den and after I sat down on the sofa, I looked Russ in the eye and said,

"Did you know about Ricky messing around wit' my old stylist, Sunshine?"

Russ looked at me for a second or two as he held my hands. Then he said, "Yeah."

I snatched my hands away from him and said, "Why didn't you tell me?"

"Because, it wasn't my place."

"Is that why she was staring you down when you walked into the shop?" I asked as I began to wipe away my tears.

"Yeah."

"So, how did you find out about her?"

"My first time seeing her was the day me and Ricky went to D.C. She called him on his cell and said she wanted to see him before he left. So, he told her to meet him in the parking lot of the Jamaican restaurant on Park Ave. When we pulled up she was already there, waiting for him. So, when she seen us pull up, she got out of her car and walked over to the driver's side and they started talking."

"What did they say?"

"Nothing but how much she's gonna miss him. And that she can't wait until he gets back."

"Did they kiss?"

"She leaned over and kissed him. And then after that, he told her we had to go."

"Did he leave her any money?"

"Yeah. He did."

"Well, at least I knew that much!" I yelled.

"What you mean?"

"Sunshine is a greedy bitch! And all she does is prey on niggas who got money. She's a hoe to her heart!"

Russ saw the pain I was going through. He

pulled me back into his arms and held me even tighter than before. "It's gonna get better. Don't even worry about it," he whispered in my ear.

"But when?" I asked.

"When you're ready to let it go."

That's when I realized he was right. It was up to me. I had complete control of my life and the decisions I made. I looked into Russ' eyes and thanked him for being by my side. And after I thanked him, I leaned over to him and we started kissing once more. This time, it was better, because my feelings for him started growing stronger and stronger. And it felt like he was experiencing the same thing, 'cause he wouldn't stop kissing me. One thing leads to another and before I realized it, me and Russ were upstairs in me and Ricky's bed, screwing each other's brains out.

"Yes. Keep doing it just like that," I instructed Russ as he searched with his tongue for the spot on my pussy. "Hmrnm, that feels so good," I moaned and groaned with every stroke of his tongue. When that part of our lovemaking was over, Russ flipped me over on all fours, then slid all eight-and-a-half inches of his dick inside of me.

"Wait! I can't take it! I can't take it!" I screamed with passion. I mean, this nigga was fucking the hell outta me. I ain't been fucked like that in a very long time. That alone was scaring me.

Now after Russ finished sucking, turning, and massaging me all over, I was convinced that my days with Ricky were officially over. And not only that, but screwing another man in the bed me and Ricky shared, was nothing but a taste of sweet revenge.

I just wished I would've thought about using

our video recorder. Seeing his boy Russ, fucking the hell outta his wife, would have done some permanent damage. And that's just what his ass needed.

"Let me get on outta here, before your husband gets back," Russ commented, as he slipped his shoes back on.

I didn't respond to his comment. I was too caught up in the moment to say anything. All I wanted to do was lay back and watch him get dressed. When he was done, Russ leaned over and kissed me right on my forehead.

"Are you gon' call me later?" he wanted to know.

"That's if you want me to."

"You know I want you to. So, why you playing?" He smiled.

I smiled back and said, "I ain't playing. You know I'm gon' call you."

"Do that," he said before he left.

Ricky walked in the house a little after ten o'clock, so, I had enough time to take a shower and sneak a nap in before he came. Now, when he came in our bedroom, I could sense he wasn't in the mood to talk about nothing. It was probably because of that problem he had with that nigga Remo. I pretended to be asleep; that way, nobody's feelings would get hurt. I'm guessing Ricky felt the same way, because after he stripped down to his boxers he headed back downstairs to the den, this was where he slept the rest of the night. But before he walked out of the room, he sniffed the air around the bed a couple of times.

I knew he smelled my juices lingering in the air but, since he wasn't the one that helped to bring them outta me, he must've assumed his mind was playing tricks on him. He never uttered a word about it.

The next morning, I got up and got dressed so I could get to work for my nine-thirty appointment. Ricky found a way to stop me on my way out.

"Did you pick up our passports yet?" he asked as I was walking to the front door.

"No, I haven't," I said shortly and sweetly.

"So, when you gonna do it?" His tone was very aggravated.

I sucked my teeth and said, "Either today or tomorrow!"

"Look, do it today. 'Cause, I don't want no last-minute mix-ups!"

"Well, why don't you do it?" I snapped back at him before I walked out of the house.

I heard Ricky call me a couple of stupid bitches, but, it didn't bother me. 'Cause while he was cussing me out, I was driving down the street, laughing my ass off about what I had in store for him.

Da' Housing Projects

I was curling the hair of one of my clients and watching TV at the same time, when a special news bulletin popped on about three people getting killed execution style, inside an apartment of a housing project in the Norview section of Norfolk.

"Oh shit, turn that up!" I instructed Rhonda. Everybody in the whole shop got quiet. And come to find out, the three people who were found dead around seven o'clock this morning were a twenty-year-old Remone Thomas; his twenty-three-year-old sister Pamela Thomas; and her boyfriend, Julius Grimes, also known to others as June.

They were found tied up to chairs by Pamela Thomas' son, who had spent the night at the next-door neighbor's house. All three of them had been tortured before they died.

The news lady said that whoever was responsible for the killings wanted them to suffer and die a slow death, because of the many stab wounds they had that were filled with salt and the smell of alcohol. She also said that it appeared that the victims were also forced to sniff gunpowder through their noses, which was an apparent sign of a drug deal gone bad. The police said they didn't have any suspects.

"Whoever did that was crazy!" Rhonda yelled out loud. "I'm so glad that li'l boy wasn't there, 'cause, they probably would've killed that poor kid, too!"

I couldn't say nothing because I was too messed up in the mind. I mean, I just called Mr. Shapiro about this very incident. And it happened. So, what was I gonna do? 'Cause I know Mr. Shapiro would have to tell the police that I told him about it. That makes me a witness, and I don't wanna be that. Damn! Why did I even open my big mouth from the beginning. Now, look what I've got myself into.

"Didn't Remo work for Ricky?" Rhonda walked over and asked me in a whisper-like tone.

"I don't know who he is," I lied.

"I bet you Sunshine knew who they was," Rhonda commented as she walked back over to her work station.

I remained quiet for the rest of the day. Rhonda sensed something was wrong with me, but she couldn't put her finger on it. So when I said that I was leaving for the day, she told her client to excuse her for a minute and then she walked me out to my car.

"Are you alright?" she asked.

I lied to her again and said, "Oh yeah, girl. I'm fine."

"Well, you don't seem like it."

"I'm just tired."

"Is it about that mess wit' Ricky and Sunshine?"

"Yeah. It's that, too."

Rhonda reached over and hugged me and said, "Girl, don't let neither one of them mutha-fuckas stress you out! You are too much of a good person to let them get you down."

"I ain't gon' let that happen," I assured her.

"Good, 'cause I would hate to pull out my boxing gloves."

I smiled at Rhonda and said, "You know you're my girl, right?"

"Yeah. I know that."

"Well, what would you say if I decided to move away and leave you my shop?"

Rhonda hesitated for a few seconds. Then she looked me dead in the eyes and said, "Are you thinking about leaving me?"

"I've already thought about it. So, all I need to do now is figure out where I'm going."

"But, why?"

"Because, I need to get away and make a new start for myself. I am so over this place." I allowed a few of my tears to fall from my eyes.

Rhonda held onto me tighter. I grabbed on to her too.

"Does Ricky know that you're leaving?"

"No."

"Are you going to tell him?"

"No."

"So, what do you want me to tell him when he comes here looking for you?"

"Just tell him you thought I was wit' him, getting ready to go on the trip."

"Well, are gon' keep in touch wit' me?"

"From time to time."

Rhonda began to rub my back. Then she said, "Just take care of yourself"

"I will," I assured her. I got in my car and left.

I didn't realize it at first, but when I pulled my cell phone outta my handbag I noticed that I had eight missed calls showing up on it. Five of them were from Mr. Shapiro and the other three were from Russ. I was too scared to call Russ because I didn't want the Feds to know anything about him. I pulled over to the nearest pay phone and called him.

"Hello," Russ answered.

"Hey, it's Kira."

"What's up, baby?"

"I'm returning your call."

"What's wrong wit' your cell?"

"The battery is dead," I quickly thought to say.

"Where you at?"

"I'm at the BP gas station on the corner of Newtown Road and Virginia Beach Boulevard."

"Did you see the news?"

"Yeah. I saw it."

"Are you getting ready to go home?"

"Yeah. But I'm trying to find a reason not to."

"Is that an invitation?"

"Why don't you figure it out?" I replied sarcastically.

"Well, do you want to spend some time wit' me?"

I told him, yeah. That's when we decided to meet up at the Ruby Tuesday restaurant off Military Highway.

The idea of somebody seeing us wasn't something we cared about, being as though we had other important things to worry about. "I'm leaving," I said to Russ the second after the hostess walked away from our table.

"What you mean, you're leaving?" he asked.

"I'm moving."

"Moving where?"

"I don't know yet."

"Well, tell me why."

"Because, I've got to."

"Is this Ricky's idea?"

"No. He doesn't know about it."

"Oh, so this is how you plan to leave him?"

"Something like that."

"So, what do you call it?"

"Look, Russ," I sighed. "There's a lot of shit going on that you have no knowledge of whatsoever. And if I tried to explain it to you, you might begin to look at me in another way."

"Why don't you just try me?"

"I'm scared."

"Well, it can't be that bad," Russ said.

Before I broke everything down for Russ, I tried to piece together all of what I was gon' say to him, just so it wouldn't sound so bad coming outta my mouth.

When I finally got up the nerve to tell him, I said, "Ricky and all the niggaz that work for him are under investigation by the Feds."

"How you know that?" Russ asked me with a puzzled look on his face.

"Because I've got a cousin who used to work for Ricky. And when she got locked up for carrying a whole lot of coke, the Feds took over her case."

"So, she's snitching everybody out?" Russ responded sarcastically.

"Well, it didn't start out that way."

"It never does."

"Will you just listen?"

"Yeah. Go 'head."

"Well, from the day she got locked up, Ricky's been giving her the cold shoulder. He doesn't even want her calling our house. I mean, it's an out of sight, out of mind thing wit' him. So, when the Feds started asking questions, she came straight to me since I was the one who set the whole thing for her to get the work from Ricky."

"So, what did you tell her?"

"At first, I was angry wit' her for even entertaining the thought of telling them crackers something. But after Ricky started showing his real colors, I told her to do whatever she gotta do."

"And when did all this happen?"

"Not too long ago. I mean, it's been about a few weeks."

"Damn! They probably got my ass under investigation, too!"

"No, they don't."

"And what makes you so sure?"

"Because, all the information they got, my cousin Nikki gave it to them."

"So, what does that mean?"

"It means that if she doesn't know anything about you, then that's some information she can't give to them."

"So, you ain't tell her about us?"

"No, I haven't."

"So, what's gon' happen now?"

"Well, I can't really say. But, I do know that Ricky had something to do wit' those murders that everybody is talking about. So, the heat is gonna be on full blast! And I ain't gon' be around to witness it."

"Where you going?"

"I told you, I don't know. But it's going to be real soon. And I ain't looking back."

"So, what you gon' do wit' your salon and the house?"

"That house was bought wit' drug money. Do you think the Feds gon' let me keep it after Ricky gets locked up? I don't think so! And as far as the shop is concerned, that's already been taken care of."

Without commenting, Russ looked at me and then he looked out of the restaurant window. There was no doubt in my mind that he was trying to consume everything I had just laid on his plate. Whether or not to trust me anymore was probably another question in his mind, too.

"Look, I know it's hard for you to swallow everything I just told you. So, if you don't do nothing else, I want you to believe that I like you a whole lot. And that's why I'm telling you all this. I mean, I could've just said the hell wit' you, and let the Feds do whatever. But, I didn't! So, that's gotta account for something. Right?"

Russ hesitated for a bit, but then he smiled and said, "Yeah. It does."

I smiled back at him and grabbed both of his hands.

"If I'm small enough to fit in your luggage, would you take me wit' you?"

I didn't know what to say. I mean, I wanted to say yes. But I didn't wanna feel cheap if he was playing a joke on me. To be on the safe side, I reversed the question and said, "Would you wanna go?"

"Damn right!" he replied and smiled.

Oh my goodness! This nigga wanna leave with me! I felt like jumping outta my damn seat, because I was so happy! But, I couldn't do that. I needed to remain cool. I couldn't let him see me sweat over his good-assed dick! All I had do now was to make a trip home so I could pack some of my prized possessions, then go to the bank so I could make a final withdrawal from my safe deposit box and close out my accounts. What a way to go out with a bang!

Me and Russ went over the last little things we needed to do before we jetted outta VA. So, after we got a bite to eat, we called it a night and headed on back to our respective homes.

9mm Glocks

By the time I got home, Ricky was nowhere in sight, which I thought was a good thing. I wasted no time as I rushed upstairs to my bedroom, with the objective of packing all of my irreplaceable items.

I only grabbed two of my furs, being as though they were the more expensive ones. Then I grabbed all four of my diamond watches. I wasn't gon' dare leave them behind. Every last one of them had a story behind it. Then I packed up all my jewelry, a little bit of my clothes, my shoes, and I couldn't forget all my important papers and pictures. Especially all the bank statements 'cause if the Feds got their hands on that information, they would have a field day. That's why I had to hurry up and clear out all the accounts. Because if I didn't, I was gon' be in bad shape.

After I gathered up everything I was taking with me, I took it straight outside to my car and hid it in the trunk. As soon as I stepped foot back in the house, the phone started ringing. "Hello,"

I answered, wondering who it was because their number didn't show up on the Caller ID.

"It's me," Ricky answered.

"Yeah. What is it?"

"Did you get them thangs this morning, like I asked you?"

"No."

"But why?" he screamed at me. "You wasn't that busy, that you couldn't pick the shit up for us. We are leaving in two days!" He continued like he was upset.

"For your information fool, I was busy! I work every day, unlike your black ass! So, if you wanted those damn passports today, then you should've picked them up yourself!" I snapped back.

"You's one stupid bitch!" he said before he hung up.

I hung the phone up right after he did. Before I could make another move, my cell phone started ringing. "Hello?"

"Kira?" Mr. Shapiro said.

"Yeah."

"Did you get my messages?"

"No. I ain't had a chance to check my voice-mail."

"Is your husband near you?"

"Nah. He's not here."

"Okay, remember what you and I discussed yesterday?"

"Yeah."

"Well, I've spoken with the U.S. Attorney about it. And since the murder did take place, she's going to need a statement from you, so she can go before a grand jury and get the indictments."

"What you mean, get a statement from me? I don't know who did the killings! All I know is that Ricky called a meeting, because he found out Remo had something to do wit' them Norview niggas robbing his spot."

"Okay. And that's fine. But, I'm going to need you to tell her the same thing you just told me."

"Look, I don't wanna get involved wit' that."

"But, you have to."

"No, I don't!"

"Okay, listen," Mr. Shapiro began to say, "Don't say no, now. Sleep on it. And I'll get back with you in the morning."

"Yeah. A'ight," I said, with little enthusiasm, and then I hung up.

After I ended my conversation with Mr. Shapiro, I went on in the den so I could watch a little bit of TV, since I wasn't hungry or sleepy. As I laid there on sofa, I couldn't help but wonder how everything was gon' play out. I mean, it was a done deal that a lot of niggas on Ricky's squad was going to jail. The question was, when? And since I didn't have the answer to that question, I just remained clueless.

Ricky came home later that night, about eleven-thirty. And he wasn't alone, either. I heard Brian's voice right after Ricky closed the front door behind them. They went straight into the kitchen. That's what Ricky normally did when he brought company home. He liked to show them he was the man by offering them bottles of Corona or Red Stripe.

"You got some lemon?" Brian asked Ricky.

"Nigga you don't need no lemon! Drink that shit straight!" Ricky told him as they both laughed. Then they got quiet. Ricky usually did that if he wanted to talk about something he didn't want me to hear. After about ten minutes, their volume picked up a little bit. I could hear Brian talking about this new chick he met a couple days ago at this party, and how phat her ass was. He also told Ricky how he got her to suck his dick in the bathroom right before the party ended. All Ricky could do was laugh.

So, Brian continued on talking about his new chicks and Ricky continued laughing until Brian's cell phone started vibrating.

"Hold up. It's Shampoo," he told Ricky.

"Yo, son," Brian said to Shampoo.

"It's done," Shampoo told him.

"Oh! A'ight!" Brian replied and then he hung up.

"It's done," Brian said to Ricky.

"Good," Ricky replied. And then I heard him gulp down some more of his beer. "Now all we gotta do is get the other two."

"Mike and them niggas working on that now," Brian said. "I'm just glad they got to that chick before the po-pos did, because she was our main problem."

"Where did they get her at?"

"He didn't say. But, she was probably at her crib."

"Man I sho' hope they got to her before she had a chance to run off at the mouth about what she told you."

"I hope so, too," I heard Brian say and then he let out a sigh of relief, which was how I figured out they were talking about the girl who used to braid Brian's hair.

Without forcing it, my mind started imagining all kinds of ways they killed that poor girl. She would've been better off keeping her mouth closed. But nah! She had to go back and tell Brian what somebody else told her. Now, look what it got her: a one-way ticket to her grave. That's why I was carrying my ass outta here.

Brian finally left around twelve-thirty. After Ricky locked the front door, he went on into the then. I turned over on my stomach in hopes of falling asleep, especially after finding out Ricky had somebody else killed. But my mind wouldn't let me. And as the minutes went by, I developed a huge knot in my stomach. I got this same feeling every time I got nervous or upset. It ate me up, too. That's why I tried not to let shit bother me. But this was different. I finally found a way to fall asleep, after tossing and turning for about two hours. But that didn't last long, because Ricky woke me up with all of the walking around he was doing downstairs. Then it sounded like he was looking for something, because of all the closet doors he kept opening and closing. Whatever it was, it had him running around downstairs like a chicken with his head cut off.

Ricky woke me up the next morning, by calling my name real loud from downstairs. I yelled back at him by saying, "What!"

"What time you leaving the house?"

"I don't know," I yelled once more.

"You ain't got nobody hair to do this morning?"

"Why'?"

"Because, I wanna know if you gon' pick up them passports today?"

"I wish you would stop worrying me about them damn things!" I told him.

"Well, damn, I did pay for the trip. So, you could at least pick up the passports."

"Look, I know what I'm supposed to do! So, stop bothering me please!"

Now after I said what I had to say, I heard Ricky cursing me out as he walked away from the stairs. But I didn't care, and he needed to recognize that, too, instead of thinking that somebody was gon' jump when he told them to. Yeah, he used to have it like that with me. But now, those days were long gone.

I got up about an hour later, which was when Ricky left the house. I overheard him telling somebody who called him on his cell phone, that he was on his way.

I figured it was one of his chickenheads calling because they needed some dough. When that happened he was without questions and was out the door in a split second. But then again, it could've been Shampoo or Mike calling him, so they could meet up somewhere, since it was against the rules to talk on the phone about anything that'll getcha locked up. Any nigga dealing drugs knew the Feds could have your phone tapped at any time. That's why if a nigga you talking to on the phone forgot about the rule and started running off at the mouth about how much money he was trying to spend with you, and then he was either a knuckle-head, or he just didn't care and was trying to get both of y'all locked up. In that situation, the best thing for that was to act like you didn't know what he was talking about and then give his ass the dial tone. Ricky would do it in a heartbeat and so far, it's been working for him.

Once I got dressed, I headed on out to my car and was on the road in less than two minutes. I went to my shop first, just so I could give Rhonda the proper paperwork; that way she could transfer everything in her name. When I walked in the shop to do that, she had just hung up the salon's telephone.

"Was that for me?" I asked.

"Nah. It was one of my clients, telling me she's going to be late."

"Did I get any calls?"

"Nah. Not since I been here. And there weren't no messages left on the answering machine, either," Rhonda replied.

"Well, here is the paperwork for the shop. So, what you got to do is change everything and put in your name on it. Oh yeah, I also typed up a bill of sale receipt, so when you go down to City Hall, they won't give you problems about getting the business license."

"Wait! Hold up!" Rhonda said. "You're leaving, for real?"

"Yeah."

"But, what about your clients?"

"They're yours now," I assured Rhonda and placed the papers down on her booth. And before I could step away, she threw her arms around me and hugged me.

"Please don't leave me," she begged.

I hugged her back and said, "I've got to."

She started crying. "So, when are you leaving?" she wanted to know.

"I'm leaving late tonight."

"So, how are you gon' keep in touch?"

"I'mma call you when I get settled."

"Have you decided where you're going?"

"Nah. Not yet."

"Well, just be careful. And don't forget to call me!" Rhonda demanded.

I kissed her on her cheek and said, "I won't."

Before I walked out of the salon for the last time, I went into my back office and gathered up all my mail, along with the rest of my stuff, and stuck it in my duffel bag.

Rhonda was standing outside in the front of the shop, puffing on a cigarette, when I walked back outta my office. I kinda figured she was going to take my leaving town pretty hard. As I made my way out the front door, I kept my head down until I got into my car.

"I'mma call you," I finally said, as I drove away.

Rhonda didn't reply at all. But, she did nod her head.

Waiting In Da' Cut

I got to the bank about twelve o'clock that afternoon. Since everybody knew me, it didn't take long at all for me to close all my accounts and empty out my safe deposit box. I walked outta the bank with more dough than I thought I had. I counted $470,000. Three hundred and fifty thousand of it was Ricky's. The other $124,000 of it came from the money I had been stealing from Ricky's stash, which was the bulk of it. And the remainder of the dough came from my savings and checking accounts. I was set and ready to go.

The next thing on my to-do list was to call Russ so we could set up a time to get outta Dodge. But before I could dial all seven numbers of his cell phone, Mr. Shapiro came through on my call waiting. I started not to answer it, but I did it anyway, just so I could set the record straight. "Hello," I said in irritation.

"Hi, Kira," Mr. Shapiro replied. "Is this a good time for you?"

"No. But, go ahead I'm listening."

"Well, as you know, I've already spoken with the

U.S. Attorney about what we've discussed. This morning, I received a conference call from the federal agents and some local detectives from the city of Norfolk. And guess what I found out?"

"What?"

"There's a woman listed in critical condition at Sentra Leigh hospital, due to a gunshot wound through her back. And luckily for her, the bullet went straight through her. If it hadn't, she would not have been able to tell anybody who had done that to her."

"So, what does this have to do wit' me?" I asked.

"Well, she has given the Norfolk detectives the names of both men who were involved in her shooting."

"Who was it?"

"She told them it was a guy who goes by the name of Shampoo and a guy named Mike, whom she knows very well. She told the detectives that they came to her apartment, acting like they came there to get their hair braided, and that a guy name Brian referred them; that's why she let them into her house."

"You are kidding me, right?"

"No. And what I'm about to say next is the big one."

"What is it?" I asked anxiously.

"Well, the woman in the hospital has also told the detectives that the only reason she could come up with why they wanted to kill her was because she knew the Norview boys robbed one of the dope houses that Brian runs. And when she told Brian, word was around the streets that their squad was weak. So, the next thing she knew, Remone, his sister and her boyfriend were killed."

"She told the police all that?"

"Yes."

"So, what's gon' happen now?"

"Well, the Norfolk detectives and the federal agents are working together to get arrest warrants, so they can round up Mike, Brian and the other guy, Shampoo. And when they do, they're hoping one of them talks and says that Ricky gave the order to kill her, as well as the other three."

My mouth flew wide open as I listened to what Mr. Shapiro was telling me. I couldn't believe it! But it was happening. Ricky was about to fall straight on his face. And the crazy part about it was that I was starting to feel sorry for him. But why should I? Shit! He made his bed by screwing every chick that crossed his path. Plus, he done robbed other cats or had them set up, just so he could get back on his feet. And since he'd been back on his feet, he's pulled in a lot of dough. Where there's dough, there come the big-booty hoes and tricks, who could care less if the nigga had a woman at home, or if he was fucking her mama for that matter; just as long as she got hers! Now after the nigga got his money straight and conquered at least two to three hoes that was when the other niggas from the street crowned him with respect. So, why risk all that 'cause some broke-assed niggas called your crew weak? Yeah, I know. There was always somebody in the game who wanted to be made an example of. And that's just how it was.

"How are they gonna find those guys? I mean, do they know where they live?"

"Don't you worry about it. Trust me, that's all under control."

"So, what's gon'happen wit' Nicole's case?"

"Well, the good thing about that is, since these guys are going to be indicted with a couple of counts of murder one, we no longer need you. Because with the woman in the hospital, and Nicole's testimony, your husband and his crew won't stand a chance."

Oh my God! I couldn't believe it. I didn't have to be involved with this mess anymore. Damn right! I mean, this was the best news of my entire life. I felt like screaming for joy. I held out, especially since them crackers could change their minds at the drop of a hat.

"So, have you talked to Nikki about this yet?" I continued.

"No. But, I plan to see her this evening."

"Well, I haven't talked to her in a couple of days. So, would you tell her that I love her?"

"Yes, I most certainly can."

"Oh yeah! Keep me posted, too."

"I will," Mr. Shapiro assured me before we hung up our lines.

I rode around Virginia Beach, trying to decide which fast-food restaurant I was gon' stop at. Popeye's Chicken was my final decision. It wasn't crowded, so I was able to get my food real fast. I took a seat in one of the booths way in the back of the restaurant so I could see everything outside surrounding my car.

As I ate, it dawned on me that I needed to get up with Russ to find out when and where we was gon' meet up. After I put my biscuit down I pulled out my cell phone and dialed his number. But, he didn't answer it. It sounded like he cut it off, because it didn't ring. All it did was go straight to his voice mail. I called it over and over, but, his phone kept doing the same thing; which, of course, got me worried.

Now I knew he was trying to handle his thing and whatnot, but my time here was starting to run out on me. So, he needed to make it snappy.

I stayed at Popeye's for about thirty minutes, and then I drove over to Nikki's apartment, just to do my usual: check her voicemail and take the mail out of the mailbox. Once that was done, I grabbed the TV remote and laid back on the couch in the living room. I went through all the channels, but nothing good seemed to be on. I turned it to the news channel, just to see if they said anything else about the murders. After I had been sitting there waiting for over an hour for Russ to call, Ricky started ringing my cell phone like crazy. So I answered it after I let it ring seven times.

"Yeah."

"Where you at?" Ricky asked me in a desperate manner.

"Why?" I asked.

"Because, I need you to go to the house."

"For what?"

"I need you to pack me up some clothes."

"Why can't you do it?" I asked him, even though I had already had a strong feeling about what he was gon' say.

"I'll tell you when we get up wit' each other

later," Ricky answered. Then he said, "Oh yeah, go get the dough I told you to put up for me."

"All of it?"

"Yeah. I'mma need it. So, call me back after you get all my shit! And then, I'mma tell you where we gon' meet. Because right now, I'm trying to make a couple moves so I can cover my tracks."

"A'ight."

"Don't forget!"

"I'm not," I said and then the conversation ended. I sat back and wondered what Ricky was planning to do, now that he was probably aware that the Feds was onto him and his whole crew? I mean, the way he was just acting on the phone, telling me I needed to get him some clothes and pick up all his money was a dead giveaway.

And if he thought I was gon' tell him where I was, he was sadly mistaken. My ties with him were unraveling pretty fast. He would see it when he finally got his eyes open.

On my way outta Nikki's apartment, I made sure everything was straight for her. Then I wrote her a brief letter, letting her know it was my time to leave and that I was gon' keep in touch, and that I loved her. I also told her in the letter that I left her some dough, so she'll be able to find it in her favorite hiding spot.

Then I left.

Sticking & Moving

I tried hitting Russ back up on his cell phone, but I kept getting his voicemail on the first ring. I stopped by a pay phone and called his cell phone again, just in case he decided to answer because he thought somebody else was calling him. But I got his voicemail again. From that point, I started getting worried. I hoped nothing was wrong with him. And I also hoped he wasn't stupid enough to be driving around with Ricky, especially after I told him what was going on. Time would tell!

For it to be February, it was kind of nice outside. To get a little bit of the breeze, I pulled my sunroof back just enough for me to block the sunlight. I couldn't take a whole lot of sunlight. It didn't work well with my skin. That's why I had to make sure everything was measured out to the T. As I continued to drive around, I realized that I had no place to go. I think I knew where I wanted to go when I left this place, but, I just couldn't figure out where I wanted to go around here while I was waiting for Russ to call me. Which reminded me to redial his number again. But, I kept getting the same damn thing. That was when my patience began to run thin.

"I mean, what the hell is going on Russ?" I screamed in frustration. But, it didn't help me none. However, it was a good way for me to let out some steam, and was my way of dealing with all the drama in my life. While I exercised my thoughts, I pressed play on my CD player and listened to Luther Vandross's latest album while I cruised around Norfolk, Chesapeake and Virginia Beach, just so I could blow off some time. Soon I realized it was three-thirty in the afternoon, which was way past the time me and Russ were supposed to meet up. I pulled over to another pay phone and called him up again. I figured this time, he would answer because he didn't recognize the number. But he didn't. When I got back in my car, I noticed I had missed a call on my cell phone. Come to find out, it was Ricky. Before I could pick up my cell phone and call him back, he was calling me again. I hesitated, trying to think of what I was gon' say to him. But my mind refused to work for me, which wasn't a good thing.

I answered him anyway. "Yeah," I said.

"Did you take care of what I asked you?" he didn't hesitate to ask.

"I did everything except your clothes."

"Well, where you at?" he wanted to know.

"Just leaving the bank," I lied.

"Well, did you get our passports?"

"Yeah," I lied again.

"A'ight! Good! So, meet me at the barbershop in about twenty minutes."

And before I could get another word in, Ricky hung up. I just sat in my car, trying to figure out what I was gon' do next. I mean, I couldn't go meet Ricky because I didn't want to be around him when they picked him up. And not only that, I wasn't trying to give him his money. Shit! I needed it! So, what in the hell was I gon' do? Then it came to me: there was nothing else to do but stall him. Have him think the po-pos got me pulled over and were running my license. I called down to the barbershop and got Ricky's barber to put him on the phone.

"What?" he asked me, the minute he put the phone up to his ears.

"Look, the police just pulled me over," I told him like I was upset.

"Which ones?" he wanted to know.

"What you mean which one?"

"Was it the narcos or the blue and white?"

"The blue and white."

"Where you at?"

"Out here by our house," I quickly thought to say.

"What they pull you over for?"

"He said I was speeding. So, I'mma have to call you after he let's me go."

"Did he know you got that dough on you?"

"No."

"Where did you put it at?"

"In the trunk of my car. And why you asking me a whole lot of questions?"

"Because, some cats out this way told me the Feds just picked up them niggas Mike and

Shampoo. And I been trying to hit that nigga Brian up, but he ain't answering his piece."

"You are lying!" I fronted like I was surprised.

"Nah, I ain't lying! That's why I need you to bring me my shit!"

"A'ight. I'mma call you right after he let me go."

"A'ight. Be careful. And please don't let that cracker take my shit from out that trunk."

"I'm not," I replied in a reassuring manner. From the time I hung up wit' Ricky, I thought about how desperate he sounded. I knew at that point that he was counting on me to bring him his dough. I mean, that was all he could get to, because the rest of his money was at the crib, divided between both of his safes. And since he just had the combinations changed on both of them, there was no way I was gon' be able to hit them up. I knew he was sick about that. That what he gets, trying to hide all his mess from me. Well, I guess the Feds were gon' have a field day when they walked up in there. They were gon' either sell it in an auction, or take some of it home to their wife and kids, which was alright with me.

An hour went by before Ricky started my cell phone up again, but I didn't answer it. I wanted him to think that the po-pos were still holding me up. That way, I could buy more time and see if I could get in touch with Russ.

As the clock ticked away, I got real bored driving around town like I was a tourist out sightseeing. And the fact that I didn't have any real close friends houses to go chill at, was bad. I pulled over to this small outlet mall in Virginia Beach, and decided to get my nails done. I mean, it was better than driving in circles and using all my gas.

One of the Asian nail techs met me at the front entrance of their shop and guided me to her table. "You want fill-in?" she asked in her Asian accent. I told her yeah and she started buffing my nails. It only took her thirty minutes to fix me up with the French manicure look. When I looked at the finishing touches, it looked very nice. I thanked her and reached into my handbag to pay her. I got side tracked for a brief second, because my cell phone started ringing.

"Hello," I said, without looking at the caller ID.

"Yo, baby. You ready?" Russ' familiar voice said.

I couldn't believe it. After all this time, he wanted to call me now.

"Where you at?" he asked.

"Out at the beach."

"What you doing?"

"Well, I just got my nails done, so, I'm paying the lady now. And once I leave outta here, I'll be ready to do whatever."

"Okay. Well, meet me at the Red Roof Inn, 'cause, that's where I'm at."

"How long you been there?" I wanted to know.

"Since last night."

"Did you talk to Ricky yet?"

"Nah. Why?"

"So, ain't nobody told you the Feds just picked up Mike and Shampoo?"

"Nah. This my first time hearing about it."

"Well, that's strange. 'Cause, Ricky is the type that'll let niggas know if the po-pos are on them."

"When did he tell you that?"

"About a couple of hours ago."

"So, what is he gon' do?"

"He didn't say. But, I know he's trying to leave the country because he asked me to go and get all his dough from out my safe deposit box."

"Did you do it?"

"Yep. But, he ain't gon' get it!"

"Yo, girl! You wicked as hell!" Russ laughed.

"Look, I'm just doing me."

"A'ight! I hear you, baby. So, are you gon' still come and scoop me up?"

"So, which Red Roof Inn you at?"

"Out Chesapeake. It's off Greenbrier Parkway."

"A'ight. I'll be there in twenty minutes," I told him, then I hopped into my whip.

Finally, my plans were coming together. With Russ in Chesapeake waiting for me to get there, and the fact that I had all the money I needed, I knew everything was gon' be a'ight.

Russ had the door to his room open when I pulled up. He was standing right smack dab in the doorway, smiling as if he was glad to see me. I thought he was gon' be dressed when I came, but he wasn't. All he had on was a white hotel towel.

"What you doing standing in the door like that?" I asked him as I smiled.

"Waiting for you," he replied and smiled back.

Before I got outta my car, I turned my cell phone off and stuck it in my glove compartment. I didn't want any distractions and since I hadn't called Ricky back, I knew he was gon' keep blowing my phone up. I got out and locked the door behind me. "What time we leaving here?" I asked, as Russ stuck his lips out to kiss me.

"After I put my clothes on," he answered.

"Well, go 'head, 'cause, I'm ready to break outta here."

"Okay. I will. But, let me make love to you first," Russ said as he pulled me into his arms.

"Not now. Let's do it later," I told him. But the more he touched and filled me up, the more my pussy got wet. "Russ, please stop," I told him, even though I didn't want him to stop. I mean, it wasn't a crime to play hard to get every now and then. But at that point, Russ wasn't trying to hear it. The next thing I knew, that nigga had me on my back and was fucking the hell outta me. Throughout the whole thing, my feelings grew more and more for him. I prayed that he was the one for me.

Russ hopped outta the bed and headed to the bathroom to take a shower. I wanted to take a shower with him, but my body wouldn't let me. I wrapped myself in the sheets and closed my eyes. I could hear Russ singing in the bathroom, but it wasn't loud enough to keep me from dozing off.

I don't know what time I fell asleep, but I do know that when I woke up Russ was standing over me, tying me to the bedpost.

"What you doing?" I asked after noticing he was fully dressed.

"What does it look like?" he replied sarcastically.

"Well, is this some type of joke?"

"Nah. But since I'm getting ready to bounce, I gotta make sure you ain't gon' be able to follow."

"But, what about the plans we made to leave together?"

"I didn't make them plans. You did." Russ stuffed my bag of money into his duffel bag.

"Wait! Hold up! You been in my car?"

"Don't it look like it?"

"But that doesn't belong to you!" I snapped at him.

"It does now."

"Come on now, Russ! It ain't even gotta go down like this," I said this calmly, while at the same time hoping he would leave me something.

It became apparent that he wasn't trying to hear nothing I had to say because after he zipped up the duffel bag, he throws it across his shoulder. And I was devastated.

I wanted so badly for all of this to be a dream. I mean, I couldn't believe that this nigga was standing right in my face, telling me he was taking my shit! How dare he!

While I was tied to the bed, this grimy-assed nigga was standing around, talking shit to me and taking my money on top on that! Now, how stupid could I be? I felt like a damn fool. I mean, how come I didn't see this mess coming?

"You know if I tell Ricky you took his money, he gon' put a bounty on your ass!" I snapped.

"Yeah! And what you think he gon' do if tell him I been fucking you in his bed, and that you planned to take his dough, too?"

"Now, I know you don't think he's going to believe that."

"He ain't got to. But I know one thing: you ain't to be trusted 'cause, anytime a nigga's wife steal his dough and fuck another nigga on his squad, she is a fucked-up broad. So, why in the hell did you think we was gon' be together? Nah, baby! That won't ever happen."

I got really angry as I heard Russ talk shit to me about what I had done. I figured I was only doing what I had to do. So, to hell with him. "How am I gon' get myself untied?" I asked him.

"A house keeping lady is coming by to bring some clean sheets. So, ask her to untie you."

"You are a cold mutherfucker!" I yelled. "Oh and don't think you gon' get away wit' this! Trust me, I know a lot of niggas who would love to fuck your ass up!"

Russ put his hand on the door knob and then looked back at me and said, "Well, just make sure they are some gangsta-ass niggas!"

"Oh don't worry about it! They will be," I replied to him as he walked out of the hotel room.

About two hours passed before the cleaning lady came by to bring the sheets Russ told me about. When the lady untied me, she kept advising me to call the police. But, I didn't. And as far as everything else went, since Russ took all the money; I couldn't go anywhere. But, I thanked God he didn't take any of my jewelry or my fur coats. And not only that, but Rhonda stood by my side. She wanted to give me my shop back, but I told her I couldn't do that. So, we decided to be partners. And business was good. Getting to the situation about my house, I kind of knew the Feds were gon' take it from me, in addition to Ricky's Benz and his Ninja motorcycle. But, they did let me keep my car and all my other personal things, since I could prove that I made enough money from my salon to buy it. And quiet as it was kept,

I hired some old safe-cracking guy to open both of Ricky's safes at the house, before I let the Feds come in and take it over.

Once I was able to get in them, I found plenty of pictures of his stinking-assed tramps posing buck naked, along with video tapes and a few rolls of dough wrapped in rubber bands. I counted $19,000 in all; which was cool. But, I understood why he wouldn't let me have the combination.

Now as far as Ricky goes, he got picked up the same day as Mike and Shampoo. His dumb ass made the mistake of using the barbershop phone to call Mike earlier that day. When the Feds got a hold to Mike's cell phone, they traced it back to the shop. Ricky was charged with conspiracy to plot three counts of murder, and conspiracy to manufacture and distribute cocaine. So, when Ricky took his case to trial, everybody and they mama testified on that ass. That's why he was sentenced to life, without parole. And when he made his first call to me, I told that bastard to kiss my ass! And if he wanted to communicate with somebody, then he'd better request to write Sunshine at the Virginia Beach jail, since that's where she was housed. I got word from one of my clients that Shampoo was the one who told the Feds he was taking a brick of coke to her once a week, to hold for Ricky. That's why she was picked up and indicted. Plus, her salon got closed down. Come to find out, Ricky got her to use it as a front to let cats come up in there to pick up their packages on certain days of the week. Penny and Tabitha asked could they come back and work for me. I told them, yes, being as though I ain't really have a problem with them.

Ricky's ghetto-assed aunt pleaded guilty to one count of distributing cocaine. The federal judge gave her eight years.

Brian got life, too, because Mike and Shampoo told the Feds that Brian was the one who told them to make those people disappear. And as far as the rest of the flunkies in Ricky's crew, all of them took a guilty plea from five to ten years. But what was so good about all this was that my cousin Nikki got outta her situation without testifying, even though that was the Feds' initial plan. I later found out that a couple of niggas on Ricky's squad beat her to the punch. However, she did get five years of probation. She's truly thankful for that.

Oh yeah, let's not forget Frances, the baby mama from hell! I ran into her at the beauty supply store about two days after Ricky was arrested. She had the nerve to ask me if I could go into Ricky's stash and get out five hundred dollars, 'cause Fredrica needed braces on her teeth.

I told her, "No, I can't go into his stash!"

Frances asked, "Why?"

I replied, "Because he ain't got one!" Then I told her not to ever say nothing to me when she sees me in public again, because me and Ricky are legally separated. So, when Fredrica needs something, then she needed to go on down to the jail and pay her daddy a visit; or pull out some paper and a pen and send his ass a kite, 'cause my days of playing step-mama were over.

I could tell Frances wanted to throw some bows after I said what I had to say. But, she wasn't stupid 'cause, with all the anger and frustration I had built up, she knew I would've fucked her ass up. That's why she sucked her tongue and got the hell outta my face.

Oh and I still saw her trick ass every now and again. But all she did was roll her eyes at me.

And as far as Russ goes, I haven't seen or heard from that nigga since he took that dough from me. When Ricky first asked me about it, I told him the police took it. Of course, he didn't believe it, but he might as well. Because we wasn't gon' ever see that money again.

**Catch a preview of Kiki Swinson's novella,
KEEPING MY ENEMIES CLOSE,
from SLEEPING WITH THE ENEMY!**

Available now at your local bookstore.

Chapter 1

Men aren't worth shit

"He better be gone when I get home. I put up with a lot of his shit, and this was the last straw," I mumbled out loud as I waited for the traffic light to turn green. The woman in the next car probably thought I was losing my mind. I was so preoccupied with my ongoing conversation I could not have cared less what she thought. And as soon as the light turned green, I left her in the dust and was immediately reminded that I was less than two blocks away from my apartment.

A huge knot formed in the pit of my stomach the instant I pulled into my apartment complex. The thick summer air smacked me in the face the moment I opened up my car door. As we all know, the summer brings out the freaks, so the parking lot behind my apartment building was crawling with people. Right after I locked my car door and began to walk toward my building, all the so-called hustlers lined up alongside their vehicles and started whistling at me, but I couldn't be bothered. *Been there done that, got the T-shirt and the hat. I'd rather work for mine. It's time for me to rise to the top and stand on my own two feet,* I reminded myself. One guy in particular kept making comments about how he would love to take me out to dinner and get to know me better. When I continued to ignore him, his true colors came out.

"Oh, bitch, you ain't all that just because you're pretty with long hair and a fat ass. I fuck with hos that look better than you!" he screamed.

But again, I refused to entertain any of their bullshit. Every last one of those lame-ass niggas had at least three baby mamas, drove a pimped-out Chevy or an Oldsmobile with 20-inch rims, and had an IQ of 105. They were immature as hell, and as soon as they ran across a half-Indian and black chick with a college degree and some class such as myself, they got all intimidated and started showing their asses. So the way I handled them was by ignoring them and keeping it moving. I sure wish I would have done the same thing with the nigga I spent damn near four years with.

When I met Todd, so-called man, I thought that he could change the world. Yes, I knew he was a hustler from Young's Park, but what did I care; he gave the money and excitement I was looking for. Not to mention he was F-I-N-E. He had a body to die for, which I later found out came from having nothing to do but work out during a five-year bid in Indian Creek State Penitentiary.

At first, blinded by Gucci bags and Jimmy Choo shoes, I overlooked his blatant infidelity. But after six trips to my primary care physician for antibiotics to cure my dripping pussy, I had

had enough. The last time he cheated, I warned
him that I would not take it anymore, but what
did this motherfucker do? He pushed the envelope, tested the waters, and started fucking with
a nineteen-year-old chick named Rema that lived
right around the block from me. And to make
matters worse, I heard the bitch was three
months pregnant. Now what kind of shit was
that? But you know what? It's okay. She can have
his grimey ass because I am done with his bullshit once and for all.

Now, as soon as I stepped into my apartment,
I immediately knew something was amiss. I was
overwhelmed by a strong odor; it smelled like
Clorox mixed with ammonia. I began coughing
and gagging. "What the hell?" I said out loud as I
continued down the short hallway toward my
bedroom. The smell got stronger the farther I
went. And when I entered my bedroom, I found
that my closet door was gaping wide open. Upon
further review, I noticed that every stitch of my
clothes were gone. "Wait, now I know this nigga
didn't steal all my damn clothes," I said to myself,
confused. By now I had my hands covering my
mouth and nose because the fumes were so
strong. I closed the closet door, noticing that the
sheets were missing from my bed, and the mat-
tress had been sliced and diced, with cotton
spilling out of it like a gutted animal. I began to
get nervous. I ran into the bathroom, which was
adjacent to the bedroom. There I noticed that my
medicine cabinet hung open and was empty; the
cabinet under the sink was also empty of my toiletries and smell-good essentials. The mirror on
the medicine cabinet was smashed, and the glass

lay in the small sink below it. Even my cushioned toilet seat had been sliced up, which would have made taking a shit impossible at that moment, although the nervous knot in my stomach was forcing me to feel the urge. Nevertheless, nothing prepared me for what I found next. Amidst all of the coughing, gagging, and eye tearing, I managed to pull back the shower curtain. "OH NO THE FUCK HE DIDN'T!" I screamed, incensed.

Todd had filled the tub with water, bleach, ammonia, Mr. Clean, laundry detergent, and any other household cleaner he could find, and put everything I owned—my clothes, toiletries, shoes, boots, expensive handbags, my mink jacket, contact lenses, bed sheets, towels, and face cloths—in the solution. All of my shit was ruined; there was no saving it. The bleach and ammonia together could make a bomb, so by mixing it, it had eaten away most of the material that comprised my belongings. Smoke was rising from the bathtub, and I was scared that if I touched anything, it would explode. I left the bathroom in shock, I ran into the kitchen to survey if he had done any other damage, and yes, he'd struck again. I found all my dishes broken and in the sink. The glasses were broken into shards so small it appeared that he must have taken his time with a spoon or a hammer to smash them. I could not even get the glass out of the drain; that's just how small the pieces were. By this time, I was hysterical. I walked into the living room expecting disaster, and once again Todd didn't disappoint me. He had sliced up the leather sofa and the love seat. The DVD player and Sony surround sound system lay in shambles. I pressed the power button on the television, and sparks started flying out of the back. Seeing this sent me running. The TV didn't explode, but I later found out that he had poured water into the back of it. I stood outside the front door of my apartment and fumbled through my handbag for my cell phone. When I finally found it through all the junk I had scattered inside, I grabbed it and immediately dialed my best friend Tenisha's number.

"Hello," she answered with a hoarse voice, pretending to be asleep.

"You sleep?" I asked, my voice quivering.

"Yeah," Tenisha breathed into the receiver.

"Well, get up! You ain't gonna believe what this nigga did to me!" I screamed.

"Mmmmm," she moaned, hoping that if she sounded like she was out of it, I would tell her I'd call her later.

"Come on, Tee, I know that fake sleep act. Now, get up and stop being selfish all of your life! I need to talk to you!" I yelled, on the brink of tears.

"Okay . . . what happened now?" she asked, reluctantly. I knew she was tired of all my Todd stories, especially after all I'd been through with him and always managed to give him the benefit of the doubt and go running back to him with open arms. But this time it was different—he was gone for good this time. So I needed her shoulder to lean on.

"Girl, he destroyed everything I owned. He put all my shit in the tub and poured bleach, ammonia, and whatever else he could find in it." I began to cry. Then ten seconds later, I broke down.

"Why did he do that?" she asked nonchalantly.

"Because I told his ass to get out."

"Well, this ain't the first time you told him to get out, so there must be something you're not telling me."

"I just found out that bitch Rema is pregnant."

"You mean that young chick he was fucking around with?"

"Yes, and she's parading around here telling everybody, too."

"Oh, now *that's* serious."

"I know. And that's why I couldn't let that one slide."

"You did right by putting his no-good ass out. But I think I would've done it a different way, like change the locks or something so he would not have gotten in to mess your shit up."

"Well, it's too late for that," I replied between sobs.

"So, what are you going to do now?"

"I don't know. But I can't stay here while the place is like this."

"Wait there, I'm gonna come by and see you," she said.

"Okay, I'll be standing outside waiting for you," I told her, and then we hung up.

Want more Kiki Swinson?
Turn the page for a preview of
I'M STILL WIFEY
and
LIFE AFTER WIFEY
Available in 2009 at your local bookstore!

From I'M STILL WIFEY

It Ain't Over

Can you believe it? After all the planning I did to leave my husband Ricky to run off with Russ, it backfired on me. It has been two-and-a-half months since the whole thing went down. Now I'm sitting here all alone, in my hair shop, thinking about what I am going to do about this baby I'm carrying.

Rhonda and Nikki both didn't believe me when I told them that I was pregnant by Russ. But after I pulled out a calendar and counted back the days from the last time we were together, it finally registered through their thick skulls.

So, what cha' gon' do about it?" Rhonda asked me the day I got the results from a pregnancy test about a month ago. The first thing that came out of her mouth was for me to get an abortion since I ain't gon' have a baby daddy. God knows where he is. But I told her that was the furthest thing from my mind because whether I had Russ in my life or not, I was gon' have this baby. And then she said, "Well, what would you do if he found out you're pregnant and wants to come back with a whole bunch of apologies and shit?"

I told her that shit ain't gon' happen because first of all, Russ ain't gon' find out I'm pregnant 'cause ain't nobody gon' know I'm pregnant by him. And second, after that stunt he pulled on me to rob me for my dough, I know he ain't gon' never show his face around this way ever again. He would be a fool to. I mean, he don't know if I told Ricky that he robbed me or not. So to play it cool, he's gon' do like any other greasy-ass nigga would do after they pull a stick-up move, and that is to disappear. And even though he thinks he got away with it, he hasn't. 'Cause whether Russ knows it or not, karma is coming for his ass. And what will give me much pleasure is to be able to see it hit 'em.

Hopefully my day will come very soon.

Back at my place, which is a step down from my ol' two-story house, I decided to pop myself a bag of popcorn and watch my favorite show, *America's Next Top Model*. Afterward, I began to straighten things up around my two bedroom, two-bath condo until my telephone started ringing.

"Hello," I said without looking at the caller ID.

"Whatcha doing?" Rhonda wanted to know.

"I was just dusting the mantel over my fireplace."

"Girl, sit your butt down. 'Cause if my memory serves me, I do remember you being on your feet all day today."

"I'm fine. But what I wanna know is, why you didn't come back to work today?"

Rhonda sighed heavily and said, "Kira, if I could kill Tony and get away with it, I would do it."

"What happened now?"

"Girl, I caught this nigga talking to some hoe named Letisha on his cell phone."

"Where was he at?"

"He was in the bathroom, sitting on the fucking toilet, taking a shit."

I laughed at Rhonda's comment and asked her what happened next.

"Well, before I busted in on him and smacked him upside his damn head with my shoe, I stood very quiet in the hallway right outside our bedroom and heard this bastard telling that hoe how much he missed her and that he was going to get his hair cut at the barbershop. And right after I heard him say that, that's when I went off."

"So, what did he do?"

"He couldn't do shit with his pants wrapped around his ankles. So, he just sat there and took all them blows I threw at his ass. And then when he dropped his cell phone, I hurried up and snatched it right off the floor and cussed that bitch out royally."

"And what did she say?"

"I ain't let her say shit. 'Cause after I told her who I was and that if I ever caught her in Tony's face, she was gonna get fucked up, I hung up."

"So, what was Tony doing while you was going off on that hoe?"

"Trying to hurry up and wipe his ass, so he can get up from the toilet and I guess take his phone back. But as soon as the bastard stood up to flush the stool, I threw his phone right up against the wall as hard as I could and broke that bad boy in about ten little pieces."

I laughed again and said, "Damn girl! That's some shit I used to do."

"Well, jackass didn't see it coming. So, it made it all the better."

"Where's he at now?"

"In the kitchen helping Ryan with his homework."

"So, did he ever go out and get his hair cut?"

"Hell nah. Shit, he knew better."

"Well, what kind of lies did he tell you about everything that happened?"

"Girl, that nigga ain't gon' volunteer no information. All he had to say was that I was crazy as hell. And then he went on about his damn business."

"Rhonda," I said before I sighed, "I know you're sick and tired of going through all that bullshit! Because I sure was when Ricky was on the streets."

"Hey wait," Rhonda interjected, "I forgot to tell you that he called the shop today while you was at lunch."

"Did you accept the call?"

"Yeah. But we only talked for a few minutes."

"What did he say?"

"He just wanted to know where you was and when was you coming in. So, I told him that you wasn't. And that's when he asked me to call you on three-way. But I told him the three-way call thing wasn't working."

"I bet he got real mad, didn't he?"

"Hell yeah!"

"So, what did he say after that?"

"Nothing but to tell you he called. And for me to tell you to come down to the county jail and see him before the U.S. Marshal picks him up and takes him off to the Federal Holding Facility in Oklahoma, because he has something very important to talk with you about."

"Well, he should already know that it ain't gon' happen. But, I am wondering what he's got so important to talk to me about."

"Girl, he's just probably saying that so he can get you to come down and see him."

"Yeah. You probably right," I agreed.

"Well, are you going to ever tell him that you're pregnant by Russ?" Rhonda blurted out of the blue.

"Nope. It ain't none of his damn business. All he needs to focus on is signing those divorce papers my lawyer is getting ready to send his ass."

"So, you're serious about that, huh?"

"You damn right!" I commented and then I said, "I'm gonna get that nigga outta my life once and for all, so I can move on."

"Look, I understand all that. But I wouldn't let his ass get off that easy. Because the next time he calls the shop, I would make it my business to wreck his muthafucking ego and tell him, *Yeah nigga, while you was running around behind my back with Sunshine's stinking ass, I was fucking your boy Russ right in your bed. And I just found out that I'm pregnant by him.*'"

"Oh my God! That'll kill him!"

"That's the idea," Rhonda told me.

I said, "Girl, that nigga gon' try and come through the phone after I tell him some shit like that."

"Well, no need to worry 'bout that. 'Cause it ain't gon' happen." Before I could comment, she told me to hold on because somebody was beeping in on her other line. When she clicked over, it got real quiet. But just like that, she was right back on the line and said, "Hey girl, one of Tony's homeboys is on the other end trying to holler at him. So, let me call you back."

"A'ight," I told her. Then we both hung up.

From LIFE AFTER WIFEY

Prologue

Barely a second after I walked through the front door of my apartment, my cell phone started ringing. I threw all of my things down on the floor and retrieved my phone from my handbag.

"Hello," I said.

"Hey, where you at?" Nikki asked me.

"At home. Why?" I asked and then I took a seat on my living room sofa.

"I'm on my way over there."

"Why? What's wrong?"

"Syncere did it!"

"Did what?"

"I just found out he was involved with Mark getting killed."

"How did you find that out?"

"Because when he was in the shower this morning, I went through his Sidekick to see if he had any messages from any chicks and that's when I ran across an old message he had received the same night you and Mark got shot."

"What did the text message say?" I asked as my heart sunk into the pit of my stomach.

"It said, 'Squad leader was with his broad, so we had to plug both of them. We got his heat, his jewels and his dough, so holla at me when you want me to make the drop.'"

"Oh, my God," I screamed. "We gotta call the police."

"I know, but what are we going to tell 'em?"

"We are going to tell them that muthafucka had my man killed," I screamed at the top of my lungs.

"But, we have no proof"

"Where is his Sidekick?"

"He has it."

"Well, it doesn't matter, 'cause I'm gon' call the police anyway. Ain't no way I'm going to let that bastard walk the streets as a free man after today!"

"Will you wait until I get there?"

"You better hurry up."

"I will. Give me about thirty minutes, 'cause I'm way out here in Newport News."

"Well, I'm going to jump in the shower, so you better come on."

"Okay," she replied and then we both hung up.

I was pissed off once again and hurt that Syncere was the one who had Mark killed. What was I going to do? How were we going to prove the allegations? We had no murder weapon or motive, as the police would say. Our best bet was to get that T-Mobile Sidekick away from him, which is going to be very hard to do. But I guess we would figure something out. I owed Mark at least that.

I got undressed and hopped in the shower because my body needed it badly. The hot water piercing the tender parts of my muscles felt great, so I took my time and bathed every inch of my body.

When I was done, I turned off the water and flung back the shower curtain.

There was a man pointing his gun directly at me. I wanted to scream. But before I could let out a single cry, he said, "Don't say a fucking word" There was no expression in his voice at all.

"Okay," I said, my voice barely audible, with my hands partially covering my mouth.

"Here, take this," the guy told me as he handed me a newspaper clipping.

I reached and grabbed it like he instructed me. He said, "Papí wanted me to give you that, so you can see that he took care of Russ."

Hearing this man tell me that this article was about Russ made me want to read it.

The article was printed in black ink in the *Washington Post*'s Metro section. It was about the execution-style murder of a Russell Hastings. He was found in his bed at one o'clock in the morning, shot in the head three times. Police detectives had no suspects at the time.

"This is Russ?" I asked the guy.

"Yes, that's him."

"So, can I ask you why you got that gun pointed at me?"

"Because my job isn't finished."

"Wh-wh-what do you mean?" I began to stutter,

trying to figure out what this man was talking about.

"I heard you talking on the telephone about calling the police and that's not good."

"But it was about something else," I tried to reassure him.

"I heard you. I know you were talking about your husband's murder."

"No, I wasn't. I swear."

"Why are you lying to me when I already heard everything you said?"

"Listen, it's not what you think. I promise you that I wasn't talking about my husband's murder. I could care less about that muthafucka."

"Well, it wouldn't matter anyway because you took money from Papí."

"But I didn't ask for it. He just gave it to me."

"You took it though. When you did that, you let him know that you were weak and could be bought at any price. So, now you got to go, too."

"Wait," I screamed because I wanted to explain myself. But it was too late because he had already pulled the trigger. That meant that my life as I knew it was running on empty and my soul began to emerge from my body.

Chapter 1

Choosing Sides

Nikki Speaks

From the time I jumped into my car and left Syncere's house until the time I pulled in front of Kira's apartment building, I wrecked the hell out of my brain trying to rationalize and make sense of the text message I had just read on Syncere's T-Mobile.

The message was clear but I could not bring myself to believe that my man had something to do with Mark's murder, not to mention the fact that Kira had gotten caught up in the crossfire and lost her baby. I didn't want to sound stupid or naïve, but there had to be an explanation behind this whole thing. I needed to find out what it was and how involved Syncere was before Kira blew the whistle on him because whether she realized it or not, I needed my man. So, I was not letting him go that easy.

Immediately after I got out of my car I stood

there on the sidewalk and took a deep breath. After I exhaled, I put one foot forward and proceeded toward Kira's apartment to confront the inevitable. Knowing she was going to bite my head off the moment I jumped to Syncere's defense was something I had prepared myself for. As I made my way down the entryway to her building, this fine-ass, older-looking Hispanic guy wearing a dark blue painter's cap and overalls came rushing toward me, so I didn't hesitate to move out of his way. But, what was really odd about him was when I tried to make eye contact and say 'hello' he totally brushed me off and looked the other way. Being the chick I am, I threw my hand up at him and said, "Well, fuck you too! You ol' rude muthafucka!" I kept it moving.

Patting my right thigh, with my hand, to a rhythmic beat as I walked up the last step to Kira's floor, I let out a long sigh and proceeded toward Kira's front door. Upon my arrival, I noticed that her door was slightly ajar so I reached over and pushed it open. "Girl, did you know that your door was open?" I yelled as I walked into the apartment. I didn't get an answer, so I closed the front door behind me and proceeded down the hallway toward her bedroom. When I entered into her room and saw that she was nowhere in sight, I immediately called her name again and I turned to walk toward the master bathroom. "Kira, where you at?" I turned the doorknob and pushed the door open.

"Oh, my God," I screamed at the top of my lungs the second my mind registered the gruesome sight of Kira's body slumped over the edge of the bathtub, while her head lay in a pool of her own blood. I couldn't see her face because of the way her body was positioned. I rushed over to her side, got down on my knees and crawled over next to her. My heart was racing at the speed of light and my emotions were spiraling out of control as I grabbed her body and pulled her toward me.

"Kira, please wake up!" I begged her and began to cry hysterically. She didn't move so, I started shaking her frantically. "Kira, please wake up!" I screamed once again. "Don't die on me like this," I pleaded. Out of nowhere, her eyes fluttered and slowly opened. Over-whelmed by her sudden reaction, my heart skipped a beat and I pulled her body even closer. "Oh my God, thank you," I said in a joyful manner and cradled her head in my lap. "I almost thought I lost you," I told her and wiped the tears away from my eyes. Meanwhile, Kira struggled a bit to swallow the blood in her throat and then she tried to speak. I immediatcly leaned forward and positioned my ear about two inches away from her mouth so I could hear what it was she had to say.

When she finally moved her lips, the few words she uttered were just above a whisper and barely audible. I was about to ask her to repeat herself and she started choking. I panicked. "Ahh shit! Don't do this to me. Take a deep breath," I instructed her as I began to massage her chest. Then it suddenly hit me that I needed to call an ambulance. I retrieved my cellular phone from the holster on my right side and dialed 911.

"911, what's your emergency?"

"My cousin's been shot," I answered with urgency.

"What's your cousin's name?"

"Her name is Kira Walters."

"And what is your name?"

"My name is Nicole Simpson."

"Okay Nicole, I need for you to stay calm. Can you tell me if Kira is conscious?"

"Yes, she's conscious. I've got her lying in my arms."

"Okay, tell me exactly where Kira's been shot."

"In the left side of her head, right above her temple."

"Is that the only place she's been shot?"

"Yes ma'am."

"Nicole, I'm gonna need you to give me the address where you are located. In the meantime, I'm gonna need you to remain calm and grab something like a sheet or a towel and press it against Kira's head to stop some of the bleeding. Has she lost a lot of blood?"

"Yes, she has," I assured the woman. Shortly thereafter I gave her the address.

The operator stayed on the phone with me until the police and the paramedics arrived. Covered from the waist down in Kira's blood, I was ushered out of the bathroom and into the kitchen by this short, white, female police officer who had a ton of questions for me. I only answered the questions I knew the answers to. Once our little session was over, another detective—this time a white male—came in and asked me almost the exact same questions as the female officer did. I found myself repeating everything over again.

My back was turned when the paramedics took Kira out on the stretcher. By the time I realized that she had been taken away, she was already in the ambulance, headed to the nearest emergency room. The white male detective informed me where they were taking her so I immediately called my family, told them Kira had gotten shot and that they needed to meet me at Bayside Memorial. After they assured me they were on their way, I hung up with them. On my way out, I noticed at least a dozen detectives and forensics investigators combing every inch of the apartment to collect evidence so there was no doubt in my mind that they were going to find her killer.

I got to the hospital in no time at all and to my surprise my mother, my father and my grandmother arrived shortly afterward. We all sat and waited patiently for one of the doctors performing the emergency surgery to come out and give us an update on Kira's condition. In the meantime, my grandmother had a few questions for me to answer.

"Nikki, are you sure Kira was conscious when she left with the paramedics?" she asked as if she was making a desperate attempt to find the answer in my eyes.

"Yes, she was," I replied in a reassuring manner. "She even tried to say something, but I didn't understand her. When I asked her to say it again she started choking and that's when I called the paramedics."

"Well, how was she breathing when they took her out of the house?"

"I don't know, Grandma. I was in the kitchen when they carried her out," I told her and then I put my head down in despair. Knowing that my cousin was in surgery fighting for her life and I couldn't do anything to help her put a huge strain on my heart. Not to mention the fact that if I would've gotten to her apartment a little sooner this probably would not have happened to her. In a sense I felt like her getting shot was partially my fault. Which was why I was feeling so terrible right now.

"What in the world do y'all got going on?" my father interjected as if the sight of me made him cringe.

"What are you talking about?" I looked at him with an expression of uncertainty.

"What kind of people are y' all mixed up with?"

"Come on now, honey, I know you're upset but this is not the time or the place," my mother spoke up.

"Yes, your wife is right," my grandmother agreed, trying to keep the peace.

But my father wasn't trying to hear them. Their comments went in one ear and right out the other. "Whatcha trying to do, end up like your cousin in there?"